JACK

LEECH: BOOK 2

james crawford

Jack Leech: Book 1
V1

COPYRIGHT 2013 by Anthony Crawford

Cover Art Credited to: Georgina Gibson.

http://www.georginagibson.com/

Edited By: There for You Book Editing, thereforyou.melissa@gmail.com

Published in the United States of America

http://jamescrawfordauthor.weebly.com/
jamescrawford_77@yahoo.com

978-1494707743.

To My Spouse David: for keeping me sane. I know it's a harder task than it sounds.

.

A special thank you to my best friend Paris, you are always there for me when I need you. From picking me up when I am feeling down, teaching me how to interact with people after closing myself off for so long, and even giving me a friendly reminder when my mask is slipping. You're the best friend I can have.

Thank you to my writing buddies: Natasha Larry, David Beem, William Green, and Nova Sparks. For all the days I wanted to give up and you guys helped pick me back up. Everyone should have a group of friends like you guys.

And finally a big thank you to all my fans reading this, you guys are awesome and make writing a blast.

.

1

Jack's stomach turned over, threatening to heave as Mickey pulled the truck into the empty parking lot just outside the private cemetery, where their adoptive grandmother's family had been buried for generations. It had been three months since the battle that had destroyed their family, and the only evidence that the fight ever took place were a few divots left in the earth made by tire tracks and the statue of Jacob Archer, toppled over with its head a few feet away from its body.

Jack shook his head, bringing his mind into focus. "Okay, you two find the hole we started last time and I will start the search for Grandma in the compound."

"Jack, I don't think you should be alone," Jillian protested, grabbing him by the hand.

He turned his head, refusing to look at her as he fought back his tears. "I don't know what condition we will find her body in."

"Jack, I'm coming with you. End of story. We can handle this together," Jillian concluded, putting her hand on her hips and ending the conversation.

"How are we getting in?" Mickey asked, pointing to the charred remains of the woods that once hid Thorn's house and the compound.

Jack glared back at Mickey for being so negative.

Jillian sighed. "Never know till we try, right?" Jillian pulled Jack along towards the woods.

"I will get started on the grave," Mickey yelled as he walked off in the other direction.

"About time he does something useful," Jack grumbled. "This whole trip he has been doing nothing except complaining."

"He has been a little grumpy today," Jillian admitted. "It's not as if it was our fault that the pharmacy had already been raided."

"Yeah, who took a poop in his litter box?" Jack teased, nudging his sister with his elbow in an attempt to lighten the mood and distract them from the task at hand.

"And, like, I got a ton of new makeup. So it wasn't a total loss," Jillian said, adopting her pampered princess voice as she held out a hand to show off her newly painted fingernails.

Jack rolled his eyes dramatically and smiled. "Who would have thought that people wouldn't be worried about makeup at the end of the world? That's the problem with people these days, they are all focused on stuff like food and water. Doesn't anyone care about beauty anymore?"

"Hey, we could totally give each other makeovers tonight!" Jillian squealed, jumping up and down in mock excitement. "Do your hair. Oh, like I picked up this wine lipstick that would totally go great with your eyes."

Jack looked over at his sister, trying desperately to keep his face stern. "You are not putting makeup on me."

"You didn't complain last month." Jillian smiled impishly as she twirled a finger through her hair, trying to look innocent.

Jack knew she was baiting him into bringing up last month, when she played makeover while he was sleeping. He walked around camp all day with them laughing at him before Mickey finally told him to wash his face, showing him what Jillian had done in a little hand mirror they found a few weeks before. He mockingly glared at her out of the corner of his eye, trying not to laugh. "Never going to happen again."

"Is that a challenge?" Jillian shoved Jack playfully. "Cause you are so waking up looking like a cl—" Jillian stopped midsentence and pulled her gun at the sound of someone running up behind them.

"I think our job is already done," Mickey yelled from a little way off.

Both Jillian and Jack turned and saw him pointing down to where the statue had fallen.

"What do you mean?" Jillian slid her gun back into its holster as Mickey just motioned them to come look. They followed him back to where two wooden crosses stuck out of the ground right beside the statue. Jack looked around, wondering how he could have missed them when they pulled up.

"Who would have done this?" Jillian asked, her voice barely above a whisper, as if now afraid that someone was watching them and could hear what they said.

Jack knelt down beside the first grave and smiled to himself as tears streamed down his face. "Whoever did it carved Grandma on it." He traced the crudely carved letters with his fingers. He hadn't even imagined this scenario when he thought about coming back to the graveyard to finish the mission they had set out to do so many months ago.

"This one says Caleo A," Jillian cried, kneeling next to the other grave marker. Mickey knelt down beside her, gently pulling her into his arms, where she buried her face in his jacket.

It's probably because they didn't know how to spell Anima. Jack felt Mickey's hand grab and tighten on his shoulder, as if offering his support. Annoyed, Jack shrugged it off. "I don't—" Jack was going to say he didn't want his support, but stopped when the hand smacked him hard on the back of the head.

Angry, Jack snapped his head towards Mickey, but before he could get a word out he noticed Mickey darting his eyes back and forth from the road back to him. Catching the hint, Jack nodded and mouthed, "How many?"

Mickey slowly patted four fingers gently on Jillian's back as she continued to cry into his coat, her back heaving up and down in her grief.

"Did they notice us yet?" Jack mouthed and Mickey nodded slowly. Jack thought about their options. *What if they are just refugees and need help? Then they would have either hidden or called out to us. The roads were empty on the way, we didn't see any sign of anyone. Maybe this is an ambush party.* Jack looked at the back of his sister's sobbing head. *I can't let them touch her. Wait, why does Mickey only have three fingers held up? Are there three people now?* Mickey lowered another finger so only two remained up. *I don't understand.* Jack's thoughts were interrupted by two rapid gun shots as Mickey dove to the right, grabbing him by the back of his sweatshirt and shoving him down behind the nearest headstone. Jillian shot a third time, shattering the passenger side window of the truck before ducking behind the fallen statue.

"Who are you and what do you want?" Jillian yelled toward the men as they all took shelter behind the truck.

"Drifters! We heard there was a refugee camp in Butler, and we were on our way there!" a deep-voiced man yelled back as two rifle barrels appeared over the bed of the truck.

"You guys are a long way from Butler. It's at least a day's walk!" Jillian replied, taking aim over the shoulder of the statue.

"We have been walking a lot longer than that," one of the men was saying as Jack heard the driver side door of the truck creek open.

"They're going to steal our truck," Jack murmured in disbelief, turning back to Jillian who was giving him a look that said 'this is all your fault' before turning her attention back to the men, just as a gun shot hit the statue beside her.

"I could be at home, laying in my bed and reading one of the books we brought home on our last shopping trip. But no, you drag me out here in the cold to get our truck stolen," Jillian yelled at Jack before firing two shots in the direction of the truck. Jack cringed as one man screamed in agony. Quickly he peeked around the tombstone and saw a man lying on the ground behind the truck, holding his ankle as blood poured through his fingers. Jack looked back at Jillian just as she pulled the trigger again, and another man fell to the ground clutching his leg.

The truck roared to life, lurching forward a few feet before stalling. Jack looked back at Jillian, who nodded her approval as if knowing what he was thinking. He jumped over the headstone, running for the truck as fast as he could. Jillian fired another shot into the truck bed as the truck struggled to start.

Good, he flooded the engine, Jack thought as he quickly hurled himself into the truck bed, took two steps, jumped off the other side, and stomped down on a man that was ducked behind the tire holding a rifle. The man collapsed to the ground as the truck started again. A small blur of fur darted past Jack and leapt into the bed of the truck.

Through the side mirror, the man behind the wheel saw Jack beside the truck and slammed on the gas. The truck peeled out, sending stones spewing out behind it as it tore off down the road. Jack went to run after him, but a gunshot got his attention. One of the bleeding men at his feet crumpled to the ground, dead, his gun hitting the pavement by Jack's feet.

"Keep your head in the game!" Jillian yelled from the behind him.

"Right," Jack agreed to himself and took stock of the other two men. The man he landed on was unconscious—or at least really good at faking it—his rifle was at his feet and Jack quickly picked it up. The other man was crawling away, leaving a trail of blood behind him on the cement sidewalk. Jack aimed the rifle at the man trying to escape. "You can just stop right there," Jack said forcefully, secretly proud of himself for sounding like a bad ass.

The man looked back, tears streaming down his face. "I'm sorry. All we wanted was the truck. We weren't going to hurt you. Please don't kill me."

Jack took a step closer. Stopping, he tilted his head to the side and looked at the man. "Mr. Thomas?" Jack asked in shock. Behind the scraggy beard and matted hair, he recognized his gym teacher as the man begging for his life.

The man questionably stared at him, causing Jack to shake his head, thinking he must have made a mistake. The Mr. Thomas he knew was a brute who enjoyed tormenting students he thought were weak.

The man happily smiled up at Jack in recognition. "You must have been one of my students."

"It's me, Jack," he said, lowering his gun. He was excited about seeing someone he knew from before this began, even if it was someone he didn't necessarily like.

Mr. Thomas looked at Jack blankly for a moment, but his smile returned a second later. "Sorry, I can't remember all my students. It's been months and I have had so many of you." His eyes flickered between Jack and the gun, as if at any moment he was going to jump for it.

"Jack Barely," Jack stated, his excitement extinguished as he took a step back, deflated that Mr. Thomas didn't even know who he was.

"Oh, swimming Jack. I hardly recognize you, with the scars and—" Mr. Thomas stopped talking, seeing Jack tense up as he remembered his scars. "And this beautiful angel must be your sister Jillian. I can see these times have had no effect on your beauty," he added quickly, sitting up at Jillian's approach.

Motioning to the man bleeding on the ground, Jack smiled at his sister. "Jillian, this is Mr. Thomas. You know, the—"

Jillian cut him off with one of her death looks, and Jack could tell she didn't give a rat's ass who the man was. She turned and glared down at the man. "My makeup and clothes were in the truck, you better hope comes it back, or so help you I will strip you naked, tie you to a tree and leave you here to die." She waved her handgun in the man's face. "ARRRH!" she screamed as she turned to Jack. "Why the hell would you leave the truck with the keys in it? How stupid can you be?"

"Don't look at me. Talk to your love kitten, he is the one who drove it here," Jack snapped back getting in his sister's face.

Defeated, Jillian let out a breath. "Well hopefully he will bring the truck back soon. Until then, we are stuck babysitting these two." Jillian looked down at Mr. Thomas, shaking her head at his sad attempt to crawl away while they weren't paying attention. "Do you really think you're getting away just because I'm not looking right at you?" Jillian aimed her gun at Mr. Thomas again and he stopped in his tracks. "Tie him up before he wakes up," Jillian said, nodding towards the other man at Jack's feet.

☽✳☾

"How long are we going to wait for Mickey before we start walking home? We've been sitting here for hours." Giving up his pacing, Jack sat on the sidewalk Indian-style with his chin resting in his hands.

Jillian desperately stared toward the road that the truck had disappeared down and sighed. "We'll just sit tight till morning. It'll be dark soon. It's not like we have a flashlight or anything to go wandering around in the dark with."

"I'm bleeding out over here!" Mr. Thomas yelled from somewhere behind them, but Jack didn't even bother to turn around. He knew Jillian was too upset with the man for shooting at them and stealing the truck to let Jack help him.

"All night?" Jack asked, pretending not to hear the man crying behind him. "I am bored out of my mind!" He got to his feet, unable to sit there listening. Pacing back and forth, he kept stealing glances at the men when Jillian wasn't looking. "Maybe I should go check out the compound for any supplies."

"Stop!" Jillian yelled, grabbing Jack and forcing him to stop pacing. "You're not going to leave me here with these two. Mickey will be back any minute and we will head home together." She glanced back down the road as if saying it out loud would make it come true.

"Don't worry, sis, I'm sure he just pulled over and got high on catnip. He'll be back as soon as he sobers up a little," Jack said, smiling as he looked at his sister hoping that the jab at her boyfriend would distract her. When she shot him one of her death stares, Jack quickly changed the subject. "So what are we going to do with these two?" Jack poked the tied up Mr. Thomas in the gut with the tip of the rifle.

"Well, we can't very well take them with us," Jillian snapped, as if she thought Jack was an idiot for asking.

"So you want me to shoot them now?" Jack asked, faking excitement to annoy his sister as he aimed his gun toward his captives.

"Please, God, no!" Mr. Thomas begged, his words muffled through a gag that Jack had made by shoving the man's own dirty sock in his mouth and securing it with a scrap of his shirt.

"I thought I told you if you said another word I was going to shoot you in the arm so you would quit complaining about your leg," Jack said, placing the barrel of the gun flat against Mr. Thomas's bicep.

Mr. Thomas started crying, his face scrunched up and his lower lip quivering as he waited for the shot. Jack couldn't help smiling down at the helpless man as he pictured him laughing when Mike pantsed Caleo during a co-ed volleyball game during his class. Jack's eyes drifted and focused on Caleo's grave in the distance.

"Jack, quit playing with the captives," Jillian said, scolding her brother and bringing his attention back to the man at the end of the gun. When Jack pulled the gun away and the captives seemed to let out their breath, Jillian added with an air of royalty, "If you are going to shoot them, at least take them into the woods a little, so we don't have to smell them while we wait."

Jack smiled weakly at his sister's sad attempt at sadistic humor. "And you call me a dork." He laid the gun down beside Jillian, suddenly wanting to be alone somewhere. He wanted to run away, run until his lungs burned and his legs couldn't bear his weight. He shook his head, knowing he couldn't leave Jillian alone. He walked towards a large tree near the edge of the cemetery where he would be able to look at Caleo's grave and cry without Jillian seeing him.

Jillian picked up the gun and got to her feet. "Where are you going?"

"I'm going to sleep before it gets too dark. You get first watch. If they move, shoot them, but try to do it quietly." Sitting down by the tree, Jack leaned back, looking up between its branches at the sky.

"Jack, wait!" Jillian hissed

Jack rolled over and looked up at his sister annoyed.

"I hear a car," Jillian said. Jack could tell by her voice that although she was cautioning him to get out of sight, she was also excited that it could be Mickey.

"What about them?" Jack asked, looking towards the two men tied up just off the road. He ran over and joined his sister, who was crouched down behind a few low bushes.

"No time." Jillian grabbed Jack's arm and pulled him down next to her just as a truck came into view.

"It's our truck!" Jillian said excitedly and went to stand up, but Jack held her firmly in place.

"But is it our cat? Wait till it gets closer, it's too dark to see who is driving it," Jack whispered, praying that it was Mickey behind the wheel so he could finally get out of this place.

As the truck got closer, Jack could see Mickey's long black hair blowing in the wind. He let his sister go and went to follow her, but decided that he didn't want to look too happy to see Mickey, so he adopted a casual demeanor and meandered over. He looked up to see Jillian standing at the passenger window, just as she started giggling like a school girl. Jack shrugged, not wanting to know what Mickey did to get one of his sister's fake embarrassed laughs.

When the engine cut off and Mickey climbed out of the driver seat, Jack yelled, "Great, it's going to take months to get all the cat hair out of the seat."

"I think that's going to be the least of your issues," Mickey retorted. As he strutted around the corner, Jack saw he was stark naked.

"God!" Jack said, shaking his head as he turned his back so he wouldn't have to look at Mickey. "Now I'm going to have to scrub the truck and bleach this image out of my head. Couldn't you at least put a pair of underwear on?"

"Remind me next time I have to jump on a runaway truck as a cat to tie a pair of shorts around my neck first," Mickey said sarcastically as he jogged down the road a bit and started looking behind gravestones mumbling, "I think I shifted around here somewhere."

"Dear?" Jillian yelled, waving her hands to get his attention. Jack snapped her a sideways glare. He hated the fact that she seemed to be madly in love with Mickey, even though she had only known him for a little over three months. "I have your clothes." Laughing, she looked back at Jack and stuck out her tongue.

"If Grandma knew you were sleeping with him under her roof, she would tear your butt up," Jack hissed, crossing his arms over his chest. He attempted to avert his gaze from the approaching Mickey, but when his eyes fell on Caleo's grave he shook his head and decided to glare at the ground by his feet instead.

"Well, I guess it's good her roof burned up. We're more under a tarp than a roof now," she snapped back tartly.

"It's still her house," Jack mumbled, feeling stung by her words. He turned around, wanting to say more, but his words stuck in his throat as he came face to face with Mr. Thomas, who had picked up the rifle and was now aiming it at Jack's chest.

Jack started to back up, but Mr. Thomas stopped him by raising the gun to point at Jack's head. "Now, I don't want to kill you, but I will if I have to. We need a place to stay, and being you have a place I think we can work something out. What do you say, Jack … friends?"

"If you wanted to be friends, pointing a gun at me isn't helping," Jack said smartly, his eyes darting around, looking for a way out of the situation.

"You're the one who threatened us first," Mr. Thomas snapped, shaking the gun to remind Jack who was in charge.

"You were going to steal our truck!" Jack yelled angrily.

Mr. Thomas's face turned purple as he growled, "And you killed two of my group."

"Wah, wah, I don't care," Mickey said. Walking up beside Jack he shoved the rifle barrel aside and grabbed Mr. Thomas's arm with his exposed left hand. Instantly Mr. Thomas fell to the ground, and Mickey turned to Jack with an annoyed look on his face. "Now either shoot the other or cut him loose." His face instantly changed to a smile as he turned to Jillian and took his clothes. "Thanks, babe."

"Can you watch the truck for a minute?" Jillian asked Mickey as she grabbed Jack by the arm and pulled him away, not waiting for a response. "Let's go say our goodbyes, then we've got to go." Reluctantly Jack followed, keeping a watchful eye as Jillian pulled him down the street away from the graveyard.

Confused, Jack dug his heels in and pulled them to a stop. "Where are we going?"

"It's getting colder out, and soon getting away from the house will be impossible. I know this is one of the reasons you needed to come up here so bad. We're going to the cliff," Jillian said softly, as if she was a kindergarten teacher explaining that the class hamster had died.

Jack yanked his arm free of Jillian's grasp as he fought off a panic attack at the mere thought of the cliff. "Why?"

"Jack, you need some closure." Jillian gently hugged her brother, who remained stiff. "Please." Taking his hand again, she started to pull him towards the cliff.

"He's in the ground, buried. What is me seeing the ..." Jack stopped, unable to say the word. "What's the point?"

"Jack," Jillian said in a low, firm voice. "You need to—"

"No!" Shaking his head, Jack yanked his hand free and backed away. "I can't. I'm not ready not yet." He ran back to the truck, climbing inside. Without saying a word, he slammed the door shut and stared out the window. He heard Mickey ask Jillian if everything was okay, but didn't hear her answer. A few moments later, Jillian climbed into the center seat and grabbed his hand, intertwining their fingers like she had always done since the day their parents died.

"I'm sorry," she whispered.

Jack could tell she was crying by the sound of her voice, but he didn't care. *Let her cry, she shouldn't have tried to force me to go,* he thought bitterly.

"What do you want to do with this guy?" Mickey asked, poking his head through the driver's side window.

Jack saw Jillian looking at him for direction through the reflection in the glass, but didn't respond.

After a long moment, she turned away and said, "Just cut him loose and let's go home."

☽ ✳ ☾

Mickey pulled the truck onto the long driveway that led back to where the Purple Rose Inn used to stand. Now all that remained were a few exposed concrete blocks, a pile of burn scared wood, and debris with tarps stretched out over the top of it. Jack sighed when he looked up at the mess that was once his home. He hadn't said a word to anyone the whole way back to what was now their house, even though Jillian kept glancing in his direction looking for forgiveness.

The second the truck stopped next to the house, Jack pushed open the door and jumped out. "I'm going for a walk. I will be back later," he called over his shoulder. Not waiting for an answer, he took off for the woods. Running full force, he let the tree branches whip him as he went. Out of breath, Jack collapsed under a tree. Curling into a ball, he bawled.

2

"Boys, let's go. Mike is going to be here any minute and Grandma wants a picture before we go." Jack smiled at the frantic sound of his sister Jillian's voice calling up from the bottom of the stairs. *Drama queen as always.* He examined himself in the mirror. Straightening his tie, he was glad he decided to go with a formal tux. "Damn I look good!"

"How do you tie this stupid thing?" Jack turned around to see Caleo toss his tie across the room as he plopped down on the bed, crossing his arms over his chest in defeat.

"Don't pout." Jack picked up the tie off the floor and straightened it out in his hands.

Caleo lay back on the bed, looking up at the ceiling. "I don't know why I even let you talk me into going to this stupid dance. I am going to look like a fool." He looked up at Jack, his eyes pleading to let him stay home.

"Because I don't want you staying home and pouting the whole time about how you wish you would could have gone. It will be fun, you'll see," Jack said, wrapping Caleo's tie around his own neck and effortlessly tying a perfect full Windsor knot. "Up." He motioned for Caleo to get to his feet.

"You won't even see me. You'll be on the dance floor with Marcy Cobben all night." Caleo stood up and Jack slipped the tie over his head, adjusting it for him. "Or maybe behind the bleachers?" Caleo raised a single white eyebrow.

"There!" Jack said. Ignoring the question, he grabbed Caleo's arm and pulled him to the bathroom to stand in front of the mirror. "We're going to be the hottest studs at the dance." He smoothed down Caleo's collar and stepped back.

"I look ridiculous." Caleo turned to the side to get a profile view, then met Jack's eyes in the mirror. "White hair doesn't look good in a black suit. Look, it already looks like we have a cat." He pulled a white hair off his pants and held it up for Jack to see. "I'm not going."

"First off, it's a tuxedo; we paid good money to look this amazing. Second, I think the white hair makes you look mysteriously handsome."

Caleo looked at himself in the mirror again, turning every which way to get a better look. Then he made eye contact with Jack in the mirror, smiling with his intense blue eyes. "Really? Mysteriously handsome?"

Jack looked away nervously. "Yeah." He hesitated, not sure why he suddenly felt awkward about giving Caleo a compliment. "Now if only we could do something about that nose. I'm sure Jillian has something in her makeup kit that might help. If she can paint her ugly face into a masterpiece every day, I'm sure she—" Jack froze as he looked up and saw the hurt in Caleo's blue eyes reflected in the mirror. *What have I done, why did I say that. He looks great, amazing even. I should tell him I'm only kidding.*

"You think my face is a masterpiece?" Jillian asked, standing in the doorway to Caleo's bedroom in her long, white strapless gown.

Jack cringed at the amount of cleavage the dress revealed and had to fight not to go into overly-protective brother mode. "No, I said you can paint a masterpiece over that scaly snake skin you've got."

A horn honked in the driveway signaling Mike's arrival, and Jillian ran to the window and looked out. "Were twins you dumbass, we pretty much look alike."

"You're just jealous because I'm the beautiful one." Smiling, Jack ran his hand over his short, buzzed hair.

"Beautiful? You wish you looked this good in a dress." Jillian twirled around so that the pearl sequins caught the light and shimmered.

"Don't we have a photo of that somewhere already?" Caleo chimed in and smiled back at Jack through the mirror.

"I was seven, and it was Halloween."

"Eight! And it was the middle of June," Jillian corrected as she made her way back to the door.

"Whatever. You're the one that forced me to do it," Jack said, sticking his tongue out at Jillian.

She rolled her eyes. "Forced? You asked for the pink dress because, and I quote, 'yellow makes my brown eyes look too big'."

"You're wrong. I definitely remember wearing the yellow one," Jack argued.

Caleo snickered and Jack turned back to him. "What are you laughing at? You are the one who was wearing the pink dress."

"I know where the photo is. I can prove you were the one in pink." Jillian smiled impishly, drumming her fingers on the doorframe as if waiting for Jack to challenge her.

"Let's go! I'd like to get a picture before you go, and Jack you're going to be late picking up Marcy if you don't hurry." They all rolled their eyes and turned to the door at the sound of Grandma calling from the bottom of the stairs.

Jillian started to leave, but stopped and poked her head back in. "I will deny this even under torture if you ever mention it, but that being said, you two actually look really dashing in those suits. Like you're secret agents or something."

Caleo went to follow Jillian out, but Jack grabbed his arm, pulling him to a stop.

"What?" Caleo said, turning to face Jack with a confused and irritated look on his face.

Jack sucker punched Caleo in the shoulder. "You laughed at her joke."

Caleo sucker punched him back. "So did you," he said, his white smile and bright blue eyes lighting up his face.

"Oh you think that's funny?" Jack poked Caleo with his index finger in the gut. He bowed in protectively as he backed away, his smile growing bigger. Jack advanced, poking him again and again.

"Don't, we're going to get wrinkled," Caleo protested as he backed away, his hands held up defensively, but Jack could tell by the smile on his face that he didn't really care about wrinkling his clothes.

"Don't, we're going to get wrinkled," Jack mocked as he took a step closer and made a jab with his finger, but Caleo smacked his hand away and backed out of reach.

"Jack, Caleo! Don't make me come back up there and drag your butts down here. I'd hate for you to be crying in the photos," Jillian's voice yelled from the bottom of the stairs and Jack looked towards the door a little disappointed.

"We will have to continue this later!" Stepping back, Jack slid his pointer fingers into his pockets as if putting away his weapons. Caleo took off for the door in a mad dash, slugging Jack playfully in the arm as he passed by. "You wore the yellow dress."

Jack rubbed the sting from his shoulder as he picked up his tuxedo jacket from the dresser and slid it on. Smiling, he picked up Caleo's and walked out of the room.

When he got to the bottom of the stairs Jack saw Jillian standing in front of the mirror that hung in the den, struggling to clasp a necklace around her neck.

"Need help?" Jack asked, tossing the coat on the back of a chair and walking up behind her.

Jillian lifted her hair off the back of her neck with one hand as she handed Jack the necklace. "Mike gave it to me. Isn't it beautiful?"

Jack looked down at the necklace, running his fingers across the golden snowflake pendent. *It must be nice to have rich parents so you can buy your girlfriend things,* Jack thought bitterly. He looked up to see his sister's face glowing with happiness, and shoved his bitter thoughts away. "It's very nice." He clasped the necklace and whispered, "Be careful tonight. If you need me, I will be nearby."

"This isn't my first dance. I don't need my little brother looking out for me." Jillian smiled at Jack through the mirror.

"I was born first, I'm the big brother." Jack smiled back, knowing their familiar game.

"I got you beat by two inches tonight, bro." Jillian raised the hem of her dress up and flashed her high heels. "Now who is jealous?"

"I told Caleo I should have worn platforms," Jack mumbled playfully.

"I can see the new fashion craze starting now. All the guys in school would be strutting around in four-inch platforms by Monday."

"You're just jealous that I would be taller than you," Jack jabbed. "Besides, you're already wider, why not let you have taller as well?" Jack jumped back as Jillian made a swing for his arm and missed.

She went to take another swing, but stopped and adopted an innocent look as Grandma walked out of the kitchen carrying the camera. "All right, everyone around the chair for the picture."

The second Grandma's back was to them, Jillian slugged Jack in the shoulder as she went to follow Grandma to the chair.

"You look beautiful. Mom would have been in tears," Jack whispered so only she could hear.

Turning, Jillian hugged her brother. Then she stepped back and wiped a tear away from Jack's eye with her thumb, hugging him again. "Okay, princess, your mascara is going to run."

"It's because you hit like a dude," Jack said, rubbing his shoulder for effect.

He had just turned to head for the chair when Caleo burst from the kitchen. "Forget it, I'm not going!" he yelled as he stormed past Jack, heading for the stairs that led up to his bed room.

"Caleo! Get your rear-end back down here right now!" Grandma yelled, pointing at the chair. "I will get a picture of all of you together if I have to call the taxidermist to do it."

"Yeah, albino boy, quit your pouting and let's get this picture over with," Mike said as he walked out of the kitchen and over to the chair. Once there, he took a seat on the armrest beside Jillian.

"Michel Karr!" Grandma snapped her fingers and pointed to the front door. "Out of my house." She snapped her fingers again. "Right now. I might not be able to whoop you, but I don't have to listen that stuff in my house."

"I thought we were going to do pictures." Mike looked up at Grandma with a dumb look on his face, then back to Jillian for support. Jack smiled, knowing that his grandmother didn't let anyone pick on Caleo about being so pale while she was near.

"I want pictures of my grandkids, not the losers they dated in high school," she said, pointing at the door again. "You know the rules, I don't care who you are outside of this house, but in here there will be no mean-spirited bullying. Learn to mind your manners before you set foot in this house again."

"I didn't mean anything by it. I was just playing, honest. I'm sorry if I offended you, Miss Ratter." Mike slowly got up and walked to the door.

"Michel Karr, don't you play me. I'm not the one you offended. You apologize to Caleo and you can stay," Grandma said, crossing her arms in front of her chest.

Mike turned to Caleo, his back to Grandma, but Jack could see his evil smile as he smoothly said, "I'm sorry, please forgive me for being rude. It won't happen again."

There was a long pause as Caleo glared at Mike from the bottom of the stairs, his fingers wrapped around the railing in a death grip.

"Caleo?" Grandma tapped her foot on the floor impatiently.

"Apology accepted," Caleo said through gritted teeth, looking like he was about to cry.

"Good, now get over here and let's get a few photos before you all go to the dance," Grandma said excitedly, but Jack kept his eyes on Mike as he continued to smile devilishly up at Caleo.

"Maybe I will see you at the dance tonight, and we could hang out a little." Mike nodded at Caleo, his smile hinting that he was planning on doing more than just saying hello to Caleo at the dance.

Jack took a step toward Mike, challenging him. Mike just shrugged, breaking his stare down with Caleo as he walked over to sit beside Jillian again.

Two can play this game. Jack looked over at Caleo, who looked like he was ready to get sick, and winked with what he hoped would be a reassuring smile on his face. "Maybe we can all hang out after the dance. You know, just the four of us."

"I don't know, we kind of had plans. There is this party at the cave tonight. Didn't Marcy tell you? I could swear she said she would be there."

"Excuse me?" Grandma asked, looking at Mike for more of an explanation. When none came, she said, "The dance is over at ten, and I expect all of you home by ten-thirty. Not a second later."

Jillian's head snapped in Jack's direction, and she glared at him with one of her looks like she was trying to stop his heart by thought alone. Jack knew he was going to regret it later.

"Okay, okay," Grandma said impatiently, "you boys in the back, Jillian sit in the chair." Mike, Jack and Caleo all took up position behind Jillian and Jack made sure to stand between Mike and Caleo.

"Wait, wouldn't it be cool if we all wore sunglasses," Jack said excitedly as he pulled out the black sunglasses that were hanging from his pocket, and slid them on.

"Hell, yeah! Like secret service agents." Mike patted his pockets, looking for his glasses. "Shit, I got mine in my car. Hold on, I'll be right back."

"Michel, language!" Grandma yelled, but Mike was already running to his car to get his glasses.

The second Jack heard the door close, he pulled another pair of glasses from his pocket and tossed them to Caleo before running to the front door and locking it.

"Whose are these?" Caleo held them up and looked through the black lenses.

Jack smiled as Jillian turned around and saw them, then whipped her head around to look at Jack a big smile on her face. "Those are Mike's, you thief."

Jack clapped his hands together happily. "Now, who's ready for this picture?" Jack took his place behind the chair, beside a now smiling Caleo. "Let's do this." He held up his hands in the shape of a gun aimed at the sky and turned sideways. Looking over his shoulder, he saw Caleo had done the same and looked like he was having the time of his life.

There was a pounding at the door, but everyone ignored it and smiled for the camera as Grandma said, "Say cheese!"

Jack tore his eyes away from the picture of the three of them all dressed up, posing as a happy family, and looked up at the darkening night sky, letting his tears fall. In the three months since they had gotten home, nothing had changed. Sure, he has gotten used to the life of little modern comforts, but the pain of losing Caleo never seemed to numb the way everyone said it would. *Caleo, I wish I could have told you how much I loved you, how I really felt about you.* Frustrated, he broke a branch off a nearby tree and threw it to the ground. A cat's meow drew his attention, and he looked up to see Mickey walking up in his all black kitten form.

"Can't I even get a moment's peace?" Reaching up, Jack grabbed a branch from the apple tree he was under and pulled himself to his feet. Turning, he greeted Mickey, "What do you want?"

Mickey meowed again and turned around before trotting off back in the direction of the house.

Jack sighed, knowing that Jillian had sent Mickey to fetch him. "What? Timmy's trapped in a well?" Mickey turned around, hissing at Jack before running off. As Jack left the woods and entered the apple orchard, he saw the crumpled remains of his home. What used to be the two-story Purple Rose Inn that his adoptive grandmother owned, was now a pile of burnt rubble with tarps strapped over the top to keep the rain out of the basement they now lived in. Jack had started to clean off some of the burnt debris in an attempt to rebuild some kind of life here, but removing any piece of what was once his home felt pointless and depressing. He hated it here, he hated staying in the damp basement, he hated waking up every morning going outside to be reminded of everything that he had lost, and he especially hated the fact that even as he passed a rotting apple on the ground he was reminded of Caleo. Jack paused, staring down at the apple and thinking back to the last time him and Caleo played a game of smear. How he and Caleo embraced their grandmother in a sticky hug and she chased them to the back yard to hose off.

"Jack." Jack looked up at the sound of his sister hissing his name. She was crouched behind the crumpled remains of the house, looking down the half mile driveway to the street that passes their house.

Not again. Didn't we just deal with the guys at the cemetery? There should be some kind of rule against having to deal with two groups of outsiders in the same week. Knowing the drill, Jack ran to his sister's side and crouched down beside her. He looked down the driveway to see it empty, then looked at his sister. Not even bothering to whisper, he asked, "What is going on?"

Jillian whispered her response, but the October wind drowned her voice out.

Jack rolled his eyes. "There is at least a half mile between whatever is out there and us. Whispering is just stupid."

Irritated, Jillian glared up at her brother. "Fine, Stinky said that there are people coming."

Jack smiled at his sister for using the name she gave Mickey before they knew he was actually a Leech and not just a kitten. "He's in cat form he can't talk." Jack looked over at the kitten, who had taken up post in a tree a few yards away. "Maybe he was just telling you he wants his cat food warmed up tonight."

Jillian's glare turned furious, and Jack took a step back out of reach. "You know damn well he wouldn't have transformed if it wasn't important." Jillian jumped at the sound of a distant voice and turned her attention back to the road. "Do you think they will just pass by?" she whispered softly.

"The last guys didn't," Jack said flatly as Jillian pulled up a rifle and aimed through the scope towards the end of the driveway. "We don't even know if these guys are looking for trouble. Maybe it's just someone who needs help."

"The last time we let someone get close enough to find out, it ended up with me tied to a tree and you knocked out."

"Yeah, but your attack cat saved the day. Besides, that only happened once." Jack pulled his handgun from its holster as he smiled at Jillian's back.

"Once? I think we are on the fourth or fifth time now, brother," she hissed, putting extra venom in the word 'brother'.

"Those other times neither of us got hurt," Jack retorted, peering around Jillian to see the road was still empty.

Jillian whipped around to face her brother. "They stole our supplies!" she said, almost shouting.

"But if I remember right, you chased them down and got every can back, plus my handgun." Jack smiled, having successfully goaded his sister into a frenzy.

Jillian sighed and turned her attention back to the road. "This is not a game, grow up, someone can get killed." She looked back over her shoulder. "I killed people, Jack." Then her walls came down and Jack could see the fear she was trying to hide. "I can't lose you."

Jack reached out for her, but she turned her attention back to the road just as a man came into view through the break in the trees at the end of the driveway. Jack took a crouching step closer to Jillian and whispered, "Easy. Don't shoot, we don't know how many there are and they may just keep walking. Hopefully we won't have to fight."

"I know, I know," Jillian said, waving him away like a fly buzzing around her head.

Jack chuckled to himself. *Who is she kidding? This is the only fun we have to look forward to.* He slowly made his way around the house, ducking behind their newly constructed outhouse. He couldn't see the end of the road from this position, but if they stepped into the yard or if someone tried to sneak up through the woods, he would spot them. He looked up at the tree that Mickey was in, and the cat was looking right at him as if he wanted to tell him something. Slowly, Mickey scratched at the bark, making the movements seem deliberate. Jack shook his head in confusion wondering what Mickey was trying to say.

Frustrated, Jack waved Mickey's efforts away. He looked back down the road. He could hear the sound of at least four men talking. A stone hit the side of the outhouse by Jack's feet, and he snapped his attention to Jillian who pointed in the direction of the road, holding up five fingers. Jack nodded as a movement caught his attention. Standing up to get a better look, he noticed four more men wearing uniforms, slowly creeping up through the orchard and carrying automatic rifles. He raised his gun, looking through the scope. *Army or Blessed?* Jack squinted, trying to see if they had a small golden ring symbolizing that they were part of the Blessed army; an elite group of soldiers both Leech and human, sworn to protect the Angel or leader of the Leeches.

Jillian looked over her shoulder and back at Jack. The look on her face was pure panic as she slung her rifle over her shoulder and ran for Jack in a sprint. "Run, you idiot!" she screamed as she grabbed him by the arm, dragging him off into the woods.

Jack looked back over his shoulder to see the four uniformed men had given up their sneak approach and now were running up the hill toward the house. *I have to think.* Jack looked around the woods, trying to get his bearings. *We're not going to out run them.*

"They're going to out run us," Jillian said, echoing Jacks thoughts as he tried to come up with a solution. "Jack!" she yelled, frantic when he didn't acknowledge.

Jack tuned her out; he knew he didn't have much time. *Hide, we need to hide. Or better yet …* Jack pulled Jillian to a halt. Jillian just looked at him confused. "This way." He pulled her to the left and they ran about twenty feet. Then he pulled her to the right abruptly and they kept running.

"Wait, we are here to help!" a man called out behind them.

Jack looked back at the men. They were close enough to shoot, but they didn't; they were just chasing after them. *Just a few more feet.* Jack smiled, coming to a stop as he heard the resounding crack of one of his pitfall traps doing its job. "Told you the pitfall trap would come in handy!" Jack shouted as he jumped into the air, raising his fist to the sky in celebration.

"You spent two weeks digging a hole in the middle of the woods telling me you were digging a swimming pool," Jillian said, gasping in the cold autumn air as she leaned against a nearby tree.

"Well there is about a foot of water and mud down there."

Jillian grabbed her rifle off her back, aiming it at the hole as if expecting one of the soldiers to jump the nine feet out of the hole and attack them. "Just shut up and let's see who these guys are."

As they cautiously approached the hole, Jack called out, "Who are you and what do you want?"

"Really? That's the best you could come up with? Like they're really going to tell us they are going to kill us and steal our food," Jillian whispered, but Jack swatted her away.

"And what would you have asked?"

There was a long pause of hushed whispers from the hole as Jack crept closer, before one of the men answered, "We are just tracking a couple of escaped criminals."

"It looked to me like you were sneaking up on us." Jack picked up a rock the size of his fist and tossed it to the ground beside the hole. Two gunshots fired and the trees above lost some leaves.

Jack waited in silence for a moment, letting the tension build as he listened to their movement. "I have two grenades. You got five seconds to throw your guns up or you're dead."

Jack waited, smiling as the first head peeked over the edge. "He is—" A gunshot rang out, and red exploded from the uniformed man's shoulder as he fell back into the hole. Jack looked back at his sister, surprised, but she just shrugged and stared down the barrel of her rifle waiting for the next one to appear. "Jillian!" Jack hissed. "They could be with the US Army. What if they are here to help?"

"We're not playing games, Jack!" Jillian yelled, but Jack couldn't tell if she was really talking to him or just putting on a show for the soldiers in the hole. "Either they do what I say when I say or I am going to kill them! It's as simple as that."

Jack cringed at the cold steel in Jillian's voice. *What would Caleo think of Jillian's transformation from pampered princess to ruthless queen?* he wondered, then realized that it was probably losing both Caleo and their grandmother that pushed her over the edge.

"Toss your guns out of the hole, and any kind of knives, blades, or other weapons you may have. God help you if I even feel the slightest hint of intuition that you are holding anything back." Jillian stepped in front of Jack and knelt to the ground, motioning for Jack to do the same, but he just nodded and got behind a large oak tree. "I said nothing about counting, do it now!" Jillian shot at the dirt by the hole just to emphases her point.

"Okay, don't shoot," a man yelled and four automatic rifles flew over the edge, landing just out of reach of the hole, followed by their gun clips.

Smart move taking the ammo out, that way we can't just run up and use their weapons against them. Jack looked over at Jillian, waiting for her to tell him to do just that, but she just stared at the ground above the hole.

"Okay, lady, let us out so we can talk," one of the men yelled again.

Jack watched as Jillian seemed to nod to herself. "I said all the weapons!"

There was a short pause and a few handguns and knives flew out of the hole, landing in a pile.

"You think that is it?" Jack looked down at his sister who glanced up into the trees then back to the hole. "Nope, they're hiding something."

"How do you know?" Jack peeked around the corner of the tree. He couldn't see inside the hole at all from where he was standing, so there was no way she was able to. He looked up into the trees, then back down to the hole and shook his head. Slight movement drew his attention back up to see a tiny black kitten sitting on a branch just overlooking the hole. "You speak cat?"

"Jack, I'm not starting this again. Mickey is clearly shaking his head no, as in no it's not safe."

"How do you know he is not shaking his head as in are there any more weapons?" Jack shook his head to emphasize his point. "Nnnnooo."

"I know," Jillian said with a smile as she pointed to the kitten again.

"Is he sticking his tongue out at me?" Jack pointed to Mickey high in the tree and Jillian let out a giggle, then snorted trying to conceal it. "Oh so it's okay if he plays games? Not fair at all."

Jillian coughed, telling Jack to refocus. "Okay, boys, since you are not following my instructions, strip down and throw everything out." Jillian looked up at Jack and must have read the surprise on his face "What? Once they are unarmed I'll give their clothes back." She smiled brightly as she looked back down the scope of her gun. "Maybe."

Jack saw four coats and pants. "What's the end game here, Jillian?" Jack asked nervously. "If you're just going to kill them then do it already."

Jillian looked up at Mickey, ignoring Jack's question. "All of it now!" she screamed.

"It's forty degrees, we will freeze," a man yelled.

"You should have thought about that before you kept a weapon. Up with everything, including the weapon!" A lonely pistol was tossed over the edge, followed by three T-shirts and four pairs of boots. "That's enough. Now don't move!"

Jack looked up to see Mickey noticeably bobbing his head up and down.

"Don't kill us, we're not here to hurt you," a man yelled again.

"Jack, go check their clothes for weapons. Then they can have them back."

"We were after a group of Leeches that raided the compound. They stole our food and took one of our people hostage," one of the men called from the hole.

"What are we doing, Jillian?" Jack looked over at the hole. "We need a plan. What happens if they are telling the truth?" Jack looked back to see a man standing right behind her, his right hand squeezing Jillian's shoulder. Her body was rigid with pain, her eyes wide with fear.

"Don't even think about it!" a man said, running up to Jack and grabbing his gun from its holster. He then aimed it at Jack's back.

"Where is your camp?" another man asked, stepping from the trees with an aluminum bat resting on his shoulder. "All we want is your supplies, tell us where they are and you can live." Smiling, the man pointed the bat at Jack's chest.

"It's that way, just through the trees." Jack pointed with his nose, not daring to move his hands with Jillian in danger.

"Good, now get in the hole with your friends." Jack slowly reached for Jillian, but she gasped in pain, and Jack took a step back. "Just you," the man sneered, poking Jack in the chest with the bat and shoving him back another step. "The girl's coming with us."

"Over my dead body," Jack barked, and the man with the bat took a swing at his head. Jack ducked to the side and lunged at the man before he had a chance to recover. The two fell to the ground, wrestling for the bat. He heard a gunshot go off and looked up to see the guy who stole his gun aiming it shakily in Jack's face.

Laughing, the man with the bat climbed to his feet. "On your knees, scar face!"

The guy with the gun is too far away to attack. But if I attack the guy with the bat, the one with the gun will shoot me. Jack slowly climbed to his knees. *This is it. I'm coming Caleo. I just got to do what I can for Jillian then I'm on my way.* The man with the bat took a step closer, raising it to strike, and Jack prepared to duck left under the man's blow. A screeching sound, followed by a man screaming, told Jack that Mickey had attacked the man assaulting Jillian. Even though his back was to them, he could tell by the sounds that Mickey was winning the fight. The man glanced up at the scene, and Jack sprang into action. Drawing his knife from his boot, he leapt forward, burying the knife into the man's chest. The man staggered backward, dropping the bat to the ground as he pulled the blade free.

A gunshot filled the air and Jack winced. When no pain registered, Jack looked over to the man who had taken his gun and found him dead on the ground a bullet hole in his head. Two more shots rang out, and Jack turned in time to see the man who had attacked Jillian hit the ground as well.

"Spread out … there is one still missing, and he has the girl. Shoot to kill." Jack turned to see that all the men had escaped the hole, picked back up their automatic rifles, and were now running through the woods in their green army boxers and combat boots. A lone man was left standing in front of the hole with blood running down his chest from a bullet wound in his shoulder.

Jack stood there, eyeing the man for a moment, then asked, "Who are you?"

"Captain Herbert Brooks, United States Army." The man smiled at Jack weakly. "We *are* here to help." Captain Brooks took a few unsteady steps towards Jack before collapsing on the ground.

3

Jack sat in the basement of their old house. The room wasn't much. Jillian and Mickey's bed was at the far end of the room, a blanket hung across a clothes line the only privacy they had managed so far. Canned goods and other food supplies lined all four of the walls. They were well stocked, and Jack figured it would last them at least until spring even if they ate three meals a day. He sat at the table, aimlessly poking at his can of beef stew. Jack stared across the room at the man lying in what he had learned to call his bed; a few cushions covered by a mountain of blankets, and a few couch pillows. The man had been asleep for three hours. While Jillian cleaned and stitched up the bullet wound, the man had explained that they were part of the refugee camp the government had set up at the old high school, and that they were chasing down the four men who had taken off with their supplies and kidnapped one female civilian. Soon after the pills Jillian had given him for pain started to make the man drowsy, she told him to rest in Jack's bed until his buddies got back.

"It's okay, Jack, he is part of the army," Jillian whispered over her own soup can.

Jack shoved a spoonful of soup in his mouth, saying, "The Blessed have an army, remember?"

"He is not part of the Blessed," Jillian insisted.

Jack rolled his eyes and sat back in his chair. "How do you know?"

"I don't." She dropped her spoon into the empty bowl, shoved it away, and looked down at the table. "It doesn't matter if he is or not, Jack. This isn't our war ... it never was."

"But—"

Jillian held up her hand to stop him. "I just want things to go back to normal. I am tired of all of this." She motioned around the room, as if unable to find the proper word that would sum everything up.

"Our family is dead, it can't go back to normal," Jack spat, dropping his own spoon in his half empty bowl, suddenly unable to take another bite. He looked towards the stairs—wanting to escape into the woods again, where he could be alone in his grief—but looked back at his sister, knowing he couldn't leave her alone with the soldiers so near.

Jillian looked into Jack's eyes and the pain on her face was too much for Jack to bear, so he averted his gaze to the man sleeping in his bed.

"I mean safe ... I want to be safe. I don't want to worry about falling asleep and getting attacked," Jillian whispered. A soft meow drew Jack's attention to the bench beside Jillian, to see Mickey rubbing his head against her leg, purring. Jillian picked him up and hugged him close.

"Get that stinky thing away from the table," Jack barked, trying to change the subject.

Both Jillian and Mickey looked up at him; Jillian smiling and Mickey glaring through squinted eyes. She put him down before looking back up at Jack without saying a word.

"How long before Mickey can get back to normal?" Jack asked, picking up his spoon again. Instead of taking a bite, he dropped it and pushed his bowl away.

Jillian looked down at Mickey and back up to Jack, whispering, "I don't think he wants to right now." Jack raised one of his eyebrows as he kept an eye on the sleeping Captain Brooks, watching his breathing to try to discern if he was asleep or faking. "I think it has something to do with that army man. Those were all Leeches that died, and he absorbed all of their energy, so he should be more then capable of turning back. He just ... isn't."

Jack looked down at Mickey, and Mickey stared back up at him, as if trying to tell him something just through their eye contact. "Scaredy cat."

Mickey bristled the hairs on his back and moaned his argument.

"Boys, boys, settle down." Jillian picked up her and Jack's bowls, put them in an empty tote, and snapped the lid on to keep the vermin from getting a free meal. "We might as well go to bed and get a few hours of sleep."

Jack slid his chair out, standing up. Then he froze, wondering where he was to sleep with Captain Brooks already asleep in his bed. He looked down to see Mickey looking up at him, and Jack could swear that the cat was smiling.

"Now I don't speak cat, but I think he just said you get to sleep with the big hulking army man," Jillian whispered, winking at Jack. Mickey purred his affirmation.

"I'm not—"

"Gay?" Jillian cut Jack off, smiling.

Jack glared at his sister. He wanted to argue that he wasn't gay, he wasn't attracted to males or females for that matter; it was just Caleo. It didn't matter what gender Caleo was, Jack had just wanted to be with him, to spend the rest of his life loving him in any way he could. But that point was harder to make than what was important right now. *Besides, that dream is gone*, Jack thought bitterly. He gritted his teeth, trying to hold back his frustration. "Not sleeping with him."

Mickey hissed and Jack looked down at the pint-sized kitten, wanting to punt him across the room.

"I believe that he said there is no way his stinky butt is sleeping in my bed," Jillian translated, laughing as Mickey flicked his tail and strutted toward the bed.

"That's a great idea," Jack said and ran for the bed. He heard a moan just as he reached the pile of kindergarten nap mats that they salvaged from a preschool two months ago. "I know what he said and I don't give a rat's ass," Jack stated, making sure to emphasize the word rat as he threw himself across the bed. He looked up at his sister, a big challenging grin on his face as he wrapped the blankets around himself, snuggling in.

Jillian stood beside the bed, Mickey meowing pitifully next to her leg.

"Scram cat," Jack said, throwing a pillow at him. "You get first watch." He rolled over, facing the wall to hide the smile on his face.

"Jack," Jillian whined.

"Scram woman." Playfully, Jack tossed another pillow over his head at his sister. "You can take watch with the smelly old—"

The radio attached to Captain Brooks coat squawked and everyone fell quiet. "Brooks, what's your location?"

Both Jillian and Jack jumped, turning around to see Captain Brooks reach around for the radio. He grunted in pain, grabbing his wounded shoulder. Jillian ran over and handed him the radio, then stood there watching him as if waiting for him to ask for something.

"This is Brooks." He paused as he met Jack's eyes from across the room. "I'm okay, did you find the Leech and the girl?" He nodded briefly, giving Jack a faint, awkward smile.

A feeling of uneasiness came over Jack with that smile. *Something is off about this guy.* He climbed out of bed and took a few steps so that Jillian was blocking his direct line of sight. When Captain Brooks made no move to see what he was doing, he looked over the room for the nearest weapon.

"We have the girl."

"And the Leech?" Captain Brooks shifted on the bed and Jack looked back to see that he had just sat up.

"Dead. We are on our way back. We're about a half mile out from where we left you on the road. E.T.A. three minutes."

Jack tilted his head to the side in confusion. *A half mile out?* Something about what they said made no sense to Jack, but he couldn't figure out what it was. Jack spotted his gun across the room on the table. "Damn it," he chastised himself for being so stupid.

"I'll meet you there." Captain Brooks stood up, pulling on his coat over his one arm. Jack saw the golden ring of the Blessed Army on the shoulder of the coat that he hadn't noticed before and his blood went cold. "We are going to head back to base." The man looked up to the stairs, then back to meet Jack's eyes, snapping him out of his thoughts. "Could I interest you both in coming along? There is food, water, and guards for safety."

Safety? He was awake; he heard Jillian and now is playing to her. Jack looked at Jillian for a moment, trying desperately with his eyes to get her to say no. However, when she looked back at him the excitement was plain on her face, and he knew that she wanted to go with them. *Maybe she hates this place as much as I do.* Jack gave her a half-smile and nodded. *Maybe she's right, this isn't our war. They were after Caleo, not us.*

"Yes," Jillian said excitedly. "Just give us a few minutes to pack and we will be ready to go."

Jack shook his head, hoping he was doing the right thing even though he had a hard time stomaching the idea of trusting Caleo's killers.

"You have ten minutes." Brooks looked between Jack and Jillian to the cat perched on the bed, who was twitching its tale in irritation. He raised his hand and pointed to the cat, looking like his was about to say something, but Mickey jumped off the bed and ran out of the basement before he had a chance.

"Mickey!" Jillian yelled, chasing after him to the bottom of the stairs. Stopping, she looked at Jack for help.

"We have to get packed up, I'm sure he will turn up before we leave." Jack grabbed his backpack and filled it with two pairs of jeans, a T-shirt, a pair of underwear, and two sweaters. He picked up his smear stick and smiled as a memory of him and Caleo playing in the orchard ran through his head. He kissed the end of the stick before shoving it through the straps, then pulled the whole thing onto his back the smear stick resting on the back of his shoulders. "All packed up here, just got to get my—" Jack stopped short of saying the word gun when he turned around and saw Captain Brooks holding it out to him. "Thanks." Taking the gun, Jack shoved it into the waist of his jeans.

"No problem," Brooks said with a smile.

"That's all you're going to pack?" Jillian called back to Jack, not even bothering to look at him as she held up two shirts as if trying to choose which one to take.

"Pants, shirts, and a pair of underwear, what else would I need?" Jack asked, looking back at the tote full of clothes next to his bed and shrugging. "Don't pack too much, you're going to be carrying it all yourself." When he looked back at Jillian, he knew she was pretending not to hear him.

"Girls," Brooks said, smiling as Jillian let out a frustrated groan. Jack looked over his shoulder at the clearly frustrated Jillian who was throwing clothes around, obviously having trouble deciding what to take with her. He thought about going over to help her calm down, but Brooks whispered, "Why don't we step outside for a smoke?" and motioned for him to follow him up the stairs

Jack shook his head. "I don't smoke."

"Then why don't you just keep me company while I have a smoke." Walking toward the stairs, Captain Brooks pulled out a pack of cigarettes from his pocket, then turned and motioned again for Jack to follow with a wave of his hand.

What's up with this guy? He almost seems like he's flirting. Jack looked back at Jillian, unsure what to do. *I don't want to offend him by saying I'm not interested when he is going to take us to the refugee camp. It's just a cigarette, it's not like he is going*

to jump me right outside the door. Returning Brooks' smile, Jack yelled back to Jillian, "I'll be right back. Just going to get some air."

"Okay, I will be up in a minute," Jillian said robotically, as if she hadn't even paid attention to what he had said. Jack glanced back again as she held a sundress to her chest, then threw it across the room where it landed in a pile of clothes she was obviously discarding.

Jack slowly walked to the stairs, smiling because he was unsure what else he was to do. He knew how to sweet talk people in to things, but flirting was a whole new ballgame for him. He wasn't sure how to even approach it. "I think she'll be a few more minutes," he whispered over his shoulder to Brooks.

Captain Brooks laughed, slapping Jack on the back as they headed up the stairs. "Your wife seems like quite a pistol."

Jack stopped, his hand on the makeshift door to the outside. He looked back over his shoulder at the man and corrected, "Sister, not my wife."

"I see." Captain Brooks smiled again, raising his eyebrows in mock surprise. Jack rolled his eyes, knowing the man was for sure hitting on him as he pushed the door open and stepped outside.

"Look," Jack said deciding to just come clean with the guy before things got out of hand, "I don't know what you heard down there, but I'm not—" Jack stopped when two camouflaged men appeared out of the darkness, their assault rifles pointed at him.

"What's going on?" Jack attempted to back down the stairs, but Captain Brooks held a gun to his back and pushed him forward.

"I don't understand, I thought we were going to the refugee camp." Jack searched the dark for any chance of escape. His eyes stopped on the third uniformed man standing in the distance next to the girl who they said was kidnapped by the Leeches. Her arms were bound behind her back and a gag shoved in her mouth. "What is this?" Jack asked, panicked. He turned around to confront Captain Brooks just in time to see two of the uniformed men running down the stairs. Jack pulled his gun, his brotherly instincts kicking in, and pulled the trigger but it clicked empty.

"Did you think I would give it back loaded?" Captain Brooks asked, smiling that same flirtatious smile he had given Jack to get him to come outside. But his smile vanished as four gunshots rang up from the basement. "You weren't supposed to shoot her!" he yelled angrily over his shoulder.

"They didn't!" Jillian called from the bottom of the stairs before a bullet tore a chunk of wood from the door beside Captain Brooks' head.

"That's my girl!" Jack whispered to himself as he slid his smear stick from his backpack.

Captain Brooks side-stepped from the doorway, turning his back to the woods as he held the gun on Jack. "We're just going to go. We can pretend this whole thing never happened and—"

"We?" Jack asked, cutting the man off with a smile as he lifted his smear stick up like a bat, ready to swing.

Captain Brooks glanced over his shoulder to see that his third companion was now dead on the ground, lying next to the gagged woman. "What? How?" He looked around for anyone, his eyes searching for whoever had killed the man. "Listen we can—" He jumped as a naked human Mickey stepped from the shadows behind him and grabbed his shoulder.

"Just shut up! You're already dead." Mickey slapped Brooks' cheek with his left hand and continued down the stairs, not even pausing as Captain Brooks fell to the ground dead, from all his energy being snapped out through that brief contact.

Jack looked down at the dead man and he kicked him in the gut as hard as he could. "Why?!" Jack kicked him again. "Why would you promise to take us then just try to kill us?" A rustling noise behind him made Jack jump to his feet, smear stick ready to hit the first attacker that came within range. He quickly realized it wasn't an attacker, it was the poor girl tied up. Jack ran to her and pulled the gag from her mouth. "I'm so sorry."

"Are they all dead?" The girl looked around her matted hair, which was falling over her dirty face, concealing it from view.

"Four total?" he asked while he untied her wrists.

She nodded slowly. "And the others?"

Jack stood up, looking around, ready for an attack. "What others?"

"The Leeches?" The girl's voice sounded frightened, and she looked like she was going to bolt for the woods at the slightest sound.

"It's okay, they're all dead." Jack reached out his hand to the girl and she flinched as if he was about to strike her. "It's okay you're safe here." Trying to reassure her, he kept his hand out as he knelt down in front of the girl. "I won't let anyone hurt you."

She eyed him for a moment, as if trying to decide if he was telling the truth or not, then took his hand cautiously and he helped her to her feet.

She looked around nervously, and Jack could feel her shaking just through the contact of her hand as he led her toward the little bit of light emanating from the doorway. "Are you sure it's safe?" She pulled him to a dead stop a few feet short of the door. "Where are your friends?"

Jack looked back, trying to offer a reassuring smile. "My sister and her boyfriend are in the basement. As far as I know, there is no one else here." He looked down at the body of Captain Brooks, then back up at her.

She just stood there, staring at the light coming through the open door, and Jack could sense that she was fighting the urge to run. "I can't," she whispered and started to back away slowly.

"It's okay. Just wait here." Letting go of her hand, Jack walked over to the house to light a citronella candle in a little metal bucket and bring it over to her. As he approached, she backed away cautiously until she had her back against a tree. She glanced over her shoulder and back at Jack nervously. He laid the candle on the ground and sat beside it. "Are you cold? I can go get a blanket if you would like."

She stood there, not saying a word just looking at Jack through the light of the fire for a long moment. He shrugged and glanced back toward the door to the house. *I guess I've been elected for watch tonight.* He looked back at the girl, who was still studying his face. *My scars, she must think I look like a monster.* Jack scanned the woods for any movement, trying not to look at her face, afraid to see her revulsion.

"I'm not cold," she squeaked, barely above a whisper as she slowly approached.

Confused, Jack looked back at the girl. "I'm sorry?"

"You asked if I was cold." She slowly crouched down, about four feet away from Jack, keeping the candle between them.

Jack nodded, and looked off into the distance. *What did they do to this poor girl?* He watched out of the corner of his eye as she hugged her legs up close to her chest and noticed that her clothes were pretty ragged. The sound of her belly growling made Jack look back at her.

"I'm sorry, I ... I just haven't eaten in two days," she explained quietly, scooting another foot away from Jack and clutching at her belly as if telling it to be quiet.

Slowly Jack climbed to his feet and fetched his backpack off the ground. "I have a couple of Slim Jims if you would like them." He turned around, but the girl had vanished.

Bewildered, Jack looked around and saw her outline in the darkness of the woods, watching him from just beyond the tree line. "It's okay," Jack said as he laid the two Slim Jims beside the candle and retreated back to the door. He picked up the Captain's assault rifle and watched the woods, pretending to ignore the terrified girl as she crept closer to the candle. He could feel her watching him as she devoured the Slim Jims and warmed her hands over the small flame of the candle.

☽ ✳ ☾

Jack stretched lazily as the sun peeked over the horizon, bathing everything in its orange glow. It had been six hours, and the girl had finally calmed down enough to curl into a ball about twenty yards away and fall asleep. Her back was to Jack, so he couldn't see her face, but her tattered oversized clothes, thin frame, and matted hair told Jack that the refugee camp the Captain Brooks was talking about was not kind to her. He couldn't help thinking about how close Jillian was to becoming just like this poor girl. *If things had gone differently last night, I would be dead and Jillian would have been dragged back to their base and ...* Jack shook his head, trying to get the horrible images of the things that could happen to his sister out of his head. *What has the world come to?*

The girl rolled over slowly. Suddenly, she sprang awake, looking from side to side as if trying to remember what was going on and where she was. Her eyes quickly found Jack and she froze, staring at him accusingly. Jack flashed her a warm smile and she tucked her hair behind her ears, smiling back meekly.

"Good morning." He laid the assault rifle down as he stood up, stretching his back.

She sat up, pulling her knees to her chest, and squeaked, "Good morning." She looked around, as if to see if anyone else had heard her.

"You sleep well?" Jack asked, attempting to make small talk so she would feel more comfortable.

She nodded in response and looked like she was going to say something, but stopped and just stared down at the dirt by her bare feet.

After a long stretch of silence, Jack turned and looked at

the dead body of Captain Brooks and the other two dead soldiers lying beside the door that Mickey threw out last night. "I'm just going to get the shovel and start burying these guys, is that all right?" Jack looked back at the girl and she nodded. "You have nothing to worry about, I'm not even going to come near you." He reached for the shovel, but looked back at her again when she didn't respond. There was something about her that was so familiar, but he couldn't put a finger on how he knew her. "Do I know you?"

She shook her head quickly in response, hastily looking back at the ground. Jack shrugged, dismissing the thought as he grabbed the shovel. When he turned back she was gone. *She will be back*. He grabbed Captain Brooks' feet and dragged him off into the woods.

"This looks like as good of a place as any." Jack dropped the man's feet by the edge of the pit fall trap he had fallen into earlier. It was already deep enough so there would be plenty of room for all the soldier's bodies plus the three Leeches that still lay nearby.

Jack bent down and looked at the man, dreading what he was going to do next. To him, it always seem creepy to scavenge off the dead, but winter was only a month or two away and they needed all the supplies and warm clothes they could get. Pulling Captain Brooks' boots and socks off, Jack threw them away from the hole.

He had just unbuttoned the man's shirt when he heard a twig snap behind him. Jack whipped around, pulling his handgun from its holster and aiming it in the direction of the noise. With a sigh, Jack relaxed when he saw the tattered girl peeking out from behind a tree. "It's okay," he said, trying to sound calm even though his heart was racing. He put down his gun in the dried leaves and continued to strip the corpse, noticing a strange tattoo of red circle with an upside-down triangle in it just under his right arm on his ribcage. "If you want to help, pick a body," Jack said jokingly to the girl. Once Captain Brooks was down to his underwear, Jack stood up and rolled him into the hole.

Jack looked over his shoulder to see that the girl hadn't moved.

"By the way, my name is Jack," he said as he stripped down the body of the man who had the aluminum bat.

There was a long moment of silence, and Jack nearly had the body stripped by the time she answered. "Jack Barely?"

Jack spun around, looking at the girl who was now completely out from behind the tree and staring at Jack for confirmation.

Jack squinted his eyes, trying to place the face under the dirt and matted hair. "Yeah," he said, but it sounded more like a question.

"It's me. Marcy Cobben." She looked down at her feet, as if ashamed to admit who she was. "From school. We went to that dance together a few ..." She stopped, as if afraid to continue.

Jack gasped as he finally recognized her under all that dirt and grime, and tried to smile politely. "Marcy! I didn't recognize you." Jack took a step forward to give her a hug, but she backed away and he chastised himself for being so thoughtless. He tried to think of something to say but 'how you been' or 'I can't believe all the weight you lost' sounded like they could be problematic subjects, so he just smiled and nodded his head awkwardly.

The uncomfortable silence stretched out for a few minutes. Jack turned back to his work, not knowing what to say and not wanting to scare her off. Once all the bodies had been stripped and rolled into the hole, Jack picked up the shovel and stared to fill it in while Marcy watched in silence a few feet away, sitting on a rock.

"Jack, breakfast is ready!" Jillian's voice carried through the woods. Marcy winced, glancing around as if waiting for an ambush.

Jack leaned on the shovel, taking a deep breath. Looking up at the sun, he figured it had to be at least nine o'clock, which meant that he had been awake for well over twenty four hours.

He looked down at the hole. It was less than half-filled and he was running out of dirt nearby. "Mickey can finish this. Let's go get something to eat." He waited for a response, but Marcy just sat there, nervously looking back in the direction of the house. "Come on, it will be fine. Jillian will help you get cleaned up after breakfast and get you some new clothes." Jack held out his hand, hoping she would take it. "We have a shower."

Her eyes lit up with excitement, but her words sounded cautious. "A shower?" Biting her lip, she looked back toward the camp as if she was weighing her options.

"We even have a hot water heater. I made it using an old metal tub I found in the wreckage. It's probably the one from the blue room. Anyway, it is filled with water and I have it—" Jack paused when she reached up and took his hand. Smiling, Jack continued to tell her about how he made the hot water heater as he led her back to the house.

☽ ✳ ☾

Jack lay in his bed, looking across the room at the small crawlspace under the stairs, which was now Marcy's bed. It had taken three days to convince her that she would be safe sleeping in the house, but instead of taking the bed they offered, she took a blanket and hid herself under the stairs. She had come a long way in the last two weeks. She still didn't seem comfortable near Jack or Mickey so she kept her distance, but didn't appear to want to run for cover if they got close. Jillian, on the other hand, she opened right up to. They would sit for hours talking as if nothing went wrong in the world and they were still in high school.

What happened to her to make her like this? What did they do to her? Jack asked himself, staring at the poor girl curled up into a ball through the gaps between the stairs, whimpering in her sleep. He slowly climbed out of bed; it was late in the day. Jillian and Mickey would be awake doing chores, but he didn't want to see any of them. All he wanted to do was get away, leave for a few hours and get his mind away from this place.

He grabbed his backpack and silently climbed the stairs. At the top he spotted Jillian down at the apple orchard, picking what may be the last of the apples before the frost came. Mickey was a few feet away, sitting on a log and watching her; an assault rifle lying beside him. When he saw Jack he raised his head in question.

"I'm just heading out to do some hunting, probably down by the river. I will be back before night fall." Jack turned to leave, hoping to escape before Jillian saw him with his backpack.

Mickey chuckled to himself. "It's about fifty degrees today and you're going to go swimming?"

Jack shrugged. "I thought I heard the weather man predict a heat wave this week." He smiled at what was now a common joke between them, thinking it would actually be nice to be able to get a weather forecast for the week or even just hear music on the radio. Unfortunately all that had stopped months ago, after the bombs went off.

Mickey laughed. "Should I tell her after you are out of sight, or wait till she notices you are gone? You know she won't be happy I let you run off again."

"Give me about fifteen minutes and I should be far enough away not to hear her chew me out." Jack ducked into the woods and took off running, not waiting for Mickey to agree or not. He wanted to get as far away from this place as he could today to clear his mind. Ever since the trip to the graveyard, he just couldn't help thinking about how different things might have been, if he had only told Caleo how he felt back when they had time to be together. Would Caleo's life have been happier? Would he have had an easier time at school? What would their home life have been like? He wished more than anything he could go back and find out.

Jack slowed down to a walk as he approached the clearing up ahead. The bramble and dead trees still made the wall he was hoping for, when he made it, but the big gap in the center that Will blew up proved that it was a wasted effort. Although the woods had reclaimed the area, Jack could still see the scorch marks on the branches from where the Blessed army had blown the wall apart, and the tiny tin shelters near the river, now buried in overgrown grass that other survivors had used as tents.

Shaking his head, Jack took a deep breath and looked up at the cave that they had called their home back when all this began. This was the first time Jack could bring himself to come back here since Caleo's death, and he wasn't sure it was a good idea now. As he looked around, his mind played out all the memories—Caleo and him sitting down on a rock by the stream talking, or looking up from working on the bramble wall to see Caleo emerging from the cliff waving, or working in the garden with Grandma. "Grandma," he said, his eyes landing on the spot that she died. "What would you think of us now? Are you disappointed that I couldn't protect Caleo?" He swallowed hard as he pushed back the memory.

Slowly Jack made his way into the cave. Everything was untouched, exactly the way it was left as they fled from his grandmother's killer. Jack pressed his hands to his face as he tried to drive the memory of his grandmother being shot away again, but it was too strong this time and his emotions overtook him.

Tears poured down the sides of Jack's face as he fell to his knees, slamming his fists into the hard rock floor. "I miss you both so much," he finally croaked once he regained some control. Crawling into a corner, he sat down and wept into his shirt sleeve, happy that no one was around that he had to pretend to be strong for.

"Don't cry." Shocked, Jack picked his head up and looked around. He could swear he just heard Caleo's voice, but knew that was impossible.

He slowly drew his gun from its holster, expecting it to be some kind of Leech trap. "Who's there?" Jack waited for an answer as he looked around and didn't see anyone, but he knew that with Leeches invisibility was not impossible, so he kept his guard up. "This isn't funny, if you are going to kill me just do it. Quit playing games!"

"It's okay, Jack, it's me." Jack whipped around to the entrance of the cave to see Caleo leaning through the opening a bright smile on his face, but something seemed off.

"Caleo?" Jack sat there, shocked. "I thought you were dead." When he climbed to his feet and took a step forward, Caleo vanished.

Jack ran for the opening as he tried to fight back the feeling that he was going insane. "Caleo, don't leave me again!" Jack screamed, staggering through the opening into the bitter cold wind outside. He slipped down the sloping ledge to the ground a few feet below, where he landed on his hands and knees. "Please don't leave me," Jack muttered, knowing that Caleo wasn't really there and he had imagined the whole thing. "I don't want to be alone. I don't think I can take this."

"I'm not going anywhere." Jack opened his eyes at the sound of Caleo's voice and saw him standing a few feet away, smiling.

Jack rolled over to sit on the ground, afraid to take his eyes off of him for fear that he would disappear again. After a long moment, where Jack just sat there looking at Caleo, he said, "I can see through you."

Caleo smacked his own forehead, giving Jack a look that could only be described as 'duh' then said with a smile, "No shit, Sherlock, I'm a ghost."

"Oh." Jack forced himself not to cry as he stood up. "Caleo, I've missed you so much." He reached out to embrace him, but Caleo vanished before his hand could reach him.

"You don't have to keep saying my name, I know who I am." Jack turned around to see Caleo by the tree line. "I have missed you, too. I've been waiting by the bottom of the cliff, but you never came. I thought you would have at least come to find me."

Ashamed, Jack looked at the ground as he fought back more tears. "I was scared. I didn't want to get there and see your—" Jack gulped as the word got stuck in his throat. "I don't think I could handle that."

"It's okay. I'm not there anymore. You don't have to cry for me, I'm fine now," Caleo said, sounding almost happy.

"Did it hurt?" Jack asked, not sure if he wanted to know, but he couldn't stop the words from escaping.

Caleo was quiet for a moment, but softly answered, "A little." He quickly added, "It was fast and I don't remember much of it, though."

Jack looked back up at Caleo and wiped away his tears. "There is something I've got to tell you."

"It's got to wait, I need you to do something for me and I don't have much energy left to tell you right now." Caleo looked off into the woods, then back at Jack. "You need to go to the school; there is a Blessed camp there. They are keeping human prisoners."

"Prisoners?" Jack shook his head, thinking about Marcy. "We ran into a few people from there already. They tried to say they were with the Army"

Caleo looked at Jack, worry evident on his face. "They know where you are staying?"

"No, we killed them," Jack said softly, adverting his eyes from seeing Caleo's reaction to him being a killer now. "I think they tortured Marcy"

"Marcy?" Caleo asked, a look of confusion briefly crossing his face. It was replaced by a blank stare right before he disappeared completely.

"You know Marcy, the one I took to that winter dance thing a while back!" Jack yelled, not knowing whether Caleo could hear him or not. When Caleo didn't reappear, Jack went and sat with his back against a rock and waited, hoping that Caleo would come back if he just waited long enough.

The sun was setting when Jack finally stood up. "I will be back in the morning. Please wait for me." Jack walked to the woods, wondering if he imagined the whole thing. *Why would he want me to go to the school? I'm just one human. What chance do I stand against an army of Leeches?*

☽ ✳ ☾

"Just who do you think you are?" Jillian yelled as Jack emerged from the woods. "I have been worried sick. Do you know what time it is?"

"No, and neither do you since your watch died last week," Jack said matter-of-factly as he brushed past Jillian and went into the house.

"You can't just run off like that." Jillian stopped at the bottom of the stairs, glaring at Jack, who was lying on his bed smiling.

He couldn't help it. He was so happy to have Caleo at least somewhat back in his life. Jack broke from his daydream at the complete silence and looked up to see Jillian looking at him as if he had lost his mind. *Well, I am seeing ghosts, so maybe I have.*

"What?" Jillian finally asked, tired of waiting for her brother to say something.

Jack thought about lying to his sister, knowing the truth would cause him problems. Jillian would never believe him, but she knew him better than anyone and would know if he was lying. "I saw Caleo's ghost today."

Jillian stared at him, as if waiting for the punch line, but already had the 'this isn't funny' look on her face.

"I went to the cave and he was there," Jack explained, avoiding his sister's gaze.

Jack felt his sister grab his hand and tried not to cry, because he knew she was going to give him the 'you're crazy' speech. "Jack," she said softly. "I know you want Caleo back, but there is no such thing as ghosts."

Jack glared up at his sister. He knew it was crazy to think that Caleo was a ghost hanging around the caves, but he didn't want to let go of his only chance of having him back in his life. "Just like there is no such thing as a man who can turn into a cat?"

Jillian took a step back, clearly frustrated. "I want him back, too. You know, the other day I tripped going up the stairs and could have sworn I heard Caleo call me a klutz."

"Klutz?" Jack couldn't help smiling. "I don't think he has ever said the word klutz before." He started laughing at his sister's sad attempt at a joke, perhaps more than he meant to, but he couldn't help it as he pictured Caleo pointing and calling her a klutz.

"That's not the point. The point is ..." Jillian started laughing, too, as if suddenly forgetting what her point was. "Stop it," she said between fits of giggles, then coughed and composed herself. "You're up for watch tonight, don't get caught sleeping. I know it's been a few weeks since the attack, but we have to keep our guard up just in case someone comes looking for them."

"Okay." Jack lay back down on his pillow and smiled at the blue tarp above his head, barely visible in the darkening room.

"I got tuna patties cooking. Your watch starts in an hour," Jillian said, picking up the lantern on the table.

Jack grumbled and rolled over just as his sister ran up the stairs.

)∗(

Jack threw another log into the furnace, which helped heat the basement room below, and shut the door. The air was bitterly cold and it stung the scars on the side of his face even through the hoodie.

"Kind of cold isn't it?" Jack turned back into the wind to see Caleo's ghostly form emerging from the woods. He looked down the stairs to the house and back at Caleo. "I told you I would be back in the morning," he hissed, hoping that Jillian didn't hear him talking to himself up here.

Caleo walked up to stand a few feet away and stuck his hands out as if warming them by the furnace. "I got bored," Caleo whispered back, looking around. "Why are we whispering?"

"Jillian is sleeping downstairs." Jack looked down at the steps, then back to Caleo. *If she sees him she will believe me.* He went to yell for Jillian but stopped. *What if I am just imagining the whole thing? She would think I am nuts.* He looked up to see Caleo smiling.

"So you don't want your sister to see me? I can understand that," Caleo said, taking a step back from the fire and vanishing.

"No, it's not that," Jack called, stepping forward as if to chase after the vanished Caleo. "I'm just afraid she won't see you. She thinks I'm crazy." Disappointed, he sat down in his seat next to the heater. "And maybe she's right."

"It's okay, I'm not going anywhere." Caleo reappeared out of the darkness and knelt down in front of Jack. "We have a mission to do and I can't—" Caleo paused, as if at a loss of words.

"Move on," Jack offered, knowing what Caleo meant.

Caleo nodded. "That's it. I can't move on till I put you on the right path."

Jack looked up at Caleo in confusion. "Path? What path?"

"To get vengeance on the Blessed of course." Turning, Caleo motioned to the house and the yard. "They have you shacked up in this dump when you could have been living a normal life. We would still be in school and I would still be alive."

"And how am I going to do that?" Jack asked, trying to wrap his head around what Caleo was telling him to do. "I'm human. I don't have powers and they have an army."

Caleo shook his head. "Go to the school. See what they are doing to humans. Then head south and tell the government what is really going on. Have them step in and kill the Blessed for us."

"Government? Caleo, look around you. There is no government! It's all been destroyed. Now it is just the Blessed," Jack said, frustrated.

"There is a government. They just need to know how to fight back. Tell them what you know and help them get control back," Caleo pleaded

Confused, Jack looked at Caleo. "What I know? I don't know anything about fighting Leeches. Jillian is the fighter, not me."

Caleo's face changed to a look of annoyance and anger that Jack had only seen him use toward Mike. "The cuffs?" he said flatly, like Jack should have known what he was talking about.

Jack still looked confused and couldn't figure out what Caleo wanted him to say. "The thing they dug out of your and Nolan's chest?" Jack tried to remember what they looked like, but didn't remember actually seeing one. All he could remember was the damage they left when they were dug out.

"Really?" Caleo asked, making Jack feel like an idiot. "The cuffs work like a stun gun, rendering the Leeches unable to use their powers. All it takes is a constant current and they are as useless as a human."

Jack looked a Caleo, surprised by the words 'useless as a human' but shrugged them off. "So you want me to tell them how to fight back against Leeches?"

"Bingo!" Caleo yelled. Jack glanced at the door, waiting for Jillian or Mickey to come running out at any moment. "Look, I will meet you tomorrow morning on the road. We can head to the school and check it out. Maybe get our hands on one of their cuff guns, and you can take it to the US Army."

"Wait." Jack looked back to Caleo to argue, to say he wasn't comfortable with the plan, but he was already gone, vanished into the night.

"Who are you talking to?" Mickey appeared at the top of the steps with a blanket wrapped around his shoulders.

Jack shook his head. "No one, go back to sleep."

"Well your shift is over if you want to hit the sack." Mickey stepped out into the cold air, stretching lazily as he placed an open soup can on the wood furnace to be warmed.

"Really? It has only been about an hour or two." Jack looked down at his watch and frowned. He had forgotten that it died about two months ago and they hadn't been able to find a battery to replace it.

Mickey looked at Jack, a surprised look on his face. "It's been about seven hours, buddy. Are you okay?"

He genuinely looked concerned and Jack had to smile. "I think so." He stood up, looking around for anything that would have told him how many hours had passed. *There is no way it's been that long.*

Mickey glanced down the stairs before whispering, "Did you fall asleep again?"

Jack shook his head. "I don't think so, I swear it's only been an hour. I filled up the furnace then sat down."

Mickey opened the furnace and worriedly glanced up at Jack. "Dude, I could have covered for the sleeping, but you let the furnace go out."

"No way." Jack looked into the furnace to see that all the wood had burnt down to just a few glowing embers. "Maybe I dreamt the whole thing?" Jack muttered to himself as he thought about Caleo's visit.

Mickey just shook his head. "I wouldn't tell your sister that. You know how she gets with security around here. We better get this restarted before—"

"Again! You let the fire go out again!" Jack and Mickey looked back toward the stairs to the basement and frowned at the sight of Jillian standing in the doorway. "I told you not to let the furnace go out," she chastised him. "We only have so many matches! Once those are gone, we are screwed. How do you think we'll start a fire then?"

"I know." Jack looked at the furnace and still couldn't believe that he had fallen asleep last night when everything had felt so real. "I'm sorry."

"Just go to bed. You're obviously useless," Mickey growled at Jack, turning his back to Jillian so she wouldn't see his face he whispered with a wink, "I will soothe the beast. Just go get some sleep."

Jack nodded once in response, taking on a chastised look.

"You owe me big time," Mickey mouthed. Turning back to Jillian, he put on an angry expression as he pointed down the stairs like a father telling his son to go to his room. "You're not running off today either. I want you back on watch in nine hours. So get some sleep."

Jack ignored Mickey's over the top ranting and ran down the stairs, pushing past his sister as he remembered Caleo's words 'I will meet you tomorrow morning on the road'. He threw some of his clothes into a backpack as he heard Jillian fuming at the top of the stairs to Mickey about how irresponsible he was being and how he could have gotten them all killed. Jack just shrugged it off, knowing she would be down to talk to him herself when she cooled off. He walked over to the wall where they kept the easy travel food, and shoved it into his backpack: a Ziploc bag of full of instant mashed potatoes, two packs of beef jerky, and six packs of apple cinnamon instant oatmeal.

"You going somewhere?" Jack turned at the sound of Jillian's voice to find her watching him from the bottom of the stairs.

Jack nodded, and went back to packing. Throwing a few bottles of water on top of his food, he zipped the backpack closed. "I'm going to scout out the school."

Jillian looked surprised by his answer, but said nothing and just stood there waiting.

Jack knew she wanted to know why, and he debated not telling her, but sighed knowing that if he tried to walk past her without explaining she would think she'd done something wrong and would blame herself if something happened. "You see the way Marcy is, there has to be more people there who need help. I've got to go."

Jillian crossed the room in three strides, her voice cracking as she spoke. "You don't have to do anything. We don't need to stick our necks out for anyone. It's hard enough for us just to survive. We have a home here."

Jack looked away. He hated to see his sister cry, but he despised this place more. He needed to get away, needed a sense of purpose again. "No, Jillian," Jack motioned around to the cluttered room, "this is barely a shelter. Our family is dead. We lost our home when Caleo and Grandma died. All this place has is us now."

"It's all we need." Jillian hugged Jack, squeezing him tight. "You and me."

Jack stood in awkward silence for a moment, letting her hold on to him and not bothering to hold her back. When she let go, he said, "I can't stay here. Everywhere I look, I see him. I need …" Jack paused, unable to think of what exactly he needed.

Jillian sat down on Jack's bed and looked around at the room. "Give me a few days to pack and we can go where ever you like. Maybe find a house up in the mountains somewhere where no one will find us."

Jack sat down next to his sister. "We can talk about that after I get back from the school. It's only going to be a day or two, that's it," Jack lied. He knew it would take longer for him to go there, then search for the government in the south, but he couldn't tell his sister that was his plan. She would ask too many questions about why he was doing it.

"I'm going with you." She looked at Jack, determination in her eyes.

Jack smiled at her stubbornness. "Fine, do you think you can be ready by tomorrow night? I want to leave right at dusk."

Jillian bit her lip and appeared to think it over as she scanned the room. She knew as well as he did that he planned to leave earlier then dusk and was going to try to leave her behind. "I think I can manage that."

"Great, now get off my bed I need to get some sleep. I don't want to fall asleep during watch again, my sister would kill me." Lying back across his bed, Jack nudged her with his foot.

Jillian got to her feet, picked up Jack's backpack, and walked to her bed. Jack smiled as Jillian pulled her privacy tarp closed, knowing she was going to hide the bag. *Yep, she knows and she isn't going to make this easy.*

Jack caught a movement out of the corner of his eye from under the stairs. *Marcy heard every word. I wonder how she feels about me going to the school.* He saw wet eyes looking back at him and tried to smile reassuringly. *What happened to you?* Jack wondered as he closed his eyes and surrendered to sleep. *What could they have possibly done to you to make you this way?*

4

"Why couldn't you just drop me off at the school, then go pick her up?" Caleo asked, fidgeting with his tie as he tried to make it straight in the sun visor mirror of the minivan.

Jack reached over, slapping Caleo's hand away. "I told you to quit fussing with that thing. It was perfect and now you have gone and messed it up."

"It was crooked." Caleo tried again in vain to straighten it before giving up. He flipped the visor back up and sagged into his seat.

"It wasn't until you started playing with it." Jack glanced over, smiling at Caleo's frustrated face.

Defeated, Caleo sighed as they pulled into the driveway of Marcy's house. "She doesn't even like me."

Jack put the van into park and flipped down his own visor mirror. "Sure she does. What's not to like. Great hair, well built, a perfect smile, and big brown eyes you could get lost in."

Caleo folded his arms across his chest and Jack could tell he was holding back a smile. "My eyes are blue."

"Oh, sorry. I must have been describing this handsome guy in the mirror." Jack grinned over at Caleo in the passenger seat, who looked miserable as he stared past Jack toward Marcy's house. "Don't worry, she likes you."

Caleo rolled his eyes. "Is that why she told me I couldn't come within ten feet of her at the dance or she would drown me in the punchbowl?"

"I told you she likes you." Jack nudged Caleo in the arm.

Confused, Caleo looked back at Jack.

"Think of it like this. You know that girl who ate the worm last month in her sandwich at lunch?"

Caleo nodded and raised an eyebrow.

"Well it turns out that she was caught making out with Marcy's ex-boyfriend under the bleachers the day before," Jack explained.

"What's that have to do with me?" Caleo asked, still wearing the look of confusion. However, Jack could see the hint of a smile hiding under Caleo's worried expression as he waited for there to be a punch line.

"The point is she didn't actually put the worm there herself. She had Cindy, the new girl trying out for cheerleading, do it." Jack could still see Caleo had no clue what he was saying, so he tried to make it simpler for him. "She is a Queen Bee, she would never get her hands dirty. If she hated you, she never would have told you herself. She would have had Cindy or Tammy do it for her."

Caleo was silent for a moment, and when Jack looked over, Caleo smiled as if he somehow was winning the argument. "Mary gave me the note in English class last week."

"Maybe she just couldn't find time to tell you herself," Jack tried desperately, attempting to make this night work.

"She sits behind me in English. Mary doesn't even have any classes with me." Caleo looked back out the window, pulling his tie free from around his neck and throwing it onto the back seat.

Maybe this wasn't such a good idea. Jack looked over at Caleo and frowned, wondering why he was desperately trying to fit in with the popular crowd when they treated his best friend like trash. "Come on." He nudged Caleo with his elbow to get his attention. "There is no way that she would even risk going near that punch bowl wearing the white dress she bought for this thing. Could you imagine how cool that would look though?" Jack tried, but Caleo didn't even bother to glance in his direction. "Dude, relax. I think you're safe." Jack pushed open the door and stepped out. "If I am not back in five minutes, come rescue me." Jack winked at Caleo, tossing the keys into his lap. "You can drive."

"Is this part of your arrangement for me to come along? I have to be your chauffeur for the evening?"

"What? No." Jack looked back toward the house. He could see Marcy's mother looking out the window and she seemed to be getting impatient. He raised his hand to wave, and she disappeared as if she didn't want him to have seen her staring at him. "There is no arrangement. She told me she wouldn't go if you were coming. So I kind of lied, I told her you weren't." Jack shrugged, turning back around. "I figured by the time she knew you were, there would be nothing she can do about it."

"You did what?" Caleo got out of the van, slamming the door behind him. "Are you trying to get me killed?"

"Don't be so dramatic." Jack stood by the door to the van as he watched Caleo walk off up the road. "Caleo, come back. It's going to be okay. She'll get over it."

"No, Jack, she's a cheerleader. If she doesn't kill me, she will make me wish I was dead by Monday." Caleo took another five steps then yelled, "Or worse yet, she will have Mary kill me for her."

"You're being unreasonable. Come on, please get back in the van," Jack pleaded.

"Hey, where is your friend going?" Jack turned around at the sound of a deep voice behind him. A tall man in his forties with thinning hair stood a few yards off, wearing a blue jumpsuit stained with oil from the garage "isn't that the albino kid?"

Jack fought hard not to yell at Mr. Cobben for a moment, then looked over his shoulder and said through gritted teeth, "He's not albino." Jack flinched as he swore he felt his grandmother slap the back of his head for being rude, so he quickly tried to hide his anger by pasting on a fake smile and saying, "But yes, that's Caleo."

"Oh yes, that's his name. Marcy was talking about him the other day. I didn't know he was coming." Mr. Cobben watched as Caleo walked farther out of earshot, then whispered, "So if he isn't albino, what is he?"

Jack stared at Mr. Cobben in disbelief. *What is he?* Jack thought bitterly. *He is a kid who wants to be accepted and all you can do is pick at what makes him different. What are you? Marcy must get her hate from your side of the family.*

Mr. Cobben must have noticed that Jack was upset and tried to amend it by asking, "I mean, is there anything wrong with him?"

"No ..." Jack looked back at Caleo, who was barely visible in the distance and would be following the road around the bend out of sight any second. "He's perfect. It's everyone else that has the problem with him."

☽ ✳ ☾

Jack felt a light tap on his shoulder and rolled over. However, no one was there. He rubbed his eyes tiredly. He didn't think he had been sleeping long, but the room was now dark and he couldn't see a thing. He picked up the flashlight next to his bed and flipped the switch. Marcy's form came into view a few feet away, holding a broom down by the bristles with it pointed out toward Jack.

Jack cocked an eyebrow in question, even though he knew she couldn't see it in the dark. "Why are you poking me and what's up with the broom?"

Marcy dropped the broom and stuck a finger to her lips before whispering, "Jillian is right outside the door. I think she is guarding it so you don't leave."

"Okay?" Jack sat up in his bed, stretching lazily.

"You aren't seriously planning on letting her go with you?" Marcy asked, her voice hinting that it would be a bad idea.

Jack smiled at the question before the look of horror on Marcy's face registered. *She is actually worried about Jillian getting hurt.* He shook his head. "No, I'm planning on sneaking away right before dawn when my watch is about over. That way she is sound asleep."

Marcy shook her head in return. "No, you have to leave now while she still thinks you are sleeping. I heard her talking to Mickey and she is planning on keeping watch with you tonight."

"Figures she wouldn't make this easy." Jack glanced at the stairs, trying to think of a new plan.

"She was just down to check on you about ten minutes ago so that gives you time to sneak out now," Marcy said, following Jack's eyes to the stairs.

"But you said she is guarding the door," Jack said as his mind raced with the questions. *Why doesn't she want Jillian to go? And why does it seem like she is pushing me out the door?*

"The tarp is loose in the corner on the other side of the room, right above the canned corn. If you untie it, you can slip out easily and I can retie it when you are gone."

Jack stood up and Marcy grabbed the broom, backing away a few steps. "Why are you helping me?"

Marcy looked as if she was about to run or cry at any moment. "I'm not." She looked down at the white Nikes Jillian had given her. "I don't want Jillian to—" She burst into tears, unable to finish her sentence. Jack took a step forward to comfort her, but she dropped the broom and bolted under the stairway to her bed.

"I'm sorry. I know this is hard for you."

Jack gathered up his backpack from Jillian's bed and was just untying the end of the tarp when Marcy murmured, "My mom is in there, too."

Jack froze as he understood what she was trying to tell him. It wasn't that she was pushing him to go; she saw him as the only hope of getting her mother out of there. *She wants me to go help them escape.* He nodded his head in acknowledgement before whispering, "I will do what I can." Slowly, and as quietly as he could, he climbed out from under the tarp and into the fresh, cold air outside.

He could hear Jillian talking to Mickey around the front of the house and stayed as low to the ground as he could, hoping not to be seen. *Now for the hard part; getting out of here without Jillian mistaking me for an intruder and shooting me.* Jack crept toward the outhouse on the edge of the woods and ducked behind it. A stick broke under his foot and he pressed himself against the wall, praying that Jillian wouldn't just open fire. After a long moment, he peeked around the corner. He could see Jillian wrapped in a blanket, sitting next to the fire her face lit up with a smile as she looked up at Mickey who had her wrapped in his arms. *Thank you, Jesus,* Jack thought as he ducked back around the outhouse, running silently into the woods. He kept his hands stretched out, feeling from tree to tree as the leaves crinkled beneath his feet.

He waited till he had put a good distance between him and the house before he flicked on his flashlight. He didn't want to waste the battery, but didn't see how he had much of a choice. He needed to get well away from the house before the sun came up and he was far enough away from the house that Jillian wouldn't see the light. A rustling of leaves behind him pulled him to a stop. He flicked off his light, and crouching low to the ground he pressed his back against a nearby tree.

"What are you hiding from?" Caleo's voice made Jack sigh with relief. *Since when do ghosts make noise when they walk?* he wondered as he flicked on the light, and smiled when he saw Caleo casually standing beside a tree twenty feet in front of him.

"You heard the leaves blowing in the wind." Caleo made a few quick steps to prove that he didn't make a noise walking, then motioned for Jack to follow him as he headed off into the trees. "The moon is out once you get to the road. You won't need that light."

Jack obediently followed as Caleo led the way. They talked for a while, Jack filling him in on everything that had happened the last few months as Caleo listened and walked in front of him. Every few feet Jack would stop, as the feeling that someone was watching them crept into his bones.

"Hey, let's stop here for the night," Jack said as they came up on a small sign on the side of the road with the nearly faded letters welcoming them to Evans City.

"Why? It's only about four more miles. We could be there by dawn," Caleo said impatiently, motioning for Jack to come along as he started walking again.

Jack shook his head and remained still. "I don't want to go through there at night."

Caleo came to a stop and looked back at Jack with a smile. "You aren't afraid of ghosts, are you?" he asked, holding up his arms as he walked toward Jack like Frankenstein's monster.

"The explosions," Jack said matter-of-factly.

Caleo came to a halt and looked around, a confused look on his face. "Explosions? What explosions? I haven't heard anything."

Jack looked at Caleo in disbelief. "Don't you remember the explosions that destroyed everything? We could trip on just about anything in there. Well, I could. I'm not actually sure if ghosts can trip."

Without a word, Caleo blinked out of existence, leaving Jack standing in the dark alone.

"Caleo?" He walked to the edge of the woods and shrugged off his backpack. "Well since you aren't here to argue, I might as well get that sleep I was talking about." Jack waited for a reply, but when none came he walked into the woods a few feet to a large oak. He dropped his bag on the ground, sat down next to it, and leaned against the tree. Yawning tiredly, he looked around to make sure he couldn't see any danger. *I'm far enough away from the road that I shouldn't have to worry about anyone seeing me, and I doubt they will be walking in the woods with the road right there. So I should only have to worry about a bear or maybe a coyote at this time of year. Even though I haven't heard of any around this area for a few years.* Jack slowly lowered himself down into the dry leaves, laying his head on his pack and closed his eyes.

"Jack?" Caleo asked timidly

Jack opened his eyes and rolled over to see Caleo laying a few feet away. "Yeah?"

"When we get to the school, what are you planning on doing?

Why is all he wants to talk about this stupid mission? Jack rolled back over, putting his back to Caleo. "I don't know."

"You're not going to run in there and try to save all the humans are you?"

Jack rolled over, once again surprised at his use of the word humans. "What is wrong with you?" Jack asked angrily. "You're acting like, like … Ahh!" he screamed in frustration. "I don't know." Rolling back over, he glared at the dark bark on the tree.

"Jack?" Caleo asked, his voice sounding worried.

There was a long moment before Jack responded, his voice shaky as he fought back tears. "You know I love you, right?"

"Yeah, and I love you, too, but—"

"No," Jack cut him off. "I really love you. I have wanted to tell you for a while, but I just didn't know how."

Caleo was silent for a moment before responding with an awkward, "Okay. So you're telling me you are gay?"

Jack ignored the question. "That day you found me at the pool … the day the president got shot. I had been in there all day."

"Why are you telling me this?" Caleo asked, his voice sounding annoyed. Jack knew his fears were right; that coming out and confessing his love to Caleo would have ruined their friendship.

"I just thought you should know that I was planning on telling you that day. I was so nervous, I spent all morning swimming, trying to get my thoughts in order. Then you just walked in and my mind went blank. I know I should have told you sooner, but I was afraid that you would—"

"Dude, calm down, it's okay. I don't care that you're gay," Caleo said happily. "It's your life."

"What?" Jack rolled back over and looked at Caleo, confused.

"I said it's okay. I don't care if you're gay. You're my brother and I love you." Caleo smiled reassuringly. "See, you had nothing to worry about."

Jack sat up slowly, pulled his gun from where he had stashed it under his backpack, and aimed it at Caleo. "Who are you?"

"What do you mean? I'm Caleo," he said, holding his hands up to show he was unarmed. "We grew up together, you're my brother."

"You're not Caleo. Who are you?" Jack yelled, but Caleo vanished leaving him alone in the dark

☽ ✳ ☾

"Wake up!" Jack's eyes instantly flew open at the sound of fear in Caleo's voice and saw Caleo's face inches from his own.

Jack grabbed his gun and aimed it at Caleo. "What do you want now?" Jack pushed himself up into a seated position as he searched the darkness for what might be the trouble. "I don't see anything." He climbed to his feet, keeping his gun pointed at Caleo.

"It's the Blessed. They're coming." The sound of dry leaves being crumbled underfoot alerted Jack of someone running towards him. He turned his gun towards the noise, waiting for his target to emerge from the darkness, but Caleo stepped in front of him. "Don't shoot, it's just a girl. They're chasing her. You have to run." A small, hooded figure burst through the foliage and Caleo vanished. Her panicked eyes looked Jack over for a moment before she ran past him, disappearing into the trees behind him.

"What was that?" Jack said as he watched her go. The sound of fast approaching steps forced Jack's attention back to the bushes in front of him. Quickly, he ducked behind the tree. The sound of leaves crackling stopped abruptly a few feet away from where he had been sleeping.

"She left her pack here," Jack heard one guy whisper and the sound of his backpack being unzipped.

There was a long pause as Jack heard the contents of his bag get dumped onto the ground and a man searching through them.

"Is it in there?" another man hissed as Jack caught the movement of two more men approaching the tree out of the corner of his eye.

"No, but this is Captain Brook's knife," the man digging through Jack's pack announced and all the men turned in his direction.

It's them, Jack thought, running through possible scenarios in his head. He took a deep breath. If he was going to do anything about the base he had to start here. These were Blessed soldiers, they were hurting people. The image of Marcy's face flashed through his mind; first as the snobby, self-assured cheerleader, then it morphed to the mousey, broken girl who hid under the stairs. *Shoot two, drop to the ground and shoot the third guy, roll to the right taking out the final one.* Jack let out his breath, content on his plan. Just as he was about to step out from behind the tree, his gun flew from his hands and sailed into the woods. A gloved hand grabbed him by the throat, pinning him to the tree.

The man holding Jack's throat smiled from behind his long, black hair. "Got you!"

The smile quickly vanished as he let go of Jack, staggering backward, grasping at a knife handle that Jack had shoved into his chest. Jack grabbed the knife handle, and using his foot as leverage he kicked the man freeing the knife with a sickening pop. The man took two staggering steps backward and dropped to the ground. Two Blessed soldiers rushed forward, guns raised, searching the woods for the attacker.

As they ran past him, Jack swung behind the closest man, slamming the knife into his back and burying it five inches deep up to its hilt. The man screamed out in pain and Jack dropped to the ground as two popping sounds went off to his left, like something being shot out of an air cannon, then a thud sounded as whatever it was slammed into a nearby tree.

What the hell was that! Jack rolled to his left as two more objects hit the ground he had just been on. He rolled over two more times until a tree in his path forced him to stop.

"Get up!" Jack heard the sound of a gun cocking and looked up to see it hadn't been a tree he had rolled into, but one of the men, and this one was holding onto a real handgun. "Get up!" he barked again.

Jack slowly did as he was told. Accepting defeat, he raised his hands in surrender.

"Turn around," the man said, motioning with his gun.

Again Jack complied, thinking that at any moment he would feel the bullet enter the back of his skull.

Jack smiled as he saw Caleo emerging from behind a tree, happy that it would be his face that he would see before he died. *He's coming to take me to the afterlife with him.* Jack imagined a large apple orchard, him and Caleo sitting under a tree smiling as they talked the day away in their ratty old smear clothes, running through the woods, or swimming in a lake floating on their backs staring up at the sky.

"Stop where you are!" the man with the gun yelled, and a soldier across from him shot a burst from his gun, but the object passed right through Caleo and into the darkness beyond. "I said stop!" The man held his gun up, ready to fire again, but hesitated.

"Wait, you can see him, too?" Jack asked, then whipped around as the man behind him screamed in pain.

Jack staggered back as a girl, who looked to be in her early twenties, slit the soldier's throat. She shoved him to the ground, where she stabbed another knife into his back and looked up at Jack like it was somehow all his fault.

The sound of a lion's roar caused Jack to glance over his shoulder, to see the ghostly image of a lion had taken the place of Caleo and was slowly stalking toward the last man standing near Jack's bag. When Jack looked back; the girl had vanished, and the only evidence of her existence was the dead man by Jack's feet.

"Stay back!" the last soldier yelled, his gun shaking at the lion's approach. Jack cringed as the man shot four blasts into the specter; all of which passed right through the lion, sending dirt and dried leaves into the air behind it. The man backed away as the lion approached closer and closer.

Jack caught a quick movement behind the tree and saw the girl with her knife in her hand, moving in for the kill.

"Don't, I need him alive!" Jack yelled, stepping forward with his hand outstretched.

The man saw Jack's movement and turned his gun on him. There was another popping sound and Jack collapsed to the ground, shock wave after shock wave of electricity pulsing through his body, radiating from his chest. He wanted to turn over, but all the muscles in his body were too tight to move, forcing him to bury his nose in the moist dirt. *Is this one of those things Caleo had in his chest? What did he call it? A cuff. I see why this makes it impossible to move at all.*

The pulsing stopped abruptly and Jack gasped for air as his muscles slowly relaxed, leaving them aching like he had just swam a mile.

"You should have ducked for cover," a deeply accented English female voice said sternly from somewhere nearby.

Jack rolled over to see a specter image of a tall, dark woman in a long, plain white dress looking down at him. "Who are you?" Jack looked around for the girl and found her hog-tying the last remaining uniformed guard beside the oak tree. He looked to be unconscious, but Jack wasn't sure with the amount of blood that now covered his face.

"Excuse you?" the specter woman said hotly, waving her index finger at Jack. "I just saved your good-for-nothing human existence, and the first words that come out of your mouth are 'who are you?'" The specter woman in the dress crossed her arms across her chest and tapped her foot impatiently.

"Thank you." Jack climbed to his feet and looked at the specter woman, trying to figure out who she was and why she had been impersonating Caleo. He looked back over at the girl who was going through the dead soldier's pockets, not even bothering to look up to see why he was talking to a ghost. Jack turned his attention back to the specter. Something about the two looked very similar, like they could be sisters or something. "I'm sorry, are you a ghost or a Leech?"

The girl stopped digging through the pockets of the dead man, and she and the specter gave Jack a look that shouted, 'stupid human'. Then their expressions changed to a look Jack could only describe as challenging. "Boy, you have got to be the dumbest kid I have ever met," the specter said, laughing, and the girl went back to looting the dead. "Of course I am a Leech, did you really think that ghosts existed?" the woman slapped a hand on her thigh as she laughed at Jack's expense. "I mean, really, it took you this long to put that together?"

Jack nodded. He knew he should be mad at the girl for using Caleo to trick him, but he needed to know why she was doing this and starting an argument with her wasn't going to get him the information he wanted. Frowning, he took a deep breath and focused on the task at hand. "We need to get away from the road. I want to get some information from him about the school and I can't have him drawing attention."

The girl's eyes darted to Jack and a smile broke across her face as the specter asked, "What are you going to do, beat it out of him?"

"Exactly." Jack took a step forward and felt the device that was imbedded in his chest pull at his skin. The specter watched him uncertainly as he pulled at the device, trying to figure out how to remove it. "Do you know how I can get this thing off?" Jack asked, motioning to the device in his chest.

Without prompting, the girl got to her feet, pulled a stick like object from her belt, and walked toward Jack.

The specter took a step backward at her approach and said, "Hold still." The girl took the stick and tapped the bottom of it to the round device in his chest. Jack gasped as he felt the hundreds of tiny needles retract and the device fell to the ground, landing between his feet.

"It's called a cuff. As I am sure you felt, it sends pulses of electricity through your body, enough to incapacitate a human. When it's in you, they can adjust the levels up or down. Usually it's only used on Leeches, though. The electricity makes us incapable of using our powers. This is what you need to take to your leaders," the specter explained.

Jack picked the object up, flipping it over and examining it as best as he could in the low light. He looked up at the unexpected information. He had already known about the electricity trick from when Caleo explained it. *Why was this woman offering the information freely and why does she want me to go to the government. She can't be working for the Blessed. Maybe she's part of Thorn's group, but Thorn was captured.* He looked around, wondering who he should speak to about what's going on, but the girl had disappeared. "Where's the girl?" he asked the specter, who had turned to keep an eye on the hog-tied soldier.

"I went to get the Blessed's Hummer about two minutes ago. I'm on my way back now," the specter woman said, looking over her shoulder at Jack.

"Wait, you're the girl?" Jack regarded the ghostly figure carefully, then tentatively stuck his hand out and it passed through the figure with no resistance. "Wow. So this is like a hologram?"

"You touch my mother again and I will slit your throat," the phantom said angrily, its eyes glowing red as she glided back out of reach.

"Sorry," Jack muttered as he turned from the ghost and walked over to his backpack. Ignoring the man lying hogged-tied, he repacked his stuff, placing the cuff at the top of the pack.

The Hummer pulled to the side of the road and Jack watched as the girl got out.

"You could always stop watching me and start loading up your shit," the apparition growled from behind Jack.

"Okay, okay." Jack picked up his pack, shouldered it, then turned to the Blessed soldier on the ground. The girl walked up and stopped on the opposite side of the man without saying a word. Jack looked up and could just make out her face for the first time. She looked to be about sixteen, but he knew better then to assume she was that age. Leeches never seemed to look their age. Her face was a soft light brown and framed by thick, black hair that hung in frizzy curls. She glared at him, her eyes seeming to be challenging him to say anything.

Feeling like if he made any signs of aggression she would pounce on him and rip his throat out with her teeth, Jack looked away.

"He's your prisoner," the spirit announced and Jack could still feel the girl's eyes drilling into him as she continued to stare him down.

Jack nodded. *I wonder why the ghost does all the talking.*

"You can carry him," the spirit said as the girl turned, picked up a cuff gun off the ground, and walked back to the car.

Maybe it's a power trip kind of thing, Jack thought as he grabbed the man under his arms and started dragging him towards the road. "Do you have a name, or should I just call you ghost girl or something?"

"Go ahead and call me ghost girl and see what happens!" the apparition of the woman challenged, growing in size. "My name is Paris. You call me ghost girl again and you will wake up dead in a bathtub," Paris's mother said, getting into Jack's face as Paris got behind the wheel of the Hummer and slammed the door shut.

You can't wake up dead. And what the heck does a bathtub have to do with anything? Jack thought about correcting her, but decided that after seeing her slit a man's throat, and barely blink an eye, it would be better to tread carefully around her till he had the upper hand.

He awkwardly maneuvered the soldier's body into the back seat of the Hummer and slammed the door. He pulled open the passenger door and stopped as Paris's mother looked down at him impatiently. "Child, don't stand there letting all the heat out. Shut the door and get in the back."

He looked over at Paris in the driver's seat, to see her glaring down at him. Jack bit his tongue. "Definitely a power trip," he mumbled as he slammed the door shut.

Five minutes later Paris pulled into the driveway of a large, blue house just outside of the town. The small patch of grass in the front yard came up to Jack's waist, making it hard for him to see the stone walkway that led to the large porch. Paris quickly got out of the car, as if she couldn't stand being in it any longer than she had to, and headed for the porch. Jack noticed that her ghost was not following her. He turned around, expecting to see her still sitting in the car, but she'd vanished as well. With a sigh of relief, Jack pushed opened the back door and stepped out. The soldier was now awake, but looked disorientated and afraid lying across the seat.

Jack frowned. *There is no way I'm going to be able to drag him into the house like this.* He knew what he had to do, but he didn't like it. "I'm going to cut your legs free." Jack slowly pulled the knife from his belt and cut the rope around the man's ankles. He watched carefully as the man sized him up, then looked at the yard behind Jack. *He is trying to decide if he can make a run for it,* Jack guessed. "Sorry, but if you run I promise you I will shoot you in the leg and drag you back here. Do you understand?" Jack said, reaching for his gun, then remembering it was lost somewhere in the woods. The man nodded slowly and Jack took a step back to allow him to climb out of the car. Watching Jack carefully, he pivoted in his seat then placed his feet on the ground, standing up to his full height. For a moment Jack could see the tension in the guy's posture as he contemplated running. "Walk to the front porch." The man hesitated briefly and then slowly walked through the grass, onto the porch, and into the house with Jack following closely behind.

The sun had just barely come up, filling the over-sized kitchen with an orange glow as they entered the house. The man stopped just inside the door and Jack whistled as he looked around at all the expensive beauty that was the kitchen; the giant sink, marble countertops, all stainless steel appliances, and the largest gas stove Jack had ever seen. "I wonder who lived here. It had to be the mayor or someone important."

Unimpressed, the man just shrugged in response. Jack refocused on the task at hand, shoving the man forward. "We might as well get this out of the way now."

"Get what out of the way?" the man asked as Jack pushed him down a hallway and into an empty bedroom. The man stopped in front of the enormous king-size bed, turning to face Jack. Even with his hands still tied behind his back, he looked like he was ready to put up as much of a fight as he could.

"I'm needing some information and you are going to tell me what I need to know." Jack shoved him onto the bed, but the effort was lost because it just looked like the man sat down.

"And if I don't talk. What exactly are you going to do?" The man looked around the bedroom and back to Jack, his expression hard.

"Oh God, nothing like that. Geesh!" Jack shook his head. "I figured I would start by throwing you in the shower."

"The shower?"

Jack jumped at the sound of Paris's phantom's voice and turned around to see her hovering in the doorway.

"You kept him alive to give him a shower." She pointed at Jack and laughed. "Boy, you are two tons of a special kind of stupid. What the hell is a shower going to do? We don't even got any hot water."

Rolling his eyes, Jack turned to face his prisoner.

"Did you roll your eyes at me?" Paris's mother spat.

Jack whipped around and snapped, "Look, lady, if you want to talk to me, stop whatever you are doing and get your ass in here. I'm getting tired of this power trip you're on. Come talk to me yourself or you and your mother can go haunt another human. I am tired of dealing with all this bull."

Paris's mother looked stunned for a moment, then her eyes flashed red and she said, "Fine. I will leave you boys to get your shower together or whatever you—"

"Do you feel how cold it is in here? I would say it's probably just a monkey's butt hair above freezing. Do you know how much pain he will be in soaking wet as the water saps his heat and his body temperature drops into hypothermia levels? It's going to hurt like hell."

The phantom looked surprised and dumbstruck for a moment, then smiled politely. "Just keep the noise down." She disappeared into thin air, seeming satisfied.

Jack turned back to the man, feeling happy about his exchange of words with Paris. It saved him having to explain everything to the man and he thought it sounded way more intimidating then if he had to play badass and explain it to the guy directly.

"So, let's start simple. Name?" Jack asked, shutting the door to the bedroom and dropping his bag on a nearby dresser.

"Nathanael Larry," the man said without hesitation.

Jack nodded his encouragement. "Are you part of the Blessed?"

The man stayed silent for a moment, then swallowed hard and looked Jack in the eyes. Jack couldn't tell if the man was afraid or just playing along. "Yes."

Panic gripped at Jack's throat as he asked the next question, because he hadn't even thought about it till he got the answer to the last question. "Are you a Leech?"

The man glared at Jack for a moment, obviously sensing Jack's fear, before saying, "Yes."

Jack took a step backward, pressing his back against the dresser, telling himself to remain calm. *The man is tied up, I have nothing to worry about.* He reached for his gun finding his holster empty again. Quickly he scratched himself across his belly, trying to hide the fact that he was unarmed, and asked, "What is happening at the school?"

Again Larry answered without hesitation. "The school is military housing and a temporary jailing facility for rogue Leeches."

Jack dug his fingers into the dresser as he asked the next question. "And the humans?"

"Your government has provided us with food, shelters, and ammunition. In exchange we help them reclaim their territory and we are to protect and evacuate any humans when we can."

Questions whirled around in Jack's head. *The government is still working? Reclaiming their territory, does that mean this will be over soon? If me and Jillian head away from the fighting, would we be back in civilization and safe?* Marcy's face popped into his mind. "I ran into a girl the other day who said she came from the school. Do you know what happened to her there?"

Larry's face went blank for a moment, then paled as he nodded his answer.

"And that is?" Jack asked impatiently

Larry was silent as he stared at the wall behind Jack. "She was claimed as payment for dues." His voice sounded almost robotic as he said it.

"And what is that supposed to mean?"

"The Blessed believe in an old religion. They believe that if a debt is owed it can be paid by giving one of your children—"

Jack shook his head and screamed, "What did you do to her?"

"She was commandeered as a slave to work off her father's debt," Larry said quickly

The door to the bedroom was kicked open as Paris flew in, knife in hand, her eyes burning with rage. She kicked Larry square in the chest, knocking him backward on the bed, and she mounted his chest, pressing the knife to his throat. "You raped a little girl?" her mother's phantom screamed as it materialized on the other side of the bed. "Do you think it's fun to hurt someone who can't defend themselves? Look at the big manly Leech as he hurts a pathetic human girl. You're defenseless now, maybe I should bleed you out on this bed!"

Jack watched in horror as blood trickled out from beneath the knife and rolled down Larry's throat. He hated the man, he wanted him dead for what he had done to Marcy, but he still needed answers. "Paris!"

She gritted her teeth, pressing harder on the knife at Larry's throat.

"Paris!" Jack reached out, grabbing her shoulder in an attempt to get her attention.

"Don't touch me human!" Paris shrugged Jack off and pushed him away, as her mother screamed and flew at Jack, backing him against the nearby wall.

"I didn't touch the girl," Larry pleaded. "I didn't touch any of them!" The powerful odor of a skunk filled the air and Jack had to cover his nose with his sleeve as he fought to keep his last meal down.

"Oh that's just f'ing great! He's a scenter," Paris's mother yelled as Paris jumped off the man and ran for the door, holding her hand over her mouth. "If I smell like skunk I'm going to kill you!" Paris's mother vanished as Jack dry-heaved in the corner.

Jack ran over, throwing open a nearby window. "What the hell was that?"

The man shuffled uncomfortably and sat up. After a moment the air cleared and Jack could smell the scent of fresh baked apple-pie filling the room.

The man noticed Jack sniffing the air and a smile spread across his face. "My power is to change my scent." He looked over at Jack with an almost grateful look on his face. "I thought she was really going to kill me," he explained, lowering his head to stare down at his shoes.

Jack nodded his agreement and noticed blood still running down Larry's neck. "Hold still." He opened a drawer to a nearby dresser and pulled out the first thing he could grab.

With a small smile on his face, Larry looked at Jack questionably. "You're going to use a pair of underwear to stop the bleeding?"

Jack looked down and saw a pair of white men's briefs in his hands. "Why not? I'm sure they're clean." Holding them out so they dangled from his fingers, Jack turned them. "No skid marks at least. Plus, I think you got bigger problems to worry about."

Jack eyed the door nervously as he carefully wiped away the blood and held the underwear to the cut to help stop the bleeding. *Why am I being so nice? I am supposed to be interrogating him for information on the school? When did I become the good cop?* Jack sighed and took a step back. "Look, I suck at this whole interrogation business."

Larry smiled softly but didn't say a word.

"I know a girl who came from the school. Something is wrong with her, seriously wrong. I don't know what you guys did to her, but I'm not going to let it keep happening." Jack looked back to the door and then to Larry. "We have two choices. You tell me where I can find the people responsible and how I can get the humans out, and I will let you live. Otherwise, I tell Paris you raped that girl and she can do whatever she wants with you."

The man hung his head in shame. "Most of the guards have slaves. The whole place is corrupt. I don't understand what is going on. I know we're at war with the rebels, but everything seems strange. The Angel shouldn't approve of the actions at the school, but he appears to be encouraging it, and it just seems to be getting worse."

Anger rose up in Jack at the word Angel. "The Angel is dead. He died at the bottom of a cliff, because your Blessed hunted him down."

Frowning, Larry looked up. "Alix is alive. He is the true Angel. That boy was a fake. He was just pretending to be the Angel to get support for the rebels."

"That boy was my friend, he wasn't faking anything. All he wanted to do was live, to have a normal life." Jack clutched the edge of the dresser for support. There was a long pause as Jack fought to keep his temper from allowing him to kill Larry. He took a deep breath before continuing. "I don't care about your world. I would be happy if I never heard the word Leech again. All I care about are the people in the school, nothing more."

Larry sighed as he looked up at Jack, sadness in his eyes. "There are seven guards on watch at all times. Some of them are my friends. Can you promise me you won't kill them?"

Jack shook his head. "If you know a way I can get the people out without killing anyone, I am all ears."

"What if I go in and talk to them. I might be able to convince my friends to let you get the humans out between their watches."

"No." Jack walked to the window and closed it, feeling a bitter cold wind.

"You're not going to let me walk out of here, are you?" Larry looked back at Jack, a pleading look in his eyes.

"I will make you a deal. Tomorrow morning when I leave, I will tie you up and lock you in the bathroom." Jack stopped at the obvious look of dismay on Larry's face. "If I survive, and once I get the people on their way to safety, I will come back here and let you go."

"And if you don't come back?" Larry asked, but when Jack didn't reply he sighed, defeated. "At oh-four-hundred is when Ken takes over on the west side near the back entrance around by the gym. He is one of the guys you're looking for, and that's where most of the humans are bunking. In the gym there are two guards standing watch. Both are good men. If you can take them out with a cuff ..." As the man talked, Jack nodded just to reassure him as he tried to piece together a plan in his head. Absorbing his intel while he formulated a plan of his own, knowing full well that Larry could be lying.

I know the school better than most people, having escaped from it more times than I can remember, he mused to himself. This time he just had to escape with a group of people, while the Blessed watched the exits. "Your biggest problem will be if the Angel," he stopped and looked at Jack as if waiting for a reaction, "Alix ... is still there."

Jack almost jumped out of his skin. "Wait, he's actually alive? You have seen him?"

"Well, he would have to be if I'm standing here."

Jack looked at him questionably.

"It's only a legend really, but it's said that when the last Angel dies so do we. It's why us Blessed protect him. Without him, us Leeches would simply keel over."

Jack looked up at the man, smiling as he tried not to freak out at the news. "And this legend is it real?"

"Well, as I said, it's just a legend, but it's been around for a while. There are more official words to it written in a book at the library of Atlantis, but it's written in Latin or Hebrew, or something. But we are told that's what it says and everyone knows that Alix's child was killed by the ghost."

"He is alive!" Jack said smiling. "I can't believe he is alive." Tears started streaming down his face. He knew there was a chance the legend could be wrong, but he pushed those thoughts aside as he focused on the slim hope that his angel was alive.

"There is no way I'm going to let you kill the Angel." Larry started struggling with the rope binding his hands.

"Calm down, I don't care about Alix," Jack said, putting a hand on Larry's shoulder. "My angel is alive." He couldn't contain his happiness as he yelled, "He's alive!" at the top of his lungs.

Paris's mother appeared just inside the doorway and looked at Jack quizzically "Who is alive?"

Jack looked at her blankly as something clicked in his mind. *She was making Caleo appear to me. Why? And if Caleo is alive how is she making his ghost? I need to find out more about her power.* Turning back to Larry, Jack ignored her question. "When did Alix get there?"

"He teleported in the other day, right before those rogue Leeches broke out and took that girl of yours."

"So, he can teleport?"

"No, he can manipulate shadows. He showed up with two soldiers. I'm guessing they were his guards. One of them must have teleported them?"

Jack shook his head as his thoughts immediately went to Steve. *But why would he be with the Blessed?* he asked himself as he paced the room, trying to piece everything together. "Was one of them named Steve Roberts?" Jack asked, just to satisfy his suspicions. He glanced over his shoulder and the ghost was still there, her arms crossed over her chest.

"Steve Roberts is the rebel who started all of this. There is no way he would be with the Angel," Larry said, clearly upset with the accusation.

"But he can teleport."

"Teleporting isn't that uncommon. The Blessed breed them by the hundreds," Larry argued

Breed them? Jack shook his head, as he wondered what he was getting into. *I don't need this now that I know Caleo is alive, I should be focused on finding him. But what about the people? I can't just leave them.*

"We caught his brother a few days ago. It's only a matter of time before he shows up to rescue him, though."

Jack snickered. "You obviously don't know that family." He looked up to see a confused look on Larry's face, like he had somehow burst his happy bubble. Jack looked behind him to see if Paris's reaction was the same, but her ghost had vanished. "They hate each other. The only reason Steve would show up would be to kill his brother before you guys got a chance." He walked across the room and opened up a door ... it was a closet full of men's cloths. "Let's get you set up for the day, then I will find you something to eat." Jack opened up the hallway door and found a bathroom one door down. "Get up. Let's move you into the bathroom." Jack grabbed his bag off the dresser and escorted Larry down the hall.

The bathroom was a small, windowless room with just enough space for a toilet, sink, tub, and a narrow strip as a walkway.

Jack pointed to the toilet with the closed lid. "Sit." Once Larry did what he was told, Jack dumped the contents of his backpack on the ground in the hallway and rifled through it.

"What are you doing with that?" Jack looked up to see Larry pointing to the cuff that had been embedded in Jack's chest.

"I am going to take it apart when I have a chance. I like to see how things work." Jack shoved the cuff back into his bag and started to repack his clothes. Stopping, he picked up the screwdriver he was looking for.

"You know that if you're not careful, the power source in that thing could kill you, right?" Larry said, and Jack had to smile because the man actually sounded worried.

Jack unscrewed the door knob, turned it around with the locking mechanism on the outside and screwed it back into place. "You wouldn't happen to know if it's booby trapped, would you?"

Larry looked at Jack with a smile. "Not that I know of, and that's the honest to the Angel truth. If you up and died on me I would be left with her to deal with." Jack stopped looking at the door and turned around, expecting to see a phantom behind him, but saw Paris glaring down at him instead.

"Hello, it's good to see your smiling face again," Jack said, offering a smile. Paris rolled her eyes, walking away. "I wonder what her story is."

Larry leaned forward, a surprised look on his face. "You don't know who that is?"

Jack shook his head. "No, why? Should I?"

"Her name is Paris. The Blessed have been hunting her since the thirties. She has killed more of us than any criminal on the Blessed's list. Every man we have sent against her, she has killed. She never speaks. It's said that when she was a girl her tongue was cut out, and that's why she only speaks through her ghosts." Larry leaned toward the wall as he tried to look down the hallway, as if to make sure she wasn't listening.

"Don't worry, she's upstairs." Jack stood up, pressed the locking mechanism, and tried the knob on the other side to make sure it worked.

"She can see and hear everything her ghosts can. Be careful, female Leeches are unstable. They will turn violent at the drop of a hat."

Jack laughed. "I think the hat has already dropped on this one, let's hope someone picks it back up real soon." He looked down at the man, seeing the dried blood smears on his neck. Jack grabbed a towel hanging by the sink, and turned on the water. After a moment he stuck the towel under the running water to wet it and jerked his hand back in surprise.

Larry looked up at Jack, who was smiling as the steam rose up from the sink fogging the mirror. "Hot water?" Larry asked, surprised.

"It must be run by gas or a propane tank on the property," Jack said excitedly as he looked at the shower then frowned knowing the problem. He was alone with a prisoner. He couldn't get a shower if no one was there to watch Larry.

"Please, just let me stand under the water for one minute. It has been so long since I've had a hot shower," Larry begged.

Jack looked at the shower and then back down at Larry. "How am I going to get you out of your coat and shirt?"

Larry appeared to think about it for a moment. "Do you still have my cuff gun?" Jack nodded, knowing he saw it propped against the door when they first walked in. "Unbind me. If I run, you can shoot a cuff into me."

Jack thought about this for a moment before shutting the door and locking it. "Stay seated."

He went to the kitchen and found an unopened box of Captain Crunch. Slowly he turned around and glanced to where the cuff gun was. Paris was upstairs and the gun was still propped against a chair. He walked over to the gun and was strapping it over his shoulder when he heard a male's voice coming from upstairs. Jack crept closer. Although he couldn't make out what was being said, he knew the voice. *Steve.*

Jack listened as Paris's mother's voice rang loud and clear. "I'm done. I can't just take him into the Blessed Camp. They will kill me without even knowing who I am. I agreed to get him to the base for you. We said nothing about fighting."

Jack backed away from the steps and walked back down the hallway. *She is working for Steve, but why would Steve want me to go to the school? That coward wants me to bust out his brother. But that doesn't make sense, they hate each other.* Jack put his foot behind the door as he slowly opened it a crack. Larry was still sitting in the same place, unmoved. "Stand up, turn around, and back up to me." Larry did as he was told and Jack could see that his left hand was still gloved. "Now step away and throw me your clothes as you take them off. Don't reach into any pockets, just remove and kick them over here." Larry did as he was told and stood waiting for further instructions. "Ten minutes, then you're done and get tied back up."

Larry didn't waste any time getting into the shower and pulling the curtain closed. Jack picked up the man's clothes and shut the door, locking it behind him. He walked down the hall and tossed them into a closet. He found a pair of sweatpants that looked like they would be a little big on Larry but shrugged. *He should be happy I am giving him anything.* When Jack got back he opened the door without knocking. Larry poked his head out briefly as Jack laid the sweatpants on the sink and backed out.

5

"What are you doing with my gloves?" Jack was pulled out of his train of thought at the sound of Larry's voice. He knew Larry had fallen asleep, but he had no clue how much time had actually passed since he started playing with the cuff.

"It's not your glove; it was Captain Brook's glove." Climbing to his feet to stretch, Jack noticed the sun was setting out the window and that the room was dimly lit. It must have been hours since he had escorted Larry back to the room and tied him to the bed. "I dissected that cuff thing. The power source is unlike anything I have ever seen; it's small and very light weight for the amount of power it can produce. I have been running the lamp off that one there for at least four hours now. Do you know what it is called?"

Larry shook his head. "It's Leech technology, we have had those for at least the last thirty years that I have been working for the Blessed."

Jack held up the glove like an eager child ready to show off his school art project. "I have made my own design of a combat glove. It works almost like a cuff. I have the power source here." Jack turned the cuff of the glove inside out to show where he had stitched in the small, circular blue power source that was the size of a quarter. "And I have wired this puppy to shock on impact. So anything I grab or hit with my palm gets a constant jolt."

"And what if you don't want to shock the object you are grabbing?" Larry scooted up in the bed to a sitting position to get a better look at the glove.

"I have planned for that as well." Jack pointed to a place where the side of the index finger knuckle would be on the glove "I took apart that stick thingy you use to control and disable the cuffs and have it wired into this glove here. I can turn it on or off with a flick of my thumb. I think I can even deactivate actual cuffs if I'm close enough." Smiling, Jack ran his fingers over the small button, then slid it on. He held out his hand experimentally, hoping to see sparks or anything to add to the cool factor, but sighed when nothing happened.

"Is it working?" Larry asked

"I'm not sure," Jack admitted. "I guess I'm going to have to try it out." Jack turned to leave, but noticed a look of concern on Larry's face. "Don't worry, you have answered all my questions. Now, I need to figure out what kind of game someone else is playing." Jack closed the door and walked up the stairs to the second story of the house.

"Paris?" Jack called out as he reached the top of the stairs.

Paris's mother's ghost appeared at the end of the hall. "What do you want?" it demanded, crossing its arms over its chest.

"I need to talk to you." Jack walked down the hall. He saw three doors; one on the left and two on the right. He knocked as he pushed open the first door he came to. The room was empty except for a desk and a book shelf.

"I'm here! So talk already," Paris's mother's phantom sounded angry, but Jack ignored it and walked to the next door, pushing it open.

Empty. Jack pulled the door shut and turned to the last door only to see that the phantom had put herself between Jack and it. "You might as well come out. I'm not talking to your ghosts anymore." Jack took a deep breath and walked right through the spirit.

"I told you not to touch my mother," the ghost screamed as Jack pushed open the door, only to find this room empty as well.

"Steve, you might as well come out, too. I heard you two talking."

Paris stood up on the other side of a twin size bed that was concealing her from view, her mother appearing beside her. "He is gone," her mother, said regaining her calm composure.

"So he is the one who told you to trick me into going to the school?" Jack crossed the room and stood on the other side of the bed, waiting for Paris to attack at any moment. *What if it's a trick and Steve is going to teleport behind me*, he thought as he took a few steps back so that the wall was against his back to prevent the attack.

"What other choice did I have? I am tired of running. Steve promised to take down the Blessed, and without them, I won't be hunted anymore." She turned to the side and Jack could see her eye was bruised, as if someone slugged her. She must have seen the shock on his face because she turned her head to conceal it. "Don't. I'm not one of your human women. I'm stronger than any man or Leech that you know."

"I think you underestimate a few human women." Jack looked up at Paris's mother, then back to Paris. "Can I ask you a question?" Jack waited for confirmation, but none came. "Is she a real ghost or just like a hologram or something ... I mean, do you control her or does she actually think and feel on her own."

Paris gave a half-smile, obviously happy with the change of subject. "She is just a puppet, I pull all the strings," Paris's mother said as Paris pointed to her.

"And you can make it anything you want? I mean, I saw that lion earlier and it was awesome, but can you make it into say an airplane or dinosaur?"

"Anything that I have had time to study long enough, I can recreate." The phantom turned to mist then formed into a snake, which changed into a small blue bird, then back into Paris's mother.

"Why your mother?" Jack asked and the look on her face changed to the normal angry look that Jack had gotten used to. "I don't mean why her. I mean, does it have to be something that has died, or can you do living people as well?"

Paris's mother morphed into Jack's form, which slumped forward and walked around the room like a monkey, only to stop right in front of Jack. Once there, it stood up straight and asked, "Are you dead?"

Jack raised his hands up in surrender. "You haven't killed me yet," Jack teased, and was rewarded with a choking-laughing sound from Paris. He noted that it was the first sound he heard her make.

The sound of engines outside caused Jack and Paris to fly to the window to investigate. "The Blessed," Jack heard his own voice whisper, and looked back over his shoulder at the specter. "They found us!"

"You have to get out of here. If they find you, they will kill you." Jack ran into the hallway, Paris right behind him. At the sound of the front door crashing in, they came to a stop at the top of the stairs. Jack looked around desperately and noticed the pull string for the attic hatch. "Get up there and hide," he pleaded, but she just stood there looking at him. "You have to or they will kill you."

"Wait, your friend he is alive. Steve has him." The ghostly image of Jack vanished as Paris disappeared into the attic, pulling the hatch closed behind her.

He really is alive! Jack smiled to himself as he took off down the stairs, coming face to face with a soldier dressed entirely in black on his way up.

"Hold it right——" the man collapsed to the ground as Jack slammed the palm of his left hand into his forehead, sparks arcing across the man's helmet at the contact with Jack's hand.

Three more men dressed in black raised their guns from the bottom of the stairs. "I surrender." Jack raised his hands, turning off the glove by running his thumb up over the inside of his knuckle. Two of the men grabbed him, jerking him down the stairs and throwing him to the floor.

"Not him! Get the girl! The ghost is here! Find her!" Larry yelled, emerging from the back of the crowd, where he pulled Jack to his feet. "You're coming with us." He pushed Jack firmly against the wall, snapping a pair real handcuffs around Jack's wrists, and pinning Jack's arms behind his back as he was pressed face first into the wall.

The men in black rushed up the stairs. Two stayed behind, guarding the bottom, and one stepped forward, leveling his gun to Jack's chest ... "All Leeches must be cuffed before transport."

"He's just a human." Larry stepped between Jack and the man protectively. "He is not to be harmed."

"I saw otherwise, he will be cuffed for processing!" The man shoved Larry to the side and Jack felt a sharp pain shoot through his left butt cheek. He crumpled to the ground, losing control of his muscles as wave after wave of electricity pulsed through his body.

Jack heard some arguing above him but he couldn't focus through the pain.

The pulsing abruptly lessened, and although Jack could still fill the constant pulsing going through his body, it wasn't causing his every muscle to contract beyond control.

"He is my dog. You can process him, but if any harm comes to my human you will be held accountable to the law," Jack heard Larry yelling above him.

Jack looked up at him in surprise. *Dog? Is that some kind of slave? Is he turning me into his slave?*

One of the men pulled up the left side of Jack's shirt, exposing his ribs. "He doesn't have your mark. So he isn't yours."

"Not yet." Larry bent down to him and placed a hand on Jack's shoulder. "You are going to be drugged. Don't worry, your master will stay with you until you wake up." Jack felt a small needle prick and a warm sensation traveled up his arm.

"Master? Bullshule ..." Jack's shout of outrage slurred as the drug took control of his body and he fell limp to the floor.

"We're going to be late if you don't hurry," Marcy said again, as she checked her makeup in the visor mirror for the third time since she got into the van.

Jack stuck his head out the window of the van and drove up next to Caleo, who had been walking on the side of the road with Jack following close behind for the last mile."Caleo, just get in the van. I've said I'm sorry like twenty times now. Can't we just get this over with?"

Caleo stopped and turned to Jack angrily. "You should have told me."

"You know now, and look, Marcy wants you to get in the van. Right?" Jack turned to Marcy who looked like she was turning as red as her lipstick.

Carefully she leaned over Jack so she could look right at Caleo. "If you don't get in the car right now, I will have the whole cheerleading squad spread the rumors that you were caught playing with the football teams jockstraps after school."

"Marcy!" Jack yelled, slamming on the brakes and causing her to smack her head against the steering wheel.

Marcy sat back in her seat and smiled at Jack as she muttered, "It's not like I'm that far from the truth. The little pervert has probably been watching you shower, too."

Jack shot her a warning glare as the door to the back seat of the van rolled open. When the door closed and Jack started driving again, Marcy turned and looked at Caleo. "By God, if I even see you after this car is parked, you will wish you weren't born. You are not to come within fifteen feet of us at all."

Jack looked back in the mirror at Caleo's angry, embarrassed face, and wanted to slam on the brakes again, demanding Marcy get out and walk. He slowly took his foot off the accelerator as he envisioned it; her red face, him and Caleo going to the dance stag, having a great time, maybe even just sneaking into the pool for a swim in the dark. But then the images of his social suicide replaced the happy thought; becoming the outcast, losing his title as captain of the swim team and in doing, so losing his scholarship chances. Jack pressed his foot back down, already wishing the night was over.

Just when they were pulling into the driveway of the school, Marcy put her hand on Jack's knee. "Jack, sweetie, why don't you let Caleo out here. I'm sure he doesn't want to show up to the dance looking like a third wheel." Jack looked over at Marcy, not believing what she was saying. "Isn't that right, Caleo?" she asked, looking back between the seats.

"Jack, just pull over," Caleo pleaded, his voice sounding so sad that Jack wanted to give him a hug. "She's right, I wouldn't want anyone to think that I am actually with you guys," he added bitterly.

Jack slowed down, but didn't stop as he drove up the long driveway of the parking lot and looked over at Marcy. "This is ridiculous—" He slammed on the brakes, bringing the van to a stop as he heard the back door open and saw Caleo jump out. "Caleo, get back in the van."

"I'm walking, have fun tonight," Caleo said bitterly.

"You heard him. Let's go, we're already late." Marcy reached over and put her hand on Jack's thigh and smiled suggestively. "Besides, this night is about us."

Jack felt sick. He wanted to pull away from her, the mere thought of them being together made him feel ill, but he smiled back because he knew that's what he was supposed to do even if it felt wrong.

"Fine." Jack stepped on the gas and watched in the rearview mirror as Caleo disappeared into the crowd of teenagers waiting to be announced for the dance. Jack pulled the van into one of the last open parking spots and got out, not even bothering to do the gentlemanly thing and open his date's door.

"Jenny says that if we go around to the side of the gym, she can cut us in somewhere to be announced before everyone else." Marcy put her cell phone back into her bra, grabbed Jack's hand, and dragged him to the side of the gym. Jenny was waiting, holding a door open and motioning for them to hurry as if she would get into trouble for doing this.

"Come on," Jenny hissed. Both the girls laughed as Jenny led them behind the large, baby-blue drapery that was hung on all the walls to help change the gym into something more than the drab room it was every other school day. Jack couldn't help thinking how close the color was to matching Caleo's eyes. They were pushed into a place near the front of the line and Jenny disappeared back into the gym. Jack heard someone comment about cutting in line, but after Marcy whipped her head around the complaining stopped. An announcer called out two sets of names and the line stepped forward robotically.

"Whenever we get called, take three steps forward stop and smile to the left. That's where the camera man will be." Marcy rechecked her makeup in her compact and stuck it in her little clutch purse.

Jack took a deep breath and glanced behind him, looking for Caleo, but he couldn't see him through the masses of teenagers.

"Are you paying attention?" Marcy pulled at Jack's arm, forcing him to look back at her.

"Yeah, I heard. Three steps, look left, and smile," Jack repeated, standing on his tiptoes as he looked back through the crowd, searching for the white hair.

"Are you looking for your sister? She is already in the gym. See, right there." Marcy pointed toward the gym.

Jack didn't even bother looking to where she was pointing. "No, for Caleo. Do you think he is all right?"

"What's up with you lately? Who cares if he's all right? He's a freak." They stepped forward as another set of names were called. "You are here with me. Why are you paying attention to anyone else?"

"Jack Barely and Marcy Cobben."

Jack heard his name announced and stepped forward. He felt a tug at his arm and stopped. *Why am I doing this? I should be having fun hanging out with Caleo. Why do I care what these people think?* Marcy started walking again and Jack followed robotically as they stepped off the platform and down into the crowd on the dance floor.

"Let's go get some punch while they announce the rest of the names. Oh look, there is Jenny and Miranda. You see that dress." Marcy pointed to the one Miranda was wearing and Jack didn't even bother to look at it as he scanned the crowd for Caleo. "My mother had to let out the seam around the hips so much she had to add a piece of fabric. See that yellow lace? That wasn't there when she bought it. A whole extra inch."

Jack zoned out of the conversation as Marcy greeted her friends and poured herself a cup of the red punch. *Ha, apparently I lied to Caleo, she is risking the punch.* Jack smiled as he envisioned shoving her face first into the liquid and smiling as red stains poured down her dress.

Jack looked up as he heard the girls laughing and pointing toward the stage just as the announcer said, "Caleo Anima with no date whatsoever."

Jack looked over at the announcer's corner and saw that Mike had taken over the stand and was laughing hysterically. He started for Mike, ready to punch him in the face, not caring about any of the trouble he would get in with the school or Jillian,

Marcy grabbed him by the hand and pulled him to a stop saying, "Wait."

Jack looked back at her angrily, ready to shove her away, but everyone in the crowd took a collective gasp and burst out laughing. Terrified about what could have happened, Jack looked back to the stage just in time to see the last three water balloons explode. A soaked Caleo was standing dumbstruck on the stage, looking down at the laughing crowd and scanning the faces as if looking for an answer as to why.

Furious, Jack turned back around to face Marcy. "You knew about this?"

Marcy let go of Jack's arm, still laughing smugly. "Well, yeah."

"It was partially her idea," Jenny said proudly.

Jack turned back to the stage and saw Caleo running out the side door. "Why? What did he do? You couldn't just let him have one normal night?"

Marcy crossed her hands over her chest triumphantly as Jenny and Miranda came up beside her. "He's not normal, he's a freak and you need to decide what you want. If you want to date me, you can't have friends like him hanging around."

"He's not a freak!" Jack grabbed the punch bowl off the table and upended it over Marcy's head, letting the bowl drop to the floor where it shattered. The whole building went quiet and everyone turned to see what Jack had done. Marcy screamed and ran from the gym into the girls' locker room. Smiling, Jack walked in the opposite direction toward the door leading to the parking lot.

"Mr. Barely, may I speak with you a moment?" Jack turned to see Miss Hayman, the school's French teacher, standing behind him; her face hard with fury. "I saw what you did back there and I expect to see you in the principal's office first thing Monday morning."

"It was an accident. I didn't mean—"

"First thing Monday morning!" she yelled, cutting him off. "Now go home Mr. Barely. I will be calling your parents."

"Didn't you see what they did to Caleo?" Enraged, Jack pointed to the platform where a janitor was already mopping up the water. "Why are you not talking to them? Why aren't you calling their parents? Did you kick them out?"

Miss Hayman looked back towards the stage where Caleo had just been pelted with water balloons, and Jack could tell that she was trying to hide a smug smile. "I wasn't in the room when it happened. I don't know who did it. If you know some names, bring it up with the principal on Monday. Now out!" She pointed to the door dismissively.

"Whatever," Jack muttered. *Stupid teacher thinks that she can buy popularity with the in crowd, good luck with that.* He turned around to see Jillian standing next to the door.

As he approached, she gave him a sad smile and shook her head. "You're in big trouble, you know?"

"You don't know the half of it. Come Monday I will have detention and I can kiss my swimming scholarship goodbye. No more Captain Jack of the swim team either. I may even have to turn in my Speedo," Jack joked, feeling oddly relieved that he didn't have to pretend to be someone he wasn't anymore.

Jillian wrapped her arms around Jack's neck. "She's never going to forgive you for this. If you're lucky, she will just never talk to you again. At worst, you will be tormented worse than … well, Caleo, the rest of the school year."

"If you're trying to make me feel better you're doing a crappy job," Jack whispered in her ear.

Behind them Miss Hayman coughed and Jack turned to leave. Jillian pulled back on his hand, asking, "Was it worth it?"

Jack smiled weakly in return. "It felt good at the time. Ask me in a few days and I'll let you know." He pushed open the door and stepped out into the cold night air, pulling his suit jacket tight to help block out the wind. He scanned around, looking for any sign of Caleo as he fished out his keys, thinking more than likely Caleo was already walking home. Jack pictured Caleo soaked, and crying as he walked down the street in the freezing cold air.

As he unlocked the van door, he noticed four guys coming around from the side of the school laughing as they walked to the back door of the gym, which was propped open with a brick. Jack's stomach sank and he tried to convince himself that they just snuck out for a smoke, but as he watched them he noticed blood on one of their knuckles as the guy brought it up and shook it in the air and heard them talking about hearing a sound when someone hit the ground.

"Caleo," Jack whispered to himself, running for the back side of the school. One of the guys saw him and they all sprinted for the opened door, slamming it shut behind them as the last one entered.

"Caleo!" Jack screamed the second he rounded the corner, but he couldn't see anything except darkness. "Caleo!" he yelled again, running down the side of the school desperately searching the shadows for any signs of movement that would tell him where he was as he followed the footprints in the snow.

"Here." Jack turned his head to the sound of Caleo's voice and found a dark spot that resembled a human blob slumped against the wall.

"What happened?" Jack asked, trying to feel Caleo's body for anything that could be damaged.

"Before or after the water balloons?" Jack grimaced at the bitterness in Caleo's rough, pain-filled voice.

"You've got to be freezing." Jack pulled off his jacket and wrapped it around Caleo's front in hopes of blocking some of the wind.

"Don't, you'll get blood on it." Caleo pushed the jacket away and cringed. "Oh crap!"

"What?" Jack searched the darkness for any sign of someone approaching.

"The deposit!" Caleo whined.

"What deposit?" Jack asked frantically, confused as to what was the matter.

"For the suit," Caleo said. "There is no way I'm going to get the deposit back now. I think they ripped the sleeve off my jacket, and I don't even know where my tie is."

Jack smiled, knowing Caleo couldn't see it. "Your tie is still in the van, and don't worry about the suit. I'll help pay Grandma back." Extending a hand, Jack helped Caleo to his feet. "Let's see if I can get you home without Grandma flipping out."

"I think she is actually getting used to me coming home looking like this," Caleo said and spit. Jack looked down and even in the dark he knew it was blood against the white snow.

"I think she's just not making it a big deal in front of you. I can guarantee she will be at the school Monday wanting to know what happened and trying to get the chaperones fired." Jack extended his arm, stopping Caleo as they approached the corner and he made sure the coast was clear. "Okay, it's safe." Jack helped Caleo to the side door before running around to jump into the driver's seat. He started the engine and took off down the road, heading for the house. "Let's get you home, and we can watch a movie like we should have done instead of going to this silly dance."

"What about your date?" Caleo asked meekly, staring out the window.

"It's not going to work out between me and Marcy." Jack looked over at Caleo and smiled, hoping it would cheer him up.

"Why, what happened?" Caleo asked, turning to look at Jack.

"She just ran off with her friends, leaving me on the dance floor by myself." Jack smiled, picturing her with the red punch dripping down her gown as she took off for the locker room, her two lackeys in tow.

"Just like that? Not even a word?" Caleo asked in amazement.

Jack thought about it for a moment, wondering if he should tell Caleo the whole story, but decided it would just make him worry and he had enough to stress about tonight. "Not that I can remember anyway. But who cares, I am done with her. She's too boring. I'm just not into all that cruel gossip stuff."

They sat in silence for a while. Jack could see Caleo smiling even though the cab was dark. Caleo shifted uncomfortably and Jack realized he had been caught between glances.

"What?" Caleo asked, laying his head against the window.

"I was just trying to think of a way to get you past Grandma without her seeing how dinged up you are," Jack lied as he turned on the overhead light and glanced over to get a better assessment of the damage. Caleo's eyes looked like they would both be black, his cheek already looked to be swelling, his lip was busted open and still bleeding, and that was only what Jack could see. He cringed at the thought of the damage that Caleo's clothes could be hiding.

"She is going to see it anyway, it's not like I can hide in my room for the next few days." Caleo flipped down the visor and winced at his own appearance.

"I know, but it may cut into our movie time. She would be like, 'Oh my poor baby! I'm going to march right down to the school and demand to scold every student in there'," Jack said dramatically as he adopted his best Grandma impression.

Caleo laughed and clutched his side in pain.

"Do you need a doctor?" Jack asked seriously and Caleo just shook his head. "Well, good, then. Grandma can see your ugly mug in the morning. We have a movie to watch." He raised an eyebrow at Caleo and smiled to show he was kidding about the ugly part.

Caleo smiled back, his blue eyes seeming to light up with an idea. "Well, if you got wet and went in the front door, she would be too busy getting onto you that I could sneak in the back door and run up the stairs."

"I can tell her we got bored at the dance and jumped in the lake. She will be pissed we ruined the suits, but wouldn't question it at all and the trail of water leading in the back door from your clothes would just make it that much more believable." Jack turned off into the driveway. "It's going to have to be quick. We don't need to be outside catching hypothermia or anything."

Caleo nodded and they ran around to the back side of the house. Caleo grabbed the hose and sprayed Jack down quickly.

Not waiting for Caleo to even turn off the water, Jack quickly ran around to the front of the house while Caleo stayed at the back door.

"Grandma, I'm home!" Jack took five steps into the house before Grandma came strolling out of the kitchen drying her hands on a dishtowel.

"What are you doing home so early? The dance just started less than an hour … Jack Barely! What have you done to your suit?" Grandma yelled, running to him and looking out the door. "Where is Caleo? Is everything okay?" Jack saw Caleo run up the stairs and heard the back door slam shut behind him. Grandma turned around and that was Jack's cue to run up to Caleo's room, but he just stood there, unable to move.

Jack reached out and touched his grandma on the shoulder. "Grandma, I need you to do something for me. Promise not to make a big deal about it?"

"Jack, you're dripping all over my floor and I am guessing Caleo left a river behind him as well," Grandma scolded "What did you do, jump in the pond?"

Jack shook his head, looking at the puddle forming under his feet. "It's about why we are wet. He got beat up pretty bad at the dance and I didn't want you making a big deal about it tonight." Grandma looked back over her shoulder to the stairs and looked like she was debating on whether she should run up them to check on him. "Just let him have tonight. I want to make it up to him for forcing him to go to this stupid dance in the first place."

She looked at Jack, worry clear on her face, and he could tell she was debating yelling for Caleo to get his tail down here.

"I promise I will watch him all night, and in the morning you can tear us a new one for not telling you tonight," Jack pleaded.

Grandma nodded once with a grimace before yelling loud enough for Caleo to hear in his room. "I'm not cleaning this mess up!" She winked at Jack then whispered, "Take care of my boy. I will get a mop."

Jack nodded and took off up the stairs for Caleo's room.

"And I'm not paying for those suits!" Grandma called from somewhere in the kitchen.

When he made it to Caleo's room, he pushed open the door and saw him sitting on the edge of his bed in his boxers, crying as he looked down at the bruises that prominently colored his snow white ribs, legs, and arms.

Jack walked over and knelt down next to him, trying not to cry himself. "I'm sorry. I should never have made you go. It's my fault."

Caleo wiped his eyes with his hand and lay down on the bed, rolling over to face the wall. Jack reached out to touch Caleo's shoulder, wanting to reassure him to tell him he didn't have to hide his tears, but he couldn't get the words to come up.

Slowly Jack got to his feet, peeled off his wet clothes, tossing them into the tub in the bathroom, and slipped into a clean pair of Caleo's sweatpants and a T-shirt.

He had just picked up the remote control for the TV when Caleo asked, "Why do they hate me?"

The sound of Caleo's words made Jack want to cry. He wished he could tell him everything would be different when they graduated, but he doubted anything would change in college ... it might even be worse. He couldn't think of a single thing that could make things better. He grabbed a blanket, pulling it over Caleo's body as he climbed up onto the bed and wrapped his arms around him. *I will be different. I don't care about any of those losers. This is where I belong.* Jack flicked on the TV and sung softly as he watched Caleo cry himself to sleep.

Startled, Jack rolled over. Caleo's room had completely vanished, and was replaced with the white walls of the Nurse's office at school. Confused, Jack sat up. His head spun and he thought he was going to fall over. "Nurse Wha..?" Jack called, desperately trying to think of her name. He knew it began with a Wh, but couldn't get his brain to focus enough to remember the rest. "How did I get here?"

Shaking his head, he pinched his eyes shut trying to clear the fog in his mind. When he opened them, he saw a man in an army uniform standing in the doorway looking down at him. *Blessed.* His head started to clear he remembered the fight, and being cuffed in the butt. Jack closed his eyes again to get the room to stop spinning. "Why can't I focus?"

The uniformed man walked into the room, took a plastic cup from beside the sink, and filled it with water. "It's the drug. It's wearing off, but it will take some time before you are back to normal."

Jack looked up at the man in surprise. "Can you hear my thoughts?"

"No." The man laughed "You're talking out loud. You have been doing a lot of that in the last hour."

Opening his eyes, Jack looked at the man, confused. "I what?"

"You've been talking in your sleep," the man said, smiling. "Don't worry, most of it was gibberish." He chuckled.

Jack rubbed the back of his neck and looked up at the man as he held out the cup of water to him. "Larry?" Jack asked, suddenly remembering the man's name.

"Yeah, take these." Larry handed Jack two red and blue pills, and Jack stared at him suspiciously. "If I wanted you dead, I wouldn't have saved your butt back at the house."

Jack popped the pills into his mouth and washed them down with the offered water. "If I remember right, I got shot in the butt."

Larry smiled. "Just with a cuff, which has been taken out and should be almost healed. The prongs don't do much damage if the cuff is removed before the site can become infected."

"Really?" Jack shifted his weight, and aside from sticking to the vinyl bed he didn't feel any pain. He looked down for the first time, and realized that aside from a paper hospital gown he was naked. "Do I want to know what happened?" Jack asked, pulling on the gown to conceal his nakedness.

"It's standard procedure. They thought you were a Leech, and had to look for a mark. Apparently two of the Blessed guards saw you take down a man with just your palm, and they swore they saw sparks running across your hand." Pulling a glove from his back pocket, Larry tossed it to the bed beside Jack. "Well after a day of testing and examining, they decided you are not a Leech and that the guys must have imagined it."

"They didn't find my glove?" Jack looked at Larry in surprise.

Larry shook his head. "I took it off you right after you were drugged."

"Why?"

"Consider us even. You stopped the Ghost from slitting my throat, I stopped the Blessed from torturing and possibly killing you for making a weapon using our technology."

Jack smiled. "Even? I think I am still owed a hot shower." Jack slowly stood up, the effects of the drug had all but vanished. "I saved you from both death and torture, and you still got a hot shower."

"Well, we have showers but they are not hot," Larry offered. "And there is a five minute time limit."

Jack grimaced. "We could always go back to that house."

Leaning back against the wall, Larry crossed his arms over his chest. "You would go back to that house and forget about all these people, all for a hot shower?"

Jack paused to think about it for a moment before he shook his head. "I couldn't go back; a girl is expecting me to rescue her family."

"You're married?" Larry's voice sounded surprised but his face didn't show it.

Why does everybody think I'm married? Jack shook his head again. "No, she is just a girl I went to school with."

Larry raised an eye brow in question. "A girl you're interested in?"

"No, we only went to this one school dance, but things didn't ..." Jack stopped and looked down at the paper gown that barely covered him. "Do you think we can have this conversation a little later when I am wearing more clothes?"

"I gave you your glove." Larry looked down at the glove, still sitting on the bed.

Oh great, a joker! Jack smiled, feeling especially exposed. As the man looked at him, he pulled down on the paper gown, hoping to stretch it a little to provide more coverage. He glanced back over his shoulder at the glove. "I don't think it will provide much protection."

"Well there was more to the glove before you cut the fingers off." Larry turned and walked out of the room, returning a few seconds later carrying an arm full of clothes. "I got these out of your bag." Larry dropped them on the bed. "I'm assuming your name is Jack." He picked up a pair of red Speedos, with the name Jack across the back, but it was almost all worn off.

"I never told you my name?" Jack asked, trying to think back on the events.

"Well I was going to threaten you with a cold shower, but your underwear kind of took all the fun out of that." Tossing them back on the bed, Larry turned around, allowing Jack some privacy.

Jack slipped out of the paper gown, and was just pulling on his Speedo when he noticed the red circle under his left arm. "What's this?"

Larry didn't even bother turning around. "I'm assuming you mean the tattoo? It's kind of like a brand used on cattle. It shows which Leech you belong to."

Jack stopped running his fingers over the design and looked at the back of Larry's head. "Excuse me?"

Larry chuckled. "Relax. I had to do something. If I hadn't said that you were my dog, they would probably have killed you for attacking those men."

Jack lifted up his arm and looked at the tattoo in the mirror above the sink. It was a ring, which looked like it was the exact size and shape as Caleo's, except where his was a bright golden color this was blood red with an upside-down triangle in it.

"Don't worry, it just sounds a lot worse than it is. Think of a dog as more of a knight's squire. Most of you become our soldiers and fight under us in battle. In fact, two of the people the Ghost killed in the woods were my last dogs."

"I'm not fighting for the Blessed," Jack said bitterly, sliding on his shirt. He was grateful that it covered up the mark, because he didn't like the idea of being Larry's anything.

"I wouldn't ask you to do anything you're not comfortable with." Larry turned around and lifted up his shirt, showing him that his Mark of the Leech was in the very spot Jack's new tattoo was. "That mark works both ways you know. Anything you do comes back on me. If you step out of line, I am the one who will be punished."

So he took a big risk claiming me as his dog. He knows what I plan on doing, but he still did it. Sitting back down on the bed, Jack took a deep breath. "So, what now?"

"Well I figured I'd give you a tour of where the humans are allowed." Larry started walking towards the door and stopped. "Oh, before I forget, you are my dog. It means you have to obey me no matter what I say. If someone here sees you not following my orders, and me not punishing you, they could take it upon themselves to do so. When you are in the compound, you are my servant. So be careful."

Jack glared at Larry. "Servant?"

Larry smiled. "When we are in front of the Blessed. Oh, and you have to call me sir." He took a few steps forward before looking over his shoulder with a smile.

Jack tried to tell himself that this was just for show, but something felt wrong about it.

"Or master if you prefer," Larry offered with a smile.

"I think I will stick with sir," Jack grumbled.

"Follow me." Larry took a few more steps then coughed. "Do I need to whistle?"

"No, sir," Jack said, biting back his pride as he got to his feet, following Larry out the door.

"Good boy." Larry took a few more steps and pointed down a hall as two guards came walking in the other direction. "Those two belong to General Boone. They are dogs, but they carry his rank and so are considered your superiors." As the uniformed humans got closer, Larry abruptly switched topics. "Down there is the cafeteria. You are allowed to fetch my meals, but you must eat in the gym with the other humans."

Jack rolled his eyes. "I went to school here; I know where the cafeteria is."

Larry stiffened for a moment, coming to a complete stop before turning to Jack, a look of outrage on his face. "You say yes sir! Nothing else! Do you understand me?"

Jack watched as Larry's eyes darted between Jack and something behind him. "I'm sorry." Jack bowed his head in shame, hoping he wasn't over acting. "Yes, sir."

Larry nodded his approval and continued walking. Jack glanced behind him to see if they were being followed, and saw two men in Blessed army uniforms turn to head down the hallway towards the auditorium. Something seemed very familiar about them, and Jack turned to get a better look. Just as the last man was about to disappear around the corner, he turned his head and looked back at Jack his piercing blue eyes appraising him.

"Caleo!" Jack couldn't believe his eyes. "Caleo!" he called again. The soldier with milky white skin, bright blue eyes, and white hair peeking out from under his hat stared back at him. His head was tilted slightly to the side, as if trying to figure out who had called his name.

It really is him. What is he doing here? Jack went to take a step forward, but hesitated. *Something is wrong. Why is he looking at me like that? He should have recognized me by now.* A hand reached out from around the corner, yanking Caleo down the hall. Jack took off running after them. "Caleo wait!" He rounded the corner, but Caleo and another man in uniform were already at the end of the long hallway in front of the auditorium doors. *Damn, they're fast.* He watched as they pushed open the doors and stepped inside. *How did they get from here to down there in a few seconds? Unless they ran at super speed or teleported.* "Steve," Jack said as if the name was a curse.

"Jack, what are you doing? If the Blessed see you—"

"Did you see them?" Jack asked, cutting Larry off and pointing down the hall to the auditorium doors.

"Yeah, they are the guys that came with Alix. Now let's get going before they decide to punish us both for—"

A screech came over the radio attached to Larry's belt, followed by a voice. "This is Gaun, The Angel has issued an order. We are to push forward to the compound in Cranberry. This place is to be packed in twelve hours."

"That's good news for you. We are moving on, which means your humans are free to go once we are gone. Only dogs will accompany us to the next camp." Smiling, Larry looked over at Jack. "See, your trip was for nothing."

The radio squelched again, and Gaun announced, "The humans are a liability. By order of the Angel, the humans' energy is to be recycled for the sake of preservation of our species."

"They're going to kill the humans?" Jack asked, looking up at Larry as he backed away slowly.

"But that's against the Code. Why wouldn't we just leave them?" The look on Larry's face was troubled, as if he was trying to work through why the Blessed would be killing the humans in his head.

"Larry?" Jack looked back over his shoulder, planning out his escape.

Larry's head snapped up. "You need to get out of here. I can't let this happen." Larry turned and ran down the hallway, yelling, "We are the Blessed guard! We defend the people against our Kind! We do not kill humans. Punishment is death!"

Jack stood there, not sure what to do. *Should I run after Caleo or help save the people?* There was gun fire and screaming from down the hall; Jack assumed it was from the gym, which was only a few yards away. If he went out the back door, he could be there in seconds. Jack looked over his shoulder at the auditorium, then back down the hallway. *Caleo. I've got to get Caleo back, nothing else matters.* Jack pictured himself running down the hall, bursting into the auditorium, and escaping out the back door with Caleo.

Footsteps running down the hall drew his attention. *Are they going to help or just join in the massacre?* Jack pushed himself flat against the wall and waited, hoping he wouldn't have to find out. Two figures ran past him and Jack let out a breath of relief. *Thank you.*

The footsteps stopped abruptly, and the two soldiers came running back around the corner.

Crap! Jack swore, taking off to run down the hallway, the two men right on his heels. A hand grabbed his shoulder. Jack spun, driving his gloved hand into the side of the man's head. Unconscious, the man collapsed to the ground as the other man rammed into Jack's stomach with his shoulder. He slammed him through the auditorium doors, smashing him into something hard and causing him to fall to the floor.

Taking off his glove, the man smiled as he took a step toward Jack. "I haven't drained a human in years."

Jack looked up at the man, baring his teeth. The man stopped, his facial expression changing to a look of fear, and he reached for something on his belt. However, his hands found nothing; his holster was empty.

"Get up!" a man yelled from behind him. Jack looked over his shoulder and saw Thorn, Caleo's grandfather, standing in an iron cage behind him. He had been stripped down to nothing except a pair of black shorts; his arms were stretched out to his sides and chained to the bars, a single Cuff was embedded in his chest. Jack climbed to his feet, facing the Blessed guard. "Just avoid his left hand," Thorn said happily like he was just telling Jack to tie his shoe.

The man swung with his right, and Jack made to block it, but the man pulled back. Lunging forward with his left at the last second, he aimed for Jack's throat.

Jack rolled to the left, the man's hand missing its target by inches as he stumbled off balance. Jack grabbed his arm with his right hand and latched onto the side of the man's neck with his left. The man screamed in pain as the current traveled through his body and he crumpled to the floor.

"Quick, get the controller," Thorn ordered, struggling with his chains. "If you can get this cuff off I could get these chains myself."

Jack stood up, reaching through the bars with his gloved hand. Thorn jerked away, having seen what the glove did to the man on the floor. Ignoring him, Jack reached forward, touching the cuff with the back of his hand, and it fell to the floor of the cage with a clunk.

Blood dripped from the hundreds of little pin holes, running down Thorn's sculpted chest. "How did you do that?" Thorn looked down at the cuff by his feet, then back up at Jack.

"I have the remote signal sewn into the back of the glove. Figured it would come in handy." The man at Jack's feet groaned and Jack kicked him in the head, knocking him out. "Where're the keys?"

"We won't need them now." Thorn smiled, showing his perfectly straight white teeth as tiny vines grew from under his toenails and snaked up his arms to the chains. "Grape seeds are easily hidden, and when you are as old as I am they can be very deadly."

A gunshot sounded just outside in the hall. Panicked, Jack looked back, remembering what he went in there for. "Caleo? Have you seen him?"

There was a groan from the chains as they fell to the ground, taking the vines with it. "You brought Caleo here? You—"

"No," Jack said, cutting him off, "he came in here right before I did. Where did he go?"

"No one came in here. The door opened, but I just figured they forgot something and went back out." Thorn looked at Jack skeptically.

Jack looked around the room impatiently, realizing that they must have teleported out of here before the trouble started.

"Go help the others. I can get myself out," Thorn commanded, rubbing his wrists.

"Okay." Jack turned, pulling open the door to leave.

"No, boy, the others. In here." Thorn motioned deeper into the room with his chin.

Jack looked around in the dark and noticed seven faces staring back at him, except for one large man, who was almost too big for his cage. He was frowning, an almost ashamed look on his face. *Nolan,* Jack thought bitterly. *He knew all this time and said nothing. Even put up a grave marker to fool us.* Jack ran to the first cage. The man inside pushed his chest out eagerly, waiting for the release of his cuff. The second the cuff hit the ground, the man grabbed a hold of the bars of the cage in both hands. The metal shimmered under his touch and turned to a black liquid, which puddled onto the floor around his feet. The man eyed Jack up before stepping past him and turning Thorn's bars to liquid as well.

Without waiting for prompting, Jack ran to the next cage, which happened to be Nolan's.

"Is he safe?" Nolan asked excitedly, shoving his chest up to the bars and prompting Jack to release him.

Glaring at the massive man, Jack released his cuff and backed away. "Like you didn't know?"

"Is he safe?" Nolan impatiently asked again. His body faded as he turned into a figure of pure water and stepped through his cage. "Where is he?" He grabbed Jack by the shirt, his body instantly solid again.

"Your brother has him!" Jack pushed Nolan off.

The look on Nolan's face confused Jack, and he couldn't tell if it was relief or betrayal. "Steve has him?"

"I thought you knew." Jack shook his head, trying to piece together what could be going on, but nothing made sense. "The grave?"

"I put the grave marker there, but I didn't find his body. I figured he survived and was in hiding with you." Taking a step back, Nolan leaned against his cage.

"And you didn't come to check? You let us think that he was dead for the last six months," Jack argued desperately, wanting to hurt the man for all the pain he had caused them.

Nolan gave Jack a half smile. "I have kind of been tied up for the last few months."

"Nolan, get your pants on. We need to move," Thorn ordered as he rushed out the door, the rest of the Leeches close behind.

Pants? Jack looked down automatically and backed away, seeing for the first time that Nolan was completely naked. "Dude!"

Nolan knelt down, reaching through the cage, where he grabbed his shorts off the floor.

He must have seen Jack averting his eyes, because he said, "I can turn to water, I can't turn my clothes." Nolan slid his pants on and ran for the door, not waiting for Jack. "Go home, kid."

Jack whistled and Nolan stopped at the door.

"This way." Jack beckoned, motioning for Nolan to follow before running up the stage and ducking behind the long, red curtain. "This door leads to the hall beside the gym." Pushing through the double doors, Jack ran into the hallway.

It was a mad house. People were in the halls, pounding on the doors to get outside, while uniformed Blessed guards shot at one another inside the gym. Some using powers while others shot both cuffs and bullets.

"How do we tell one from the other?" Jack asked, scanning the crowd for Larry.

Thorn caught up with him and pushed his way past, staring into the gym. "We don't, they are all Blessed." Thorn snapped his finger and pointed into the gym. "Kill them all," he ordered. His men ran inside and started fighting without saying a word.

Jack's eyes widened as he watched them kill off the Blessed soldiers indiscriminately. "Larry!" Jack went to step forward, but Thorn stuck his hand out, stopping him and pulling him away from the door.

"This is best left to the Leeches, my boy," Thorn said calmly. Jack noticed a leafy vine wrapped around Thorn's hand, curling around his middle finger like a ring.

"My friend is in there!" Jack yelled, trying to make sure he was heard over the noise.

"If your friend is in there, he is a Blessed soldier. We don't have time to hold punches. That would get us killed." Turning around, Thorn surveyed the crowd of humans shoving at the door as they screamed for help. "Why don't you worry about your own kind and get the humans out of here? Last thing we want is one of you to get hurt in the crossfire."

Jack looked back at the humans and sighed. He didn't know why being called a human made him feel like he was being insulted, but he felt like he should be doing more to save Larry.

"Nolan, help the boy," Thorn barked when Jack didn't move.

"Yes, sir." Nolan walked away picked up a chair and threw it through a nearby window. "Jack, let's go!"

Turning back to the gym, Jack searched the remaining faces for Larry, but still couldn't see him.

"You're one of the humans, boy. I suggest you lead your people to safety. We may have saved them, but we are not here to babysit. Our only priority is the Angel." Thorn's voice was cold and uncaring as he looked over at Jack.

"You did a crap job at that if I remember right," Jack said, looking at the crowd of people still pushing at the door. *They are why I came here. Let's get them to the house and I can look for Caleo myself. I will be damned if I let them take him away from me again.* Jack ran to the window screaming, "Humans!" A few of the crowd turned to look and Jack jumped out through the broken window. "Follow me!" They only hesitated a moment, eyeing Nolan by the window before they all rushed forward. "Everyone stay together. Run north and follow the road. If you see anything that can be used as a weapon, grab it," Jack said, helping people down from the window and motioning for them to keep moving.

Someone grabbed Jack by the shoulder. He whipped around, ready to drive his gloved hand into his attacker, but stopped at the last moment when he saw it was Mike Karr, Jillian's old boyfriend

"Jack? It is you, man? What happened to your face?"

"Mike, am I glad to see you. Run ahead, lead them back to my house," Jack said, patting him on the shoulder. He turned back around to help a lady holding a toddler in one arm as she tried to help a small girl through the window with the other arm. *God, did I really just tell Mike I was glad to see him?*

"Jacky?"

Jack smiled as he recognized the little girl who was next in line. "Kylie, Miss Farns." Jack picked up the little girl, placing her on the ground by his feet, and turned to help Miss Farns through. *They have lost weight since the last time I saw them. A lot of weight.* Jack knelt down in front of Kylie. "Hop on, we have to run." Kylie wrapped her arms and legs around Jack's back and neck. He stood up and bounced her twice. "Here, let me carry Zoey." Jack reached for the child and she screamed, hugging her mother's neck.

"I got her," Miss Farns said hurriedly as people continued to file out of the window.

"Were going back to the Inn. It's only a few miles away. If you start getting tired, let me know." Jack hiked Kylie up on his back once more and they took off after the crowd.

A horn honked, and Jack turned to see Nolan driving up in a military truck. "Get in! You drive." Nolan jumped out of the truck and hopped into the back of the truck bed. Without argument, Jack climbed in the driver's seat, sliding Kylie to the center while Miss Farns and Zoey got into the passenger seat.

"Buckle up and hold still," Miss Farns instructed Kylie as Jack shoved the truck into gear and stepped on the gas. He drove to the front of the group, dodging around people, and stopped.

He estimated there were at least thirty people and there was no way they would all fit. Jack looked over at Miss Farns and she shook her head.

"They won't all fit," she confirmed, looking worriedly out the window as people piled into the bed.

"Load up!" Jack yelled out the window as he saw Mike looking at him like he was crazy. Jack smiled at the sight of Bruce, Mike's best friend, as they jumped in together. Jack looked in the side mirror and saw four people sitting with their legs hanging out the side of the truck bed and more were still trying to climb onto the roof and hood.

"Anyone who doesn't fit, stay on this road I will be right back. An hour tops!" Jack accelerated the truck up to twenty miles an hour and tried to avoid any bumps as people desperately tried to hang on.

He pulled onto the half mile driveway to his home and slowly stopped where the mailbox used to be. He honked the horn twice and got out of the cab, waving his hands around in the air toward the house.

"Jack, what's up?" Mike called from the bed and some people started climbing out and walking up the driveway.

"I don't want Jillian to think we are strangers and start shooting." Jack cupped his hands to his mouth. "Yo, ugly! I'm home!" he yelled at the top of his lungs.

Jillian stood up from behind the woodpile and flipped Jack off. Even from this distance Jack could tell she was smiling.

Just wait till she sees Mike. Mickey isn't going to be happy at all. Jack climbed back into the truck and drove up the driveway, parking the truck right next to the house. Jillian was right at the door waiting for it to be opened. *Pissed or happy?* Jack asked himself as he opened the door.

She hugged Jack before staring at the people jumping out of the truck. "What did you do?" she asked, shaking her head as she surveyed the people.

Jillian's head abruptly stopped and her face lit up with excitement. "Mike!" Jillian ran to him and wrapped her arms around his neck.

Jack thought he heard Mike say how much he had missed her, but the crowd was too noisy so he couldn't be sure. *Big moment. Does he kiss her? Does she kiss him back?* Smiling, Mike leaned his forehead against hers. He moved in for the kiss, but Jillian let him go and backed away awkwardly, rubbing her hands against his pants. "Oh rejected," Jack said softly to himself as he enjoyed the moment of seeing Mike's confused face.

"Did you enjoy that?" Mickey asked. His voice told Jack he was standing inches away behind him.

Jack turned, smiling at a very agitated looking Mickey. "Maybe a little."

"So who is Mr. Wavy Hair?" Mickey leaned against the truck and looked down at his feet, trying desperately not to seem jealous.

Jack looked back to Jillian, who appeared to be giving Mike the 'I have moved on speech', because Mike's face was suddenly serious and he kept glancing over in Mickey and Jack's direction. "That right there is Mike Karr, Jillian's ex-boyfriend."

Jillian pointed over to Mickey and Mike's face got red. Mickey smiled and nervously raised a hand in greeting.

"Hou," Jack offered, looking at Mickey with an upraised hand.

Mickey lowered his tightly clenched fist down to his side, glaring at Jack. "I'm not Indian you jerk."

"Really?" Jack asked, not caring. The joke had gotten the reaction he wanted, which was putting Mickey on edge before meeting Mike. "I thought you were. You sure look Native American to me."

Mickey shrugged, turning his full attention back to Jillian. "Let me guess, captain of the football team? The guy every girl wanted at your school?"

"Was captain of the football team. Now there isn't much of a school left to have a team." Jack flashed Mickey a quick smile as he saw Jillian approaching. "But I'm pretty sure the latter part of the statement is still correct," Jack said as he retreated to the other side of the truck where Nolan was waiting, staring out into the trees.

"So why did you come?" Jack asked, not bothering to dance around with politeness.

Nolan shrugged. "You want the reason I told Thorn or the real one?"

"Aren't they the same? You want Caleo, and you think I know where to find him." Jack kicked at a rock by his foot, glaring at Nolan.

Nolan smiled, nodding his head. "That's about right."

"I will kill you before I let you take him to Thorn," Jack said flatly.

"I'm not taking him to Thorn. I can't." Nolan stopped as if he was afraid to say more, but after a moment sighed and continued. "Thorn wants Caleo to be some kind of ruthless war hero. I can't do that. It's not in Caleo. He is too selfless and kind. I won't let Thorn change him. He is … perfect the way he is. We need to get him into hiding and hope they eventually stop looking for him."

Jack felt his face getting warm with jealousy at someone else calling his Caleo perfect. He looked away as he gritted his teeth.

"Look," Nolan said, shifting his massive weight to his other foot. A gesture that would have said he was nervous on anyone else, but for him it screamed that he was an elephant ready to stampede over Jack without warning. "I know you have feelings for him."

Jack jerked his head up in surprise. He had only told Jillian about his feelings, and through her Mickey found out. *How does he know?* Frowning, Jack looked up at Nolan, challenging him to say more.

"The constant teasing, being overly protective when someone else seems to be interested in him," Nolan answered the question Jack was thinking without it being asked. "We both just want him to be safe. Let's focus on getting him away from my brother and someplace safe. Then we can sort things out between us."

Jack nodded, hating everything about this conversation. He despised Nolan, hated the idea that Caleo liked him, and loathed the idea of working with him to find Caleo. Jack pushed off the truck and looked to the crowd of people. "Listen up!" Jack waited for everyone to turn toward him and quiet down. "This is Jillian's home." Jack pointed to the tarp-covered basement. "No one is to go there without her permission. While you are on our land, Jillian is queen. If she asks you not to do something, you better not do it. Remember, she has a gun and isn't afraid to use it." Jack looked over at Jillian and bowed. "Your majesty" he said before walking back around the truck and jumping in the driver's seat.

"Where are you going? Are you seriously going to leave me with these people?" Jillian leaned in through the truck window to prevent Jack from leaving.

"Relax, I am just going to pick up the rest of the group. I will be right back." Jack slowly put the truck in reverse as Jillian climbed back out the window. The passenger door opened and Mike jumped in, closing the door. Confused, Jack looked at him, but Mike just stared out the open window. "Jillian!" Jack turned and yelled out his window. She turned back from walking to Mickey. "He's alive!" A look of bewilderment spread across her face, and her eyes darted to Mike in the passenger seat. Her features changed to a 'you deal with it yourself' death glare. "No!" Jack yelled, shaking his head excitedly. "Caleo is alive!"

Jillian stared at him, even more confused than before, but she saw Nolan standing in the crowd and headed toward him.

"He was dead?" Mike asked from the seat beside him as they pulled out of the driveway.

Jack looked over at him, wondering why he decided to come along. "We thought he was."

"Oh?" Mike asked and looked at Jack expectantly, as if waiting for him to explain further, but Jack was focused on forming a plan as to how he could get Caleo back. *If only I knew where Steve's base was,* Jack thought to himself. He couldn't see any way of getting Caleo back without knowing where he was being kept.

"So who is this Mickey guy?" Mike asked after the silence stretched on for a minute.

Jack glanced over at him and saw he was staring out the window, trying to hide the fact that he was upset Jillian had moved on. "He is just some guy who's been helping us survive the last few months."

Mike whipped around, looking at Jack in shock. "That's it? Just some guy who walked up and you let him live with you?"

Jack chuckled. "Well there is more to it than that. He kind of saved our lives, and when I was—" Jack stopped, glanced at his reflection in the mirror, and quickly looked away before continuing, "He used to be a nurse and helped take care of me while I healed."

Mike was quiet again for a moment, then asked, "But what do you really know about him? How do you know he isn't some murderer or anything?"

"I don't. Jillian told me not to ask about his past after he got all upset when I asked him about his age a while back," Jack confessed. "But I guess it's just never been that big of a deal. I mean, he worships the ground Jillian walks on. Plus, he is handy to have around at times, and Jillian genuinely seems happy, so I guess it doesn't matter if he is in his sixties." Jack smiled internally at the last part. He knew saying Jillian was happy would be a low blow, but he enjoyed kicking Mike where it hurt for all the trouble he had caused Caleo over the years.

"How old is he?" Mike asked quickly, jumping on the age problem and completely ignoring the rest.

"I have no clue. I would say older than twenty but younger than a hundred." Jack wiggled his hand. "Give or take a year or two."

Mickey snorted gruffly. "Looks like he is in his mid-twenties."

Jack shook his head. "Yeah, but you never know with Leeches. He could be any age really."

"Wait, he's a Leech?" Mike asked angrily. "You're letting one of those monsters touch your sister?"

Jack glanced over and saw Mike's face had turned beet red. "They are not all monsters. Calm down, it's okay?"

"My girlfriend is sleeping with a Leech and you think it's okay?" Mike asked. "Just what part of that do you think is okay?"

"I learned a long time ago not to tell Jillian who she can or can't date," Jack said smoothly. "You should have seen this jerk she was dating in high school," he joked.

"Some brother you are. Don't even care about your own sister. Let her whore around with a Lee—"

Jack slammed on the brakes, sending Mike flying into the dashboard. "I'm going to tell you this once, and only once, you pathetic little boy. If you call my sister a whore again I will—"

"You will what? Cry to your freak boyfriend? Yeah, I know all about your gay love with that—"

Jack had heard enough. He grabbed Mike by the shirt, pulling him closer as he raised his fist to punch him, but just couldn't do it. Sighing, he let Mike go.

"Faggot," Mike spat, adjusting his shirt.

Jack leaned against the steering wheel, taking a deep breath as Mike continued to insult him, his sister, Caleo and even his grandmother.

"Just get out," Jack said softly, not even bothering to lift his head.

"Make me, gay boy."

Jack looked up at Mike lazily. "We're not in high school anymore. I'm tired of hearing you talk. Look around, nobody cares. There isn't a single soul around who cares enough to listen to your babbling. So get out."

Enraged, Mike turned to Jack. "Make me!" he spat.

Jack turned on his glove with a flick of his thumb and shoved it against the radio. Sparks flew and a rancid smell smoked out from it. "Get out!" Jack yelled.

"You're one of them, aren't you?" Mike said, shoving open the door and jumping out.

Jack let himself have a little smile as he slammed his foot down on the gas before Mike could even get the door closed. He looked in the rearview mirror to see Mike yelling something at him, but he couldn't hear it. "Damn!" Jack yelled happily, feeling good about himself for finally standing up to Mike. Then he thought of Jillian as he saw Mike turn around and start walking back toward the Inn. "She is so going to kill me."

6

Jack lay on his bed, staring up at the blue tarp above his head, trying to find patterns in the material where it was stained from sitting rain water. He had only been home for an hour and already he felt ready to run out and find Caleo. *Focus, Jack, focus.* A picture of Caleo's face floated in front of his mind's eye. *Where are you? You're with Steve, but where is Steve?* A creak on the steps made Jack sit up. He'd expected Jillian to come once she realized he was back. She was busy helping people get things set up and settled for the evening when he arrived and he needed to think, so he just came straight down here to avoid all the confusion.

"Jack, can I come down?" Marcy's voice whispered softly from the top of the stairs. "I know you said no one except Jillian, but I ..." She paused as if unsure what to say.

"Yeah, come down. Of course you are allowed down here." She ran down the stairs as fast as she could.

"What's been going on out ..." Jack stopped as Marcy crouched down and disappeared into her cubby hole under the steps. Jack lay back down and looked up at the tarp again, picking a particular stain that reminded him of a blow-dryer to stare at. "Too many people?"

There was a long pause before she answered in a whisper, "I will be fine."

"Are your parents out there?" Jack held his breath, waiting for the answer. He hadn't seen them, but he wasn't really paying attention, and everyone looked so different with their weight loss and the layers of dirt.

"They're there," she answered timidly.

Jack looked back and saw her head looking out from between the stairs with a slight smile.

"They're setting up in one of the tents Jillian passed out earlier."

Jack smiled at the thought of the tents. He had scavenged them on one of their shopping trips. Jillian had told him it was a waste of time because they had the basement and argued about taking them. In the end Jack won out, telling her that if it came to trading they would be valuable. They took ten tents that day, some fitting up to six people. "Can you do me a favor?" Jack asked, rolling over to his belly as he looked at her.

Marcy shrank back into the darkness and answered in a shaky voice, "Yes."

"I need you to look after Jillian for me."

"You want *me* to look after her?" Her voice sounded surprised and her face reappeared between the steps.

Jack chuckled. "She's not as strong as she seems ... if things get bad, I need you to show her how to stay hidden to stay safe."

"You're going away again?" The worry in her voice was evident, so Jack rolled over and stared back at the tarp, hoping that if he wasn't looking directly at her she would feel more comfortable.

"He's alive. I have to find him." Jack closed his eyes, envisioning Caleo in front of him smiling, healthy, and alive.

"So it's true ... you do love him?"

Jack opened his eyes at the unexpected statement. Her words didn't feel accusatory like Jack had once expected from her, but seemed generally interested in the answer.

His first instinct was to lie; it was none of her business after all. But he sighed. *I'm not going to hide it anymore. It's not like it matters if she knows anyway.* He nodded his answer. There was a long silence before Jack asked, "Why didn't you ever tell anyone? I know you knew after the dance, or at least suspected it. I went to school ready to be outed, to have my reputation destroyed, maybe even attacked by Mike and the rest of the football team. At the very least, get detention. But when I got there, everyone was saying it was an accident and even the principle told me just to be more careful."

"I was going to," Marcy said timidly. "I was in the locker room typing the text to send to everyone when your sister walked in."

"Jillian convinced you not to tell anyone?"

"Yeah, she said she would drop out of the cheer squad as long as I didn't tell anyone what happened." Marcy sounded ashamed, but Jack smiled at the thought of his sister protecting him even back then.

So that's why she dropped out of cheerleading and started taking up all that other crap. He chuckled as it all made sense. *All the extreme dance, the ballet, and interpretive dance classes; she was just trying to replace the cheerleading.* Jack looked back down at the floor. "But what about the other stuff? You could have still told everyone that I am ..." Jack stopped, unable to say the word gay. He didn't feel that was a right fit for him. He didn't like boys, he didn't even like girls. He was in love with Caleo. "... in love with Caleo," he finished, happy to have said it out loud.

"Well after I told her you were a ..." Marcy stopped, and Jack knew she was going to say fag but thought better of it. "... gay, she told me if I told anyone she would kick my butt."

"I believe my words were 'I will give you a black eye every day for the rest of your school career, if anyone ever picked on my brother for being gay'." Jillian walked down the steps and sat down next to Jack on the bed.

"How long have you been listening?"

"Somewhere around I have the greatest sister in the world and I will do anything she asks of me." Jillian leaned back against the wall, a smug look on her face.

"Yeah, I was thinking about getting her a mug, but you know I can't seem to find a store that carries them these days." Jack moved, and Jillian sat down beside him, grabbing his hand and intertwining their fingers.

"So when are you leaving?"

"As soon as I figure out where to go." Jack took a deep breath, knowing Jillian wanted him to explain how he knew Caleo was alive. "He's with Steve. I saw him, but something was wrong, it was as if he didn't even recognize me. I yelled his name and he just looked at me with that confused look he used to get when you'd talk about your interpretive dance classes."

Jillian smiled, obviously picturing Caleo's look. "Are you sure it wasn't a trick or something? Mickey told me some Leeches could turn into other people."

"No ... well, yeah it started out as a trick, but I really did see him at the school." Jack took a deep breath, knowing Jillian still had no clue what he was talking about, but she just smiled and waited. "I saw Caleo's ghost and he told me to go to the school, but it turned out that it wasn't Caleo's ghost, it was a Leech making me think I was seeing Caleo's ghost. When I was at the school, I really did see him."

"Ghost Caleo?"

"No, real Caleo."

"I'm confused."

"He was real at the school, but the ghost of Caleo that told me to go to the school was a trick by a Leech named Paris," Jack said, quickly becoming frustrated knowing that he wasn't getting anywhere closer to finding Caleo.

Jillian sat up and turned to face Jack, her face looking pissed. "Wait, are you telling me you went to the school because a ghost that looked like Caleo told you to? Jack, are you stupid?" When Jack didn't answer, Jillian blew out a breath of air. Leaning back against the wall, she said more calmly, "Why would anyone do that? God, she actually made you see a ghost of him."

"She was working for Steve," Jack said in an attempt to defend Paris, not knowing why. Jack sprang up out of the bed, smiling at his revelation. "She was working for Steve!" Jillian looked at him with a raised eyebrow, waiting for him to explain. "If she was working for Steve, there is a good chance she knows where he is hiding. I've got to go." Jack grabbed an empty backpack and started shoving some of his clothes in it.

"You're just going to leave me here again ... you left me for three days all alone. Do you know how hard that was?" Jillian yelled.

"You weren't alone, you had Mickey and Marcy." Jack smiled as he said their names, then tried to say them three times fast in his head, overjoyed at the thought of having a plan to find Caleo.

"Marcy doesn't count. All she does is hide in corners. It took me two hours to get her to come out for some breakfast yesterday." Jack glanced over to the steps and Jillian slapped a hand over her mouth. "Sorry Marcy."

"It's okay," came Marcy's meek reply.

Jack marveled at how Marcy could be so quiet that people forgot she was even around. "You won't be alone. In case you didn't notice, I kind of brought you a whole town of people."

Jillian bit her lip, obviously trying to change tactics. "You can't go alone either. What if there is trouble? Take Mike and Bruce."

Jack cringed inwardly, not wanting to tell his sister that he had gotten into an argument with Mike and left him on the side of the road. It was obvious that he hadn't told her yet, even though he arrived back at the house before Jack had. So he decided to go in a different direction. "I can't. I'm just going down the road to see if Paris is still there. If she sees anyone else she will run." *Or more likely try to kill us.*

"Take Mickey. He can be a kitten and stay in the truck, even hide under the seat if needed. That way if something happens, he—"

Jack held up his hand, stopping her. "There are laws against leaving animals in cars." Jack smiled as he lifted his backpack onto his shoulder. "I will be fine."

"Ahh! You can be so stubborn sometimes." Throwing her hands up in the air, Jillian ran up the stairs.

Jack raced to the bottom of the steps and called up, "I think we both got that from Dad!" A quick giggle from under the stairs let him know that Marcy was still listening. "I will be back tomorrow morning at the latest. If I'm not, here are directions to the house I am going to. Please don't give it to Jillian unless I'm not back by tomorrow night." Jack placed a slip of paper on the bottom step and went to his bed, picking up his smear stick and sliding on his glove. When he turned around, the note was gone. "Stay out of trouble." Jack climbed the stairs and stepped out into the cold evening air. It was already late in the day, he guessed it would be dark in an hour or two. He spotted Jillian standing in front of a tent, talking to a very angry looking Mike and Bruce who kept pointing in his direction as they yelled. He waved quickly, hoping to escape before she could stop him and ask about what happened between him and Mike. However, she didn't even turn to look in his direction as she got right back into Mike's face.

"You know where he is, don't you?" Jack turned and almost ran straight into Nolan's chest.

Jack shook his head. "No, but I know a girl who was working for Steve and I am going to see if she knows where his base is. And no, you can't come. If she sees you she will run."

"Why would she run?"

"Look at you." Jack tried patting Nolan on the chest as he tried to step by, but when Nolan just crossed his arms and moved into Jack's path, he said, "She is a Leech, and if I remember right your kind has strict rules saying you have to kill her. Call me a fool, but I don't think she wants that to happen."

"For good reason, too. They are never stable," Nolan said warningly.

"Yeah, well, they have the same rule about homosexuality if I remember correctly, but you don't seem to have a problem with that rule." Jack turned and walked to the truck, only to find Mickey sitting in the cab staring at Jillian, who was now laughing hysterically at a red-faced Mike. "Out, I got to make a run into town," Jack growled

"Do you think I am sitting here watching him hit on my girl for fun? Just shut up, and let's get this over with," Mickey grumbled, never taking his eyes off of Mike.

"He's not flirting, he is pissed. Just get out of the truck and tell her I forced you," Jack said, jumping into the driver's seat. When he looked over, Mickey was a black kitten sitting in a pile of clothes, glaring up at him. "Fine, but you stay in the truck. I can't have her thinking I am a cat person. Why couldn't you turn into a pit-bull or something?" Jack pulled out of the driveway and drove down the road, singing, "The jig is up, the news is out ..." *Renegade* by *Styx* was one of his favorite songs.

Jack pulled into the driveway of the house, opened the truck door, and stepped out. With one hand on his bag, he turned back to Mickey and raised his finger, saying, "Stay here. Stay." Mickey hissed then curled up inside his coat on the seat.

"Who are you talking to?"

Jack whipped around at the sound of Caleo's voice to see his ghost form standing inches from his face. "My cat. Isn't he just the cutest little ball of fleas you have ever seen?" Jack asked flatly, looking back over his shoulder to see Mickey yawn tiredly and stretch his back. *Yeah, it wasn't my best joke. Great, now I am speaking cat.* Pulling his bag out, Jack slammed the door shut.

"Why are you here, human? Last time I saw you, you were ..." Jack ignored the apparition, walking through it and right into the house.

"Paris, we have to talk," Jack said as he entered the kitchen, tossing his bag on to the kitchen table.

The phantom of Paris's mother appeared in front of him. "We were talking before you ran through me."

Jack pulled out a chair, sat down at the kitchen table, and pointed to the seat opposite of him. "I want to talk to you. That's you sitting in front of me. Not your ghosts."

Paris walked out from down the hall and sat down across from Jack, tapping her fingers on the table impatiently. "This better be good, human," her mother said, coming to stand behind her. They both glared at him from the other side of the table.

Jack wasted no time and got to the point. "I'm going after Steve and I need your help."

"Ha! I don't work for humans," Paris's mother announced as Paris stood up to leave.

"I'm not asking you to work for me. I want to work with you. I know you hate him for touching you, and I know that you know where I can find him."

Paris and her mother nodded smugly in unison at Jack across the table, and her mother answered, "And you want your friend. He is the new Angel, right? What makes you think I want to help you rescue your Angel? I would rather Steve be in charge."

"Caleo is different. He won't care that you're a woman, he just wants to be left alone."

Paris rolled her eyes. "Really? That's not the impression I got. What makes you think he wants to be rescued? Last time I saw him, he was all buddy-buddy with Steve."

"He what?"

"Well he wasn't being held at gunpoint or anything. In fact, he seemed to be working with Steve on this whole plan." Paris leaned against the table as she stared Jack down.

Jack shook his head. He couldn't believe Caleo was willingly staying with Steve, let alone actually allowing Paris to torture him with his image. "I don't care, I have to see him."

Paris smiled across the table at Jack. "Fine, but I am not babysitting you. If you die, you die. And don't even think about telling me what to do."

"Deal." Jack looked up. He liked this girl. In some ways she reminded him of a combination of his grandmother and Jillian; straight forward, beautiful, smart, and a 'don't take crap from anyone' personality. Well, maybe if Jillian was a pissed-off rattlesnake. He wondered what might have happened to her to get her so pissed-off at the world, but figured being hunted since the day you became a Leech would do that to a person. "So where is his base?

Confused, Paris looked up at Jack. "How the hell should I know?" her ghost snapped

"Well you're the one working with him."

"And you're in love with the white boy."

Jack just glared across the table at Paris for the low blow, and after an awkward moment of glaring each other down, Paris's mother said, "He always finds me. I have no clue where he lives." Paris got up and started pacing the floor, reminding Jack of an agitated lioness.

"What?" Jack's heart sank as his plan fell apart. "So you never actually saw his base? How did you see Caleo? I thought you said you needed to study someone before you could make their ghost shape."

Paris looked at Jack like he was stupid. "He brought him to me one day, told me to make him a ghost, and then told me that I would need to convince you to go to that school."

"But why?"

"I don't know. But he wasn't happy about you making friends with that Blessed soldier you had in the bedroom," Paris snapped.

Jack couldn't help wincing, thinking that he was responsible for her black eye, and glanced down at the wood grain in the table. "How are we going to find them now?"

"He was planning an attack on the Blessed base in Cranberry. He said that the Blessed took up residence in a hospital there."

Jack looked up in surprise. "Cranberry? That's where the Blessed soldiers were told to go to."

Paris nodded. "The school was the third base he has done this to."

"How? I mean, Alix was there. Is he working with Alix?" Jack couldn't shake the feeling that he knew the answer.

"It's not Alix. Steve has a shape shifter. As far as I can tell, he goes in, has his shifter order people around, brings in his own people, and shuts the base down from the inside. Cranberry is bigger than the others. He wanted me to go disguised as a boy. When I told him no, well you saw." She turned her back to Jack and looked into an empty cupboard above the sink.

"Why didn't you kill him? It's not like you even hesitated with the other guys," Jack asked.

She slammed the cupboard shut and the phantom's eyes glowed red. "Because, human, if his plan works there wouldn't be any more Blessed and I won't be hunted! I don't like having to look over my shoulder all the time and wonder if the Blessed have finally found me."

Wordlessly, Jack got up, pushed his chair in, picked up his bag and walked down the hall, leaving her in the kitchen.

"Where are you going?" Paris's mother asked.

Jack didn't even bother turning around as he entered the bathroom and shut the door. "We're leaving in twenty minutes!" he yelled through the door. "Get ready."

"What? Leaving? Where are we going?" By the sound of Paris's mother's voice, she was right on the other side of the door.

Jack didn't even bother to raise his voice as he turned on the water. "Steve is attacking Cranberry next. So that's where we are going." He slid his shirt over his head and threw it to the floor, excited at the chance to get a hot shower. Quickly he unbuttoned his pants and let them drop to the floor.

"I think the gas ran out this morning. There's no hot water." Paris's mother's voice was sweet and almost sounded sorry.

Jack stuck his hand under the water and quickly pulled it back, swearing at the cold water. Grumbling to himself, he pulled up his pants and opened the door, tugging his shirt over his head. "I'll be in the truck." He walked right through Paris's mother's specter and through the kitchen, where Paris was waiting by the door; her backpack strapped to her back and a smile on her face. "Don't say a word," he said as he walked past her and outside.

She followed Jack quietly to the truck and opened the passenger door. "Maybe I shouldn't have taken those two baths last night," her mother said overdramatically.

"Whatever," Jack grumbled, slamming his door shut.

Paris pulled Mickey out of his coat and cradled him in her arms, smiling as her mother's ghost asked, "So what's your cat's name?"

Jack looked over from the driver's seat to see Mickey glaring at him, as if challenging him to say something. "Stinky." Jack smiled as the cat moaned angrily from Paris's arms.

"You named your cat Stinky? He doesn't seem to like that!" Her mother laughed as she brought the now squirming Mickey up to her noise and sniffed. "You don't smell stinky to me. Do you little guy?"

"No, my sister named him. His real name is Mickey and ..." Jack looked up at her face, wanting to see her reaction. "He's a Leech, not a kitten," Jack added, trying not to laugh at the horrified look on both Mickey and Paris's face.

Paris dropped Mickey, who fell to the seat hissing and moaning. "Stupid shifters!" Paris's mother spat. "Move over, fur ball!" She pushed Mickey's clothes onto the floor of the cab, shoving Mickey to the center as she climbed in, making sure Mickey saw that she was purposely stepping all over his clothes. The second she closed the door, her mother disappeared and Jack backed out of the driveway.

As they drove down the road, Jack tapped the steering wheel impatiently, trying to break the silent tension in the air. He looked over at Paris and Mickey, both watching each other carefully as if waiting for the other to strike. Jack shrugged and started to sing, "When the lights go down in the ..." Mickey hissed and took a swipe at Jack's arm. "What, not a Journey fan? Fine." Jack smiled as he looked over at both his mute companions. "You can feel free to sing along if you want." He only paused slightly before he started singing, "I wear my sunglasses at night ..."

Jack pulled in the driveway, finishing the song *Take Me Home Tonight*. The second he put the truck into park, Paris kicked open her door and looked around, her expression hard. Jack figured she didn't like the idea of being this close to so many humans. "We aren't going to be here too long. Just long enough to get supplies, then it's back on the road."

Her mother materialized over her right shoulder, with her hand on her hip and an angry expression on her face. Paris grabbed her bag, intentionally knocking Mickey's clothes to the ground. Jack could tell by the slight movement of her leg that she had even kicked them farther under the truck so that Mickey wouldn't be able to get them and transform back without the embarrassment of everyone seeing him naked. "Do you think I'm in any hurry to get back in this cramped truck with you? You're like a jukebox. Do you even know how to shut up for just one second? Your mouth doesn't stop! Even the radio had commercials," her mother complained

Mickey looked down for his pants on the ground and mewed pitifully at Jack.

"You can pick up your own pants." Jack smiled as she kicked at them again just for good measure. "Gah! I can't believe you actually let me think you were a cat. Have some respect for yourself. Stupid shifters." Paris turned to walk into the woods, but stopped in her tracks and backed away from them suddenly. "This was a trap!" Her mother's eyes flashed red as she whirled around to face Jack. "You brought me to them!"

"What? Brought you to who?" Jack pulled his smear stick out from behind the seat, wondering who was there. Turning, he saw Thorn standing at the edge of the woods, leaning against a tree. "Go get Jillian," Jack yelled back to Mickey.

Mickey jumped out and ran off towards the house. Meanwhile, Paris had pulled her gun out and was shakily aiming it at Thorn.

"For a human, you're doing pretty well for yourself, Jack. You've just managed to help catch the one person who started all of this. To think she has been on the run since the forties and killed hundreds of Leeches, yet a human brings her down."

Without warning, a vine shot from the woods and wrapped around Paris's gun, ripping it from her grip. She turned and ran, only to get tripped up as the grass beneath her feet grew and wrapped itself around her ankles. "You're not getting away this time. We're at my house, everything here is of my own design."

Thorn emerged from the woods, walking slowly toward Paris. "Don't!" Jack screamed. He charged, his smear stick held high, ready to be brought down on Thorn's head. Thorn lifted his hand and a thicket of purple rose bushes grew into a wall in front Jack. They all blossomed as Jack forced himself to a halt inches from running into the fish hooked thorn bramble.

"It's been twenty years, Paris, but it's time you paid for your crime." Thorn raised his arm and vines sprouted from the ground, securing her wrist and ankles as they wound around her body, wrapping her like a mummy as they grew.

"Leave her alone," Jack yelled. He threw his smear stick over the roses at Thorn's head, but a tall man jumped out of the woods and snatched it out of the air effortlessly. "No, no!" Jack turned around and ran for Paris, but a man grabbed him from behind and held him in a full nelson, forcing him to watch what Thorn was doing. Jack awkwardly tried to grab at any body parts his gloved hand could land on, but it only snatched the air above his head.

Thorn straightened his back as he neared Paris. "You're being sentenced for the murder of the Angel Alix."

"But he's still alive! Alix isn't dead!" Paris's mother pleaded as Paris struggled against the vines on the ground.

"He is dead! His heart stopped beating and the Angel was passed to Caleo," Thorn announced.

"But he still lives!"

"His heart stopped! I don't care if they got it started again. He is no longer the Angel. You killed—" Thorn was cut off as a cuff embedded in his chest.

The man holding Jack let go abruptly, and Jack whipped around, grabbing him by the neck with his glove and taking him to the ground. The man convulsed under his hand, but Jack held him in place as he looked up to see that Nolan was the one who had shot Thorn.

"Nolan!" Thorn screamed. Two more pops from the gun sounded just as two figures came charging from the woods. They both fell to the ground, convulsing. "How dare you!"

The man under Jack's hand stopped twitching, and Jack looked down to see a sliver of ghostly silver liquid slide out from under him and snake its way toward Paris.

Her body shuttered as the liquid hit her and a big smile spread across her face. Jack looked back to Nolan as he whipped around and shot two more men charging at him from behind.

"That's enough!" Thorn yelled.

Jack looked back over his shoulder to see Thorn rip the cuff free from his chest, taking a big portion of skin with it. As he threw it to the ground, he seemed unfazed by the injury.

Before the cuff even hit the dirt, three gunshots sounded and Thorn collapsed to the ground. Jack looked over his shoulder to see Nolan walking towards Thorn as he fired twice more at hidden targets in the woods. A man cried out in pain, telling Jack that Nolan must have hit his target, but Nolan fired again and the cries suddenly stopped. Not even slowing his stride, Nolan pointed the gun back at Thorn, who had started to crawl away from Paris and was almost to the truck. Nolan fired once more, shooting Thorn through the back of the head. He then turned to face Jack, dropping his gun as if to say, 'Does this prove my intentions?' A quirky smile spread across his face as two tendrils of silver disappeared under his feet. Nolan fell to his knees, looking up to the sky as if praying.

Jack ran forward to help him, but as he approached, Nolan started chuckling loudly and Jack stopped. "Are you okay?" Jack took another cautious step forward, not sure what was going on. Nolan smiled up at Jack drunkenly, his head swaying slightly. "Nolan?"

"He's fine, he'll just need a moment. Thorn's men were very powerful, and now all that energy is his." Paris's phantom stood next to him, watching Nolan. Jack couldn't help but feel she wanted to slit his throat and have the power for herself.

Nolan slowly climbed to his feet, and sounding out of breath said, "Me? You're the one who absorbed Thorn's energy. You should be in a heavenly bliss for days."

Jack looked back to see Paris was smiling up at the sky as she ripped the vines from her body, but seemed less affected than Nolan. Paris's mother laughed slightly, saying, "You must not have heard. I am the ghost. Thorn was strong, but I have killed stronger."

Jack walked away, uninterested in the Leeches talking about power. He looked around at all the rest of the Rebels on the ground, clutching at the cuffs in their chests. "What are you going to do with these guys?" He looked back at Nolan.

"We'll handle them, it's Leech business." Nolan glanced past Jack to Paris, who was pulling pieces of dried vine out of her hair. "Maybe some of the old laws were made out of fear and need to be reconsidered."

"You think!" Paris's mother barked, standing beside Nolan.

Nolan whipped around, ready to fight, but only managed to swing his fist through the specter image.

"Relax, it's just Paris," Jack explained, walking away before he realized Nolan's sight didn't work the same as everyone else's, and he probably couldn't tell why the voice wasn't actually coming from the direction of the girl's mouth. He smiled devilishly to himself. *This could be fun!* Looking up, he found everyone in the camp's eyes were on him, and they all looked to be crying for some reason. "Don't worry, it's all taken care of," Jack said, smiling reassuringly. *Man, these people must not have had it as bad as we thought, if a little gun fight gets them rattled.* Nobody moved, and Jack glanced behind him to see that although Nolan was looking in Paris's direction, he kept flinching whenever her ghost spoke. "It's not a real ghost." Jack shook his head at the frightened people. *Geesh, these people aren't going to be much help if a ghost can scare them like ...* Jack stopped as he got closer to the house and realized everyone's tearful, worried eyes were still on him. "What's wrong?" Jack asked, but everyone moved away, giving him room and averting their eyes.

"Jack, honey." Miss Farns ran up to him and cupped her hands on either side of his face, her tears still flowing down her cheeks.

"What's wrong? Where is Kylie? Is she—" Jack stopped as she shook her head

"Kylie is fine," she said

Jack searched the faces in the crowd and saw Kylie holding onto Zoey's hand a few feet away. *Then what's the matter?* Jack continued looking for some clue as to what was going on.

Miss Farns hugged Jack tightly. "Jillian—"

"Jillian, where is she?" Jack asked as he shrugged off Miss Farns hands and frantically yelled, "Jillian!"

The world spun under his feet and Jack felt bile rising in his throat. *This can't be happening.* Miss Farns was saying something, but Jack couldn't piece together her words. *Jillian, where is Jillian? The house!* Jack spun around, and the second he saw the makeshift door to the basement he ran for it. "Jillian!" he screamed.

He ran down the first two stairs and stopped when he saw Bruce lying dead at the bottom of the steps, a gunshot to the side of the head. "Jillian?" Jack cried and sat down on the stair, bawling and afraid of what he might find if he went down any farther.

"Jack, she's all right." A naked Mickey appeared, standing over Bruce's body, and motioned for him to come down farther.

"She is?" Jack jumped to his feet and rushed down the steps, nearly tripping as he jumped over Bruce's body and almost landed on another. His eyes landed on Jillian crying on the end of her bed as she looked up at Jack. He ran to her, ignoring everything in the room except her. "What happened? Are you okay?" he asked, kneeling down in front of her."

"They ... and she ..." Tears streamed down her cheeks as Jillian picked up a pillow to bury her face in it.

Jack sat next to her on the bed. Wrapping his arms around her, he took in the scene. Bruce was at the bottom of the stairs, almost like he was about to run up them. A man lay on the ground a few feet behind him, his pants not quite pulled up all the way and unbuttoned. Jack looked at the man's face, but the jelled blood and the bullet wound made it hard to tell who it was. "Mike?" The moment the name escaped his lips, Jillian's body was racked in a sob. Jack looked to Mickey, who had managed to put a pair of jeans on and was crouched down in a corner, talking softly to someone in Jack's bed. *Marcy? Is she okay?* He looked down at the floor and saw that Caleo's smear stick lay in two pieces a few feet away. *That was beside my bed.* Jack rubbed Jillian's back and pulled her close to him as Mickey grabbed Bruce's body by his shoulders and started dragging him up the stairs.

Jillian cried even harder at the sound of his body hitting each step on its way up.

"Jillian, what happened?"

Jillian stared at Mike's body still lying on the floor. "He raped me, the little shithead raped me."

"What? Why?" Jack asked but his mind went back to everything Mike had said in the truck. *Oh God, this is my fault. I shouldn't have left them here with her.*

"He didn't like that I moved on, and hated the fact that Mickey is a Leech. Him and Bruce came down here and ... Oh, God, Marcy! Where is Marcy?" Jillian's eyes darted around the room, looking for her.

Jack glared at the dead body on the ground, wishing he could have done worse than just shooting him in the head. "She's in my bed." Jack rubbed Jillian's back in an attempt to get her to calm down. "Marcy, are you okay?" he asked, wondering if he should go check or if that would only cause her more stress, but then he remembered Mickey kneeling down in front of the bed and figured he was checking her out.

"I'm okay," Marcy squeaked back, hidden somewhere behind Jack's bed.

"She tried to save me, Jack, she tried to … I'm so sorry, Marcy. I—" Footsteps came rushing down the steps, and quicker than Jack could see, Jillian had raised a gun and was aiming it at Mickey, who held his hands up in surrender.

"It's just me, sweetheart," Mickey said, lowering his hand slowly. When Jillian dropped the gun, he went over to Mike and dragged his body up the stairs as well.

"I'm going to get something to clean up the blood." Jack got to his feet to search for a bucket, but Jillian grabbed his hand.

"I need to walk out of here," she said sternly as she wiped the tears from her eyes. Jack looked at her like she'd lost her mind, but she lifted her chin up to show her strength. "I need to show them I'm not scared. That I'm not weak."

"Nobody thinks you're weak." Jack looked at her and she straightened her posture as she climbed to her feet. *I wouldn't even be worried if anyone thinks I'm weak or not if this happened to me.*

"Just get me out of here for a while." Jillian's eyes pleaded with Jack. "Let's go for a walk in the orchard. I can't watch them clean this."

Jack went to argue that it was dark out, but decided it didn't matter. "Okay," he conceded, taking her hand. They skirted around the pools of blood on the ground and climbed the stairs, where Jillian squeezed his hand.

Once they reached the top and pushed open the door, everyone stopped talking and stared in their direction. A few took a step forward to offer some kind of help, but shaking his head, Jack held up his free hand to stop them. As they reached the first tree, well away from the crowd, Jillian asked, "Did you find out where Caleo is?"

Ashamed, Jack looked over at his sister. "I'm sorry, I should never have left you."

"It's not your fault," Jillian said firmly.

"I should have told you Mike was—"

"What we have to focus on right now is you getting Caleo back home to us," Jillian said, cutting him off.

Jack pulled Jillian to a stop. "I'm not leaving you again."

Jillian raised her chin up to look at the moon, and Jack knew she was trying not to cry. "You have to. You need him … we need him. I am ready for things to get back to normal, and in order for that to happen I need my brother to be happy again."

"I don't know if they ever will be normal," Jack admitted.

"Look around you. We have guests at the Inn again." Jillian pointed to the people around the yard. "Kids playing, people sitting around a campfire swapping stories, and look …" She pointed to a spot on the far side of the camp where two teens were sitting next to each other, wrapped in a blanket and looking up at the stars. "We can rebuild a little life right here. We have enough people for protection, we have food, and those guys cut down four trees today, saying they are going to start making huts in the morning. This is my place. We have the Inn back, and it's my job to run it."

"But—"

"No. I have Mickey and Marcy to watch my back here. You need to go find my other brother and bring him home to us." Jillian pulled on Jack's hand and they continued walking. "I'm tired of seeing you moping around here all the time." Jillian squeezed Jack's hand and he smiled even though he knew she couldn't see it. They walked along for a few moments, circling the orchard. "So did you find where Caleo is?" she asked again.

"I think so. Paris says that Steve is heading to Cranberry next. I figure we may be able to meet him there." Picking up an apple, Jack tossed it into the nearby woods that surrounded the Inn.

"Cranberry? You had a swim meet there once, right?" Jillian asked and Jack noticed that she seemed to be relaxing some.

"Yep, an hour ride, with you, Gran, four members of the swim team, and Caleo." Jack pictured the van full of people, the arguments between him and Jillian, and the guys from the team picking on Caleo. He sighed, thinking about how he should have stood up to the guys and defended Caleo more.

"Oh, yes, I remember that nightmare. You guys won and the whole way home I couldn't get you to stop singing *We Are the Champions*." Jillian elbowed Jack in the ribs gently. "You were always a brat."

"Me? You were the snobby cheerleader," Jack retorted.

"Yes, you. A whole hour of *We Are the Champions* repeating over and over. You didn't even sing the whole song. You're definitely the brat ... and I wasn't that snobby." They walked along some more and circled back to the house. "Why don't you sing anymore?"

Jack smiled, thinking back to the truck; Mickey hissing and Paris calling him a jukebox. "I think that person might have disappeared with Caleo."

"And now that Caleo isn't dead?" she asked calmly.

Jack laughed. "Did you know Mickey doesn't like Journey?"

The light from a nearby fire was just bright enough to see that Jillian was smiling. "Oh really?"

"Yeah, I don't think he is going to make it in this family. I mean really, how could you not like Journey?" Jack leaned in by Jillian's ear and whispered, "I not even sure he's human."

Jillian leaned over to Jack and whispered, "I know what you mean, but I think he's purrrrrfect the way he is."

Laughing, Jack shoved his sister away. "That's lame."

"He can be a real animal sometimes," Jillian said suggestively.

"Lamer." Jack snorted, barely able to breathe he was laughing so hard.

Jillian laughed and shoved him back. "Then why are you laughing?"

"I'm laughing at your lameness, not at your joke," Jack retorted.

"Whatever." Jillian stopped. They had made it back to the path that led to the Inn.

"Do you ever wonder what it would be like if things were different?" Jack asked softly.

"You mean like if the Inn didn't burn down and we were still in school? Why would I possibly wonder what it would be like to have graduated and be in my dorm room at Pitt studying for finals before I come home for fall break?"

Jack shook his head, smiling. "No, I mean what if you could go back and change something?"

"Just spill it already," Jillian said, starting back up the trail to the house.

Jack took a deep breath. He'd never had a conversation like this with his sister, and it felt awkward. "I was just wondering what life would have been like if I told Caleo how I felt before all of this."

Jillian shrugged. "I don't think you were ready back then."

"But I could have stood up for him more. I could have been there for him more," Jack protested.

Turning, Jillian smiled brightly at Jack. "You two have been dating since you were both in diapers," Jillian said proudly. "You being the blockhead that you are just never knew it." Jillian let go of Jack's hand and put her arm around his shoulder. "You were inseparable growing up and always seemed to have a secret connection that kept you together."

"But I could have defended him when he was picked on."

"Jack, he knows that you love him. The only thing that would have changed if you told him how you feel is Grandma would have put locks on both of your doors at night to keep you from doing anything in her house." Jillian reached up and tugged on Jack's earlobe, letting him know she was kidding. "The point is, you two have been head over heels in love with each other since the day you met. Sex has nothing to do with it, this is fairy tale love."

Jack thought about what his sister was saying and somehow it all made sense to him. He was in awe of the fact that she could describe how he felt about Caleo when he had been having such a hard time defining it himself. Jillian giggled beside him and he looked over at her. "What?"

"Fairy," she said, nudging him playfully again.

Jack shook his head, trying not to laugh. "You said all that just to call me a fairy, didn't you?"

"No, but it sure worked out great," she said. She took a deep breath and her posture suddenly went rigid as she grabbed Jack's hand. Worried, Jack looked around, noticing they were in front of the door leading to the basement, the expression on Jillian's flushed face told Jack she wasn't sure about going back down there.

"We can sleep in the truck tonight if you want," Jack said, pulling her in that direction. "Put a blanket down in the bed and sleep under the stars like we did in the summer."

She tugged his hand back, and Jack saw her release her breath as if she was trying to blow the stress of the situation away. "Come on, I'll read you a book while you sleep. You can leave in the morning." When they made it down the stairs, Mickey and Marcy were putting away an empty bucket and sponges in the corner.

"All cleaned up, your highness," Mickey said, bowing low.

Jillian smiled meekly. "Oh, great, not you, too. I get enough of that from Jack."

Mickey grabbed her hand and kissed it softly as he got on his knees. "You will always be my queen. My lady."

"Barf!" Jack coughed into his hand.

Jillian looked over at him with a smile. "Told you he's purrrrrfert."

"Just don't come whining to me when you have a litter of my nieces and nephews you want babysat."

"Oh shut up." Mickey kissed Jillian softly on the lips. "I'm going to get washed up, I will be right back." He bounded up the stairs in three steps.

Jillian led Jack over to her bed and sat with her back against the wall. "What would you like to hear?"

"It doesn't matter, whatever romance novel you're reading now will be fine. It feels like I haven't slept in days." Jack yawned, playfully hinting that it would bore him to sleep.

Jillian placed a pillow over her lap and patted it for Jack to lay his head down. "Do you remember when we were sick as kids? Mom would hold us just like this." Jack lay down and Jillian ran her fingers through his hair. "And run her fingers through our hair, playing with it as she read to us."

"Yeah, always Alice in Wonderland." Jack looked up at his sister excitedly. "Do you have it?"

Jillian frowned. "Not yet. Tonight we have Black Beauty."

"Black Beauty? Out of the whole stack we took from that bookstore, you pick Black Beauty to read?" Jack complained

Jillian bopped him on the head with the open book. "Hey, it's a classic."

"A classic bore. It's a good thing I was planning on sleeping."

"I happen to like Black Beauty," Mickey said as he came in and sat down at the edge of the bed where he proceeded to strip out of his jeans.

"Dude, you're going to give me nightmares." Jack kicked at Mickey, playfully shoving him off the bed.

Mickey stood up as he pulled on a pair of green Christmas tree sleeping pants. "You're in my bed, you should be happy that I am even putting on pants."

"Ah gross!" Jack looked up at Jillian, who was laughing. "Tell your cat to stay off the bed." Jack kicked at Mickey again as he tried to sit back down.

Mickey dodged around his foot, jumped in behind Jack, and snuggled up against him, wrapping his arm around Jack's chest. "Don't worry, I'm just going to snuggle for a while. Nothing to frisky."

"Jillian!" Jack said, struggling to get free. Mickey squeezed him tight in a bear hug, preventing Jack from moving anything except his legs.

"Let go, you smell. Oh God you smell!" Jack protested, trying to wiggle his way free.

"I don't smell that bad. I bathed three days ago, honest," Mickey said, shoving his armpit closer to Jack's face.

"Okay boys settle down. It's bed time." Jillian turned the flashlight on beside the bed and opened the book. Jack shoved Mickey off and turned to face the wall as Jillian started to read.

Jack closed his eyes and listened to his sister's voice as she read from the book. *Soon things will be safe. We just have to get Caleo, find a place to hide, and stay out of sight till everything blows over.*

☽＊☾

"You're quiet," Nolan said.

Jack looked over from the driver's seat to Nolan, whose enormous mass took up most of the cab to the truck. This left Paris squished up against him, and she was not looking very pleased about it.

Paris snapped a warning look at Nolan. Jack smiled, knowing she was going to punch him if Jack started singing again.

"I'm just thinking." Jack turned on his left blinker, coming to a complete stop at the stop sign. They hadn't seen a single car on the road in the hour they had been driving, but after stopping by accident at the first sign, he noticed that it was annoying Paris. She would look at him and motion wildly, like he was an idiot. Knowing this, Jack played the part and followed all the traffic laws, even stopping at a traffic light that was out. He stared up at it for a full sixty seconds, pretending the light was red.

"About Caleo?" Nolan asked frankly.

Jack glared out the front window. He didn't want to talk about Caleo with Nolan, especially with Paris wedged between them in the truck's small cab.

Nolan sighed. "Do you even have a plan? What are we going to do when we get to the Blessed camp? It's not like we can storm in, grab Caleo, and run out. We don't even know if he's in there yet."

Jack didn't even bother taking his eyes off the road as he stopped at another traffic light. He'd been thinking about this most of the night and hadn't come up with anything yet, but he wasn't about to admit that to Nolan. Paris patted him on the arm and Jack shrugged. "I figured we would start by scoping it out."

"They had at least fifty guards at the school. I'm sure that's nothing compared to what the hospital will have," Nolan explained.

Paris tugged at Jack's sleeve again and he shrugged her off. "I could always just walk in. They helped humans at the school. Maybe they would just take me in."

"They also killed them?"

Jack shrugged again. "Only after—" Jack was cut off as an elbow smacked him in the ribs. He slammed on the brakes, screeching the car to a halt before looking over at Paris. "What was that for?" Jack yelled.

Unfazed, she pointed out the front window to a large, eighteen story building towering behind a department store and a few restaurants. "Oh." Jack looked up at the structure and felt crushed. It somehow looked larger than he remembered, and he didn't think there was any way he could possibly find Caleo in a building that big.

"There is no way we are going to be able to storm into that building." Nolan's voice sounded as destroyed as Jack felt. "There are at least a hundred guards on patrol alone."

"We may be able to sneak in through a side door or something." Jack jumped at the muffled voice outside his window. He turned and saw Paris's mother leaning over, her face almost pressed against the glass.

Jack quickly rolled down the window and looked up at the specter. "Look, officer, I didn't see that stop sign back there. Can't you just give me a warning?"

Paris's mother glared down at him. "I don't think you missed a single sign."

"I doubt they are going to just leave one of the side doors unguarded," Nolan said, ignoring the banter.

"How do you think I got in to kill Alix." Paris's mother put her hand on her hip and leaned in through the window. Both Nolan and Jack looked at each other in silence. "I say we park the truck and you two can hide in one of those buildings while I scout it out. My ghost can walk right in, and if it gets seen, oh well."

"I might be able to get in through the water supply." Nolan kept his face facing out the front, as if staring at the hospital, not even bothering to pretend to see normally.

"And do what once you're inside? Run around the building naked with no gun?" Jack shook his head. "Like you said, there are a lot of guards in there, and a naked giant running around the halls would draw too much attention. The best idea we have is for Paris to scout and look for a way in."

"I don't think that we have that option anymore." Nolan pointed to the road up ahead as three black Hummers pulled out from besides a building and sped in their direction.

"Paris, drive!" Jack threw open the door and jumped out, slamming the door behind him. "I'll try to slow them down."

"Jack?" Paris's mother said, worry evident in her voice.

Jack looked over his shoulder at Paris sitting behind the wheel. "Drive! Get somewhere safe. I will distract them," Jack yelled at her.

"Jack, get in the truck!" Nolan opened his door and stepped out.

"You have to get out of here! They will kill you if you're caught!" Jack yelled to Paris.

She didn't even look at Jack as she shoved the truck into reverse, whipped the car around, and sped down the street.

"Be careful." Jack turned around to see Paris's mother still standing behind him, a worried look in her eyes. She reached out and cupped his face, and although he couldn't feel it he smiled at the gesture. "I will be back when it's safe." Jack blinked and she was gone.

He turned back to the road, the Hummers approaching fast. Glancing at Nolan, Jack saw him shaking his head. "The Blessed are not allowed to kill humans, right?" Jack slid out of his coat and dropped it to the ground.

"That's the rules." Nolan turned his head toward Jack just as he began peeling off his layers of shirts and throwing them to the ground with his coat. "What's your plan?" Nolan raised an eyebrow and Jack kicked off his boots, smiling.

"My plan was for you and Paris to speed away to safety." Jack pulled his belt free and let his pants drop to the ground. He stepped out of them, nearly tripping. "I figured at least then I would have you to keep Caleo safe if this didn't work."

"And you are getting taking your clothes off why?"

Jack looked up at the Hummers and slid his Speedo to the ground just as they came to a stop a few yards away. "I'm planning on looking as human and defenseless as possible so I don't get shot. I don't think looking defenseless is even possible for a man your size." Jack looked over to Nolan, but he was gone; all that was left was a puddle of water flowing down a service drain on the side of the road and a pile of his clothes lying on the ground where he had been standing. "But I guess you could always turn into water and run away."

All three of the Hummers' doors opened simultaneously, nine uniformed men armed with cuff guns appearing above their doors.

There was a long moment of silence as Jack stood as still as possible, his hands held up in the air in a sign of surrender. A bitter breeze blew past, causing Jack's jaw to start chattering, and he started regretting ditching his clothes. He was just thinking about reaching down for his pants, when one of the men yelled. "Don't move!"

Jack looked up at the man that spoke. "I am human." Jack slowly spun around, keeping his hands in the air. "See, no mark."

One of the men laughed but abruptly cut it off as the first man spoke again. "Okay, dog! What do you want? Who is you master?"

Dog? Jack's eyes fell to the red tattoo on his side and he cursed to himself for forgetting the mark. "I need to talk to the Angel Alix. I have some information he may want." His skin was starting to sting from the cold and he really wanted to get at least his pants back on. He looked down at his clothes wondering if he had remembered his tattoo and just removed his shirt if it would have been enough. "And I would really like to get dressed. It's kind of cold out here."

A few of the men laughed, and Jack slowly lowered his hands to hide his manhood. "Where are your friends?" one of the men yelled and all the laughing stopped abruptly.

"They saw your vehicles and chickened out." Jack reached for his pants, heard the collective cocking of the guns, and stopped.

"Drug him!" the guard snapped, motioning with his hand to someone behind him.

Jack only had time to flinch as a dart buried into his bare thigh. "Again?" Jack said and pulled out the dart instinctively. He felt his leg go numb and fell to the ground, happy that his face landed on top of his clothes instead of skidding on the asphalt.

He tried to move his arm but it wouldn't respond. A group of four uniformed men rushed forward, surrounding him, guns all aimed at his head. Jack blinked, they had already picked him up and were loading him in the back of a Hummer. One of the men said something about Larry, but Jack couldn't understand what it was. All he knew was it was getting harder and harder to keep his eyes open.

7

"I was told you wanted to see me?" a deep, soothing, velvety voice said from somewhere nearby.

Jack's eyes flew open and he was momentarily blinded by the bright hospital lights above his head. "What? Where am I?" He blinked and took in the small room; white walls, a sink, a small TV mounted in the corner. Other than a small couch by the large windows, the only furniture in the room was the standard hospital bed Jack was laying on.

"Do you have information for me or not?" the voice asked again, an impatient tone creeping in.

Jack's eyes searched and found the source of the voice to be a tall man standing in the dark corner, leaning against the door. Jack blinked, thinking his eyes were playing a trick on him. The room was bright, except for the shadows that seemed to be gathering around the door hiding this man's features.

"Look, dog, I am busy. Now you made quite a display of yourself out there just to see me. I recommend you get on with it." The man stepped forward and the lights overhead dimmed, keeping the man concealed in the shadows.

"You're Alix?" Jack sat up in the bed and squinted his eyes, trying to get a better look. "The real Alix?"

"Alix!" the man huffed. "It's been a long time since someone has called me that." Alix pointed to the red tattoo on Jack's ribs. "You're a dog of some rebel then I take it? One of Thorn's people I would guess." He turned, suddenly uninterested, and walked back to the door.

"Wait!" Jack cringed. He didn't mean to yell, but Alix had stopped so he continued, "Thorn is dead." All the bulbs in the room seemed to dim, but Alix didn't turn around. Jack took it as a sign that he was listening. "I just want my life back. This war has taken everything from me and all I want is for my family to be safe."

"So now that you master is dead, you think I should spare you because you no longer want to be a dog?" Alix asked, but didn't wait for an answer. "You should have just kept running." He reached for the door handle.

"I am no one's dog, this was forced on me," Jack said, motioning to the tattoo even though Alix's back was to him. "I just want for the Blessed to leave my family alone. We never wanted to be involved in any of your shit."

"And you came to tell me this why? Because you think I can, what? Rush in, save your family, and whisk you off to safety?" Alix shook his head. "I'm trying to win a war here, son. I don't have time to save every human that runs across the road. I have to save the world from a punk kid who decided to throw a temper tantrum."

"I don't want you to save us," Jack spat back, nearly jumping out of the bed. "Your men have already killed my grandmother. All I want is for them to leave my family alone." Jack glared across the room as Alix turned and walked back towards him.

"One of my men killed a human?" The shadows around Alix faded, revealing a tall, slender, dark-skinned man wearing dark slacks and a black button up shirt. "Was it provoked?"

"She was an unarmed, elderly woman. Your man shot her in the head." Jack couldn't take his eyes off the man's skin. It was far darker than anyone he had ever seen, and something kept drawing his attention back every time he tried to focus elsewhere. *It's moving. It's like a dark cloud rolling under his skin.*

"Was he provoked?" Alix gently asked again.

"No," Jack said, looking down at the white blanket he had covering his waist.

Alix's voice changed, sounding almost sorry as he asked. "And you are sure he was Blessed?"

Jack snapped his attention back to the man's face. "He was wearing your uniform. He said he was following your orders," he said, barely able to keep his anger in check.

Alix's face softened to one of remorse. "Yeah, well, there has been a lot of that being said lately." Alix waved his hand dismissively when Jack opened his mouth to say more. "My men have strict orders. Any humans found must go through processing and are set free in society. No human was to be killed, but as you know there is always a chance for casualties. The Blessed are here to extract the rebels involved in the attack on this country and to find this Leech claiming to be the Angel. We—"

Jack jumped to his feet, unable to take it any longer. "Caleo isn't claiming to be anything. Your men attacked us in our home. He didn't want to be a Leech or the Angel. He just wanted to be normal! He didn't want any part of your world!" Noticing the lights dimming around Alix again, Jack quickly sat back down and figured the best thing to do would be say what he came here for before it was too late. "I came here to tell you that your base camp in Butler has been wiped out." Jack looked up at Alix who had leaned against a nearby wall, folding his arms across his chest. "I know how Steve did it and I have a plan that could trap him."

Alix looked to the door, then shifted his weight to his other foot as he said, "I'm listening."

"I want your guarantee that Caleo will not be hurt," Jack demanded.

"Your friend, Caleo … you said he thinks he is the Angel?" Alix inquired, but he didn't sound angry.

"According to Thorn he is the Angel," Jack corrected, "Caleo didn't claim to be anything till they started telling him what he was."

"And why would Thorn think that he is the Angel?"

"I don't know. I am not a Leech." Jack palmed his eyes in frustration. "He said something about you giving him your son to hide or something like that? Oh, and he is Caleo's great, great, great-grandfather or something. He told us you were dead."

"Died, not dead." Alix was quiet for a moment as he stared out the window. "You've been told half-truths." He walked over to the nearby couch and sat down, stretching his arms across the back and crossing his legs. "My son was stolen from me by Thorn when I refused to go into hiding because an assassin was trying to kill me. He said he was protecting the blood line."

Jack nodded. "If she killed you then how—"

"She?" Alix looked up, surprised. "I guess Thorn would have told everyone that part, too." Alix chuckled to himself. "Yeah, I guess you could say she killed me. Leave it to Thorn to only tell the half of the story that fits his cause." Alix smiled at Jack. "She had been hunting me for about a hundred years right after her mother was killed. When she finally caught up with me, about thirty years back, well let's just say my heart stopped for less than twenty seconds. My guards revived me, but Thorn had a fit, saying it's not natural. That my life had ended and bringing me back could mark the end of the Leeches. That there couldn't be two Angels. He had already taken my son years back, but after I died he took off without saying a word and started this rebel group."

A hundred years? How old is Paris? Jack looked out the window as he tried to refocus on the task at hand.

"A lot older than me," Alix said flatly. "So you know her? Most people just call her the Ghost these days."

What? Can he read my mind? Jack looked over at Alix and raised an eyebrow, waiting for a response. Alix seemed to be patiently waiting for Jack's answer, but Jack changed the subject. "So that's when Caleo became the Angel? The day you died?"

"No, Caleo didn't become the Angel, he was born the Angel I died about thirty years ago. The Angel essence gets passed to the next born in the bloodline. My guess is he was born about ten years after."

"So you know that Caleo is the Angel?" Jack asked, surprised that Alix was actually admitting it.

"I figured if Thorn said there was another Angel, then it had to be true. For all his faults, that man was a by-the-book player. The problem is that since I have died, I think the essence of the Angel has been split between us." Alix stood up from the couch and started for the door. "Well, kid, it's been fun, but I have a meeting with the President of the United States in a few hours. I will be back in a few days we can talk more then."

"What about capturing Steve?" Jack asked, hoping to keep Alix talking long enough to guarantee Caleo's safety.

"We can discuss it another day. I can't keep the President waiting. That would be rude. He is almost as busy as I am."

"Wait, you're going to keep me here?" Jack got up from the bed. "I have to get back home."

"Sorry, son. You're going to have to stay here till I can figure out what to do with you." Alix opened the door.

"But what about Steve? He is going to attack soon."

"Steve, your friend, and the shifter already tried attacking here two days ago. They snuck in with a few of the surviving Blessed members from the Butter base. I doubt they will be trying again anytime soon."

"They what? Caleo attacked here? Is he alive?" Jack asked frantically, knowing his only plan had fallen apart.

"I don't think you know your friend as well as you think, but he and Steve escaped. The shifter was not so lucky." Alix walked out, closing the door behind him.

Jack sat in the bed staring at the door. *I was too late. They had already attacked here and who knows if they were coming back.* He got up from the bed, noticing for the first time that all he had on was a hospital gown again. *They could have at least given me back my clothes.* Jack tiptoed quietly across the cold tile floor. He put his ear to the door but only heard silence. *They wouldn't leave me here alone. Would they?* Slowly Jack pushed on the handle, but it was locked. *What am I supposed to do now?*

He turned back to the room and took a deep breath. *I've got to get out of here.* He ran to a set of cupboards by the sink and opened them. Paper towels, a few plastic urinals, and a sleeve of small plastic cups. "Nothing." Jack walked over to the windows and looked out. *Wow! I think I'm on the top floor.* Pressing his face to the glass, he looked up but was unable to see any floors above him. *Not getting out that way.* Turning around he noticed a small bathroom. Jack flipped the light switch on the wall and saw a toilet, sink, and shower stall. Four towels hung on the bar behind the toilet. Jack grabbed at the shower curtain rod and tried to pull it free for a weapon but it wouldn't budge.

Defeated, Jack leaned against the sink and stared in the mirror, not really seeing his reflection. "There's power. I wonder if—" He turned on the shower and stepped back as it spit and sputtered for a few seconds before water jetted out. "Please be hot, please be hot." Steam rose up from the water before he even had a chance to touch it. "Yes!" he said excitedly.

Not wanting to miss another opportunity for a hot shower, Jack ripped the gown from his body, throwing it to the floor as he stepped into the steaming jets. The hot water stung his skin and he adjusted the handle, laughing to himself. *I am locked in the top floor of a hospital but I have hot water,* he thought, scrubbing his face clean. "I can't decide if this is some strange kind of torture or if I'm in heaven."

"I guess that would all depend on the food they serve."

Jack whipped around at the sound of a voice behind him, nearly slipping and falling out of the tub because of the giant liquid figure towering over him.

"Holy crap!" Jack took a step back once he regained his footing, pressing his back against the shower knob to put a few inches between him and Nolan. "You scared the crap out of me."

He reached back to turn off the water, but Nolan grabbed his hand, stopping him.

"Don't, there is a guard patrolling the hall. The shower offers some cover for our voices," Nolan explained.

"How did you get in here?" Jack hissed, stepping out of the shower and wrapping a towel around his waist, wanting to put some distance between them. When he turned back to face Nolan, he stood fully materialized under the showerhead, smiling at Jack's discomfort.

"I have been in the drainage tunnels for the last ten hours. I was hoping someone would turn on a sink or something so I could at least get a view of the inside and possibly make sure you were still alive. I didn't actually think I would get a whole panoramic picture of you laughing in a shower," Nolan said, motioning at Jack's body when he said panoramic.

"Dude, you were watching me take a shower? Am I the only one who finds you on a whole new level of creepy?" Jack reached out and grabbed the white shower curtain, pulling it up to hide Nolan's nakedness from his view. *No wonder Caleo had the hots for this guy. Built like the movies portray Greek gods. Is that a nine-pack? I didn't know you could go above six. Don't look down at your own waist. Don't look.* Jack looked down and frowned at his flat but undefined stomach, remembering that he used to have a muscular abdomen before all this got started and he didn't have time to exercise or eat right.

Nolan gave Jack a weak smile with a raised eyebrow. "I was trying to see if you were still alive," he said, snatching the curtain out of Jack's hand. He pulled it shut, concealing his body with a chuckle.

Jack looked back and caught a glimpse of himself in the mirror. *Where did my six-pack go?* He turned and examined his body more closely. *When did I become so skinny?* Nolan coughed and Jack turned to see him poking is head out. "So how are we getting out of here?"

"We can't. I have no way of sneaking you out. There are too many guards for us to run, and judging by our lack of clothes, I don't think you have any weapons." Nolan tilted his head to the side as if he heard something. "You're just going to have to stay put for a while. I will be back when I can."

Jack heard the door open outside the bathroom. Quickly he dropped his towel and jumped in the shower, pulling the curtain closed and staying as close to the wall as he could to avoid touching Nolan, who took up over half the shower with his massive body. Nolan smiled, water dripping down his face as he looked down at Jack, whose face was inches away from his chest. "I never realized how small you were," Nolan whispered. The sides of his mouth quirked up in a sly smile.

Jack glared up at the man and whispered, "Can you tell Jillian I'm okay?"

Nolan nodded as his body turned to water and rushed down the drain.

Jack stayed under the hot water for a while, listening for the intruder but heard nothing. *Are they gone? Or just waiting for me?* He turned the water off and leisurely stepped out, listening for any sound outside of the bathroom. Slowly he dried off then stood back and looked at himself in the mirror again. *I've lost a lot of weight.* Jack turned to the side. *I'm almost as skinny as Jillian now. Oh, God, please don't tell her I thought that.* Jack wrapped the towel around his waist and looked up at the mirror again, freezing at the sight of his scarred face. *My face, it's ruined.* He ran his fingers over the rough burn scars and wanted to scream. He had only seen the scars through his reflection in water, or a few times in a small mirror that Jillian kept in her purse. *They're horrible. I'm a monster. Caleo isn't going to want me like this.* He wanted to cry.

Jack flicked off the light switch and stood in the dark, collecting his thoughts as he rubbed the tears from his eyes. He opened the door and walked out into the brightly lit room, expecting a trap of some sort. Luckily no one jumped out, and as far as he could tell he was alone in the room.

A pair of black basketball shorts and a white T-shirt were laid out across the bed. On the window sill, a cafeteria tray with a plate of ham, mashed potatoes, and a cup of milk sat waiting. Jack looked around the corner and saw that the door was closed.

"Well, this isn't what I expected." He walked over to the bed and slipped into the shorts, then hopped across the cold floor to the windowsill and took a deep whiff of the warm food. "I think it would have been easier if I was arrested months ago." He picked up the milk and took a quick, experimental sip. "Real milk!" Jack smiled as he looked out the window and began eating in silence.

I wonder how long they are going to keep me in here. Jack glanced back at the room and smiled as the heater in the corner kicked on. "And heat, too?" Jack jumped up and down happily, then stopped abruptly because of a Charlie horse in the back of his thigh. Rubbing the soreness out, he said, "Oh, great,

now I am talking to myself and it's only been a few hours ...
Wow. I suck at this solitary confinement."

Jack finished his last bite of food and gazed around the
room. "Now what?" He went to the bed and lay down, staring at
the white ceiling tiles. "Tonight sleep, tomorrow I guess I start an
exercise regimen. It's not like I have anything better to do, plus I
have to get into shape for when something does happen." He
pressed the lights off button on his bed remote and closed his
eyes. "Carry on my wayward son ..."

"And that was *Runaway* by Bon Jovi. Before that was
Carry On Wayward Son by Kansas," Jack said, lowering his voice
a few octaves in an imitation of an old timer radio broadcaster.
"Now for *Summer of '69* by Bryan Adams ... I got my first real
six-string—"

Someone pounded on the wall behind Jack's head. "Shut
up already, I am trying to watch Wheel!"

Jack crossed his arms over his chest, frowning. *Everyone's
a hater. Wait!* Jack sprang up in bed and looked at the wall
mounted television. *We have TV?* He searched the side of the
bed, hitting the remote control buttons on the safety rail. The TV
flickered to life with a pop. "Oh my God, I have TV!" Jack yelled
ecstatically as he flipped the channels a few times until he found
the local news.

A news anchor with white hair and a thick mustache sat
behind a desk reporting about a salmonella outbreak in dog food
and what brands were being recalled. Jack sat at the edge of his
bed staring up at the TV, watching as the news cast played out;
sports, weather, a segment on how dryer sheets can be used to
clean mirrors and repel mosquitoes.

"Is there nothing on the attacks?" Jack was just about to flip
the channel when a picture of a bunch of scorched, crumbling
buildings appeared on the screen with the caption New York
Stock Exchange across the bottom of the picture.

Jack fumbled with the remote as he turned up the volume
to better hear the broadcaster. "New photos are just in of the
aftermath of the terrorist attack that happened back in May.
These images are hard to stomach, so I do apologize. We all just
have to remember that we are rebuilding. The terrorists
responsible are being brought to justice, and as we watch we
must remain united and strong in these hard times and remember
all those soldiers fighting to win back our States." Images of New
York, D.C., and Pittsburgh flashed across the screen, every image

showing the same thing; crumpled buildings with a label of what once stood there before the attack on the bottom of the screen. "The President has announced that those areas are now free of terrorists and that the military action has moved on to the last few remaining terrorist cells. As they did with the other locations, the government is requesting that all of the civilian population stay clear of those major cities for their own safety. Once the debris has been secured and the rebuilding starts, they will give you the all clear. They ask for your patience in the meantime." The woman news anchor appeared on the screen, collecting her papers off the desk, then tapped them straight and smiled up at the camera as they zoomed out, revealing her mustached co-anchor beside her. "That concludes the ten o'clock news for Friday the eleventh of November. Thank you for watching."

"That's it?" Jack asked, stunned at the lack of coverage. "Less than four minutes on the attacks?" Jack flipped off the TV as a commercial for a cell phone company came on. "November eleventh! Caleo's birthday is only eleven days away." Jack lay back down and flicked off the lights with the bed control switch. "I wonder how hard it would be for Jillian to bake him a cake of some sort when we get back." The glow of the TV made Jack feel warm as he thought back again to lying with Caleo, watching TV the night of the dance. Hugging his pillow, Jack closed his eyes.

☽ ✳ ☾

Jack opened his eyes to the bright sun shining through his window and flicked on the TV as he crawled out of bed. The music to the morning news had just started playing, introducing the staff while two people sat behind the news desk pretending to chat happily. "Good morning, Annie … Ron." Jack nodded at the TV on his way to the bathroom. He stretched lazily and cracked his back as he looked over his shoulder and out the window at the cloudless sky.

"Good morning, and thank you for tuning into KDDKTV on this beautiful morning. It is Tuesday, July twenty-third. I'm Annie Holton." The woman announcer on the TV turned and gazed at her co-host with a big smile plastered on her face.

"What will the weather be today?" Jack watched the TV through the mirror as he relieved his bladder.

"And I am Ron Thomas. What a beautiful day it's going to be Annie, high near eighty-three and not a cloud in the sky."

"Oh, Annie, don't forget about that blood drive at the Children's Hospital this weekend." Jack looked at his own appearance in the mirror and ran his fingers through his rough beard and shaggy hair. "I wonder if I asked for a razor if they would let me have one? But that would require someone actually talking to me." Jack turned on the water and splashed a little on his face before turning out the light and starting his morning exercises. He jumped up and grabbed the door frame to the bathroom and proceeded to do pull-ups until the first commercial, then dropped and ran in place till the news started back up, where he would drop and do pushups till the commercials started again, followed by sprinting to the door and back, and finally doing sit ups. This ended when a guard opened the door, slid in his food, and occasionally dropped off clean linens while grabbing his empty tray from the night before, and quickly closes the door. Jack used to try talking to the men, but they never acknowledged him unless he got too close, and that always ended with Jack waking up a few hours later on the floor pulling a dart out of his chest or thigh.

Jack was just on sit-up number thirty-eight when the door opened and his food was placed beside the door along with a stack of clean towels. "Whoot! I'm starving." He waited till the door was shut before he climbed to his feet and retrieved the tray. "Now, Annie, you still haven't mentioned that blood drive. They are going to be so disappointed if you forget them again."

He sat down on the couch and ate his breakfast of scrambled eggs, toast, and a bowl of Raisin Bran as Ron talked about a firehouse needing donations, how there was a shooting of some movie star, and next week's picnic in the park being canceled because of the rainy forecast and how it was rescheduled for the following weekend.

"Thanks a lot for ruining the surprise, you jerk," Jack said as he chewed his last bite of eggs. "You could have at least announced the spoiler alert before telling me the weather for the whole week."

Jack pushed his empty tray onto the windowsill, retrieved his clean towels, and turned on the water for his shower. He peeked out at the TV just as Ron was telling everyone to have a fantastic day and Annie was smiling as she waved 'bye, bye' to the camera.

"Annie, you forget the blood drive. I can't believe you forgot the blood drive. You've been plugging it away every day for the last two weeks, and the day of the event you let all those people down. Shame on you!" Jack dropped his shorts to the ground and kicked them into the tub. "It's day three, my friend, time to be washed." He took a step back, examining himself in the mirror once again. "Prison life has been good to you, Jacky boy." Flexing his muscles he smiled at the definition he saw in his body. "Not too bad, not too bad at all." It wasn't body builder size like Nolan's, but he was in better shape now then he was on the swim team.

"Jack?"

Jack poked his head out of the bathroom at the sound of a feminine voice whispering his name, but the only thing he saw was the TV and that was playing a commercial of Crazy Tony's fireworks emporium. "Where our prices will blow you away!" Jack smiled as he said the catchy slogan and ducked into the shower.

"Psst! Jack, is that you?" the voice whispered again.

Jack pulled the curtain aside and looked back out. "Great, now I'm talking to the TV and hearing voices that aren't there."

"It is you!" Paris's mother stepped around the corner and entered the bathroom, a bright smile spreading across her face.

"Paris? What are you doing here? How did you?" Jack's questions came out a mile a minute and he couldn't help but smile at the sight of her.

"Shhh!" The spectral image of Paris's mother put her hands on her hips, as if to scold him. "You're going to get us caught if you keep talking that loud."

"Right, sorry." Jack looked at the floor like a chastised child.

She waved her hand dismissively and smiled back. "I've been looking up and down these windows for the last two days looking for you."

"How did you get in?"

"I'm not. I'm across the street behind a dumpster." Paris's mother pointed behind her to the window. "Once I figured out that my ghosts no longer have to follow the laws of gravity, it was just a matter of looking in the windows at night while everyone was sleeping. Of course when I heard someone singing Journey, I knew I had the right window."

Jack looked at her and raised an eyebrow in question. "But how is that going to get me out of here?"

"I'm not sure yet." Paris's mother frowned. "But I have been watching the guards around the building and I don't think I'm going to be able to sneak you out one of the doors."

Jack's heart sank, and he wanted to be mad at her for not trying something to get him out, but he couldn't. She was already risking her life just to talk with him.

"I know you have been in here a few months."

"Try eight," Jack mumbled as he let the shower curtain fall closed. He sat down on the floor of the tub, letting the water run over his face and he wanted to cry.

"I just need you to hold on for a few more days. I know someone who might be able to help get you out the window. All we have to do is pray for a distraction. Then she can fly right up here, break the glass, and fly you both away."

"And this friend will be willing to help?"

"I don't know, but she should. Us girl Leeches usually watch each other's back." Jack poked his face back out of the curtain at Paris's mother, trying to read any kind of emotion that Paris might be hiding. "Look, I've got to go. I will be back in a few days."

"You're leaving?" Jack climbed to his feet. "Please, can't you just stay and talk a little. How's Jillian? Is there any news of Caleo?"

"I don't know. I haven't been back to your house in a couple of weeks, but the pregnancy has been rough on her and no I can't stay, I've got to go. I don't have enough energy to keep my ghost going this far away from my body for too long."

"Pregnancy?" Jack asked, dumbfounded. "What? How?"

Paris's mother expression turned grim. "She is due soon and would like you to be there."

Jack shook his head, still trying to wrap his mind around this unexpected news. "I don't understand. I thought Leeches couldn't reproduce."

"I believe the father is one of the two they carried out of the basement the night Thorn died. Now I'm going." Paris's mother backed out of the door.

"But you can't leave me here alone. Please don't." Jack chased after her.

"Jack! Take a step back. I'm seeing way more of you than I want to," Paris's mother said, laughing.

Jack looked down to see that he had stepped out of the shower and was standing in the middle of the floor naked and dripping wet. "Shoot!" He pulled a towel off the rack and wrapped it around his waist, but when he looked up the ghost had vanished. "Paris?" he whispered, as he rushed out of the bathroom into the room, but the ghost was nowhere to be seen. Jack ran to the window, desperate to see her even if it was just a glimpse. His eyes searched for the dumpster and found it but he couldn't see Paris anywhere. "Damn it," he cursed.

Jack went to turn from the window, but he caught movement out of the corner of his eye as Paris's phantom ran from behind the dumpster off to the right. A few seconds later, Paris ran off to the left and ducked into the first alleyway in her path.

"Very clever," Jack said as he walked back to the shower and stepped in. "A few more days. I guess it's time to prepare." He picked up his shorts from the bottom of the shower and squeezed the water out of them. "Maybe I should have told her to bring me some clothes." Turning off the water, he got out of the shower and wrapped a towel around his waist. After hanging his shorts on the windowsill to dry, Jack turned to face the room. A soap-opera was playing on the TV and he smiled as a young guy held a gun pointed at a giant beefy guy. "No Jimmy, what have you gotten yourself into?" Jack sat down on the couch and stretched out lazily wondering what it was going to be like to not have hot showers, three hot meals a day, and TV again. He shuddered at the thought of missing Ellen in the afternoon. "But she was going to have the cast of that show next week. Oh God, what's that show called? It's going to bug me all day now." Jack pulled at his still wet hair. "Relax, it's only for a few weeks while I find Caleo. Then it's off to civilization and TV."

☽ ✳ ☾

Jack opened his eyes at the sound of the door being opened. "Is it lunch time already?" He glanced over at the door, but no tray slid in. Instead the door was opened just a crack and he could hear people yelling in the hall. "Hello?"

Jack stood up, pulling his towel tight just as two uniformed men walked into the room. They both stopped dead in their tracks and looked at Jack as if they were surprised to see him.

"Who are you and where is your cuff?" one of the men said gruffly, pointing a cuff gun towards Jack.

Jack raised his hands in the air to show he was unarmed. "Jack Barely."

"He's a dog. Just put him down," the other man barked.

"Do you work here, Jack?" the first man asked.

"No." Jack looked past the two men to see a few men in black basketball shorts running past his door. "What's going on? Is this a prison break? Are we free?"

One of the men looked to the hallway and smiled before turning back to Jack. "And just what do they have you in for, human?"

Jack smirked. *He said they, not we.* He took a step back, trying to compose his thoughts. "I know the ..." A glimpse of a soldier with white hair passed by the door and Jack lost his train of thought. He pointed to the hall, confused, desperately trying to call out for Caleo but couldn't find his voice.

"Forget it! He's useless, just recycle him. We don't have much time," the second man said.

Jack kept his eyes on the hallway, not noticing one of the men raise his side arm. "Caleo," Jack managed, but his voice sounded horse and barely came out as a whisper.

"What did he say?" the first man asked.

"Who cares?" The second man brought his gun level with Jack's chest.

"Caleo!" Jack yelled, knocking the gun away with the side of his forearm and bringing up his knee into the man's groin. The gun went off, blowing a hole in the TV and sending glass raining down behind him. Jack spun around the man and rammed his elbow into the second man's jaw. The man stumbled back while Jack rammed the first man's head into the wall. The man dropped his gun and fell to the ground. Quickly Jack dove for the weapon, but just as his fingers wrapped around the handle he heard the sound of a gun cocking beside him.

"Don't even think about it!" the second man yelled.

Jack could see out of the corner of his eye that he was pointing his sidearm right at his head. The man jerked the gun to the side a few times, telling Jack to move away from the gun, but Jack didn't move.

Someone pounded on the door and yelled, "What's taking so long? This is breakout, just uncuff the prisoner and move to the next floor."

Jack looked up at the sound of the familiar voice. "Steve?"

Steve tilted his head to the side and the two men took a step back so Steve could get a clear visual of who he was. "Do I know you?" Steve asked, squinting at Jack.

Jack stood there not sure if he should answer.

Suddenly uninterested, Steve shrugged his shoulders and barked, "Next floor now!" He turned back to the hallway and vanished.

The second Jack saw Steve had teleported, he scooped up the gun and fired three rounds; two into one of the uniformed men and one into the other's head. They both slumped to the ground before they even had a chance to turn around. Jack ran to the windowsill and quickly pulled on his still damp shorts as he glanced up at the broken TV.

"Sorry, Annie, it looks like I won't be seeing how the blood drive went. Maybe we will talk again soon though." Jack waved to the TV as he tucked the handgun into his waistband, picked up a cuff gun off one of the dead men, and stepped out into the hallway. Other than a dead Blessed guard at the end of the hall, and one dead beside Jack's door, the hallway was completely empty.

He ran down the hall to what was once a nurse's station. A man behind the desk looked up just as Jack pulled the trigger, embedding a cuff into the guy's chest. Then he bolted for the stairwell and ran down, taking the steps two at a time.

"Caleo is here! I just have to get to him before—" Jack skidded to a halt at the sight of a Blessed soldier frozen solid on the next landing; the sign above the door said tenth floor. He glanced to the Blessed soldier and back to the door. "Is he on this floor?" He looked back and peered over the edge of the railing at the staircase spiraling down. A figure of a man lying on the ground broken into pieces lay at the bottom. "Nope!" Jack said as he ran down the next flight of stairs only to find two more men dead; one frozen, the other stabbed in the back.

Not stopping, Jack descended the stairs as fast as he could. When he reached the bottom he stopped dead in his tracks. The door to the floor was propped open by another frozen corpse. Jack looked back over his shoulder and noticed that the man who he originally thought was lying at the bottom of the stairs was actually frozen solid as well, and by the looks of the body must have fallen over the edge, because his left leg and right arm had shattered off and were lying by the door.

"Holy hell, Caleo, what have they done to you?" Jack said as he slid through the door and his heart sank farther as he took in all the frozen people in the large emergency room waiting area. Eight guards were all frozen in a circle in the middle of the room, while dozens of men, women, and children, all wearing ratty clothing were frozen mid-stride as they appeared to be fleeing the room.

"Move it!"

Jack whipped around at the sound of another voice in the room. Almost completing a full circle, his eyes landed on a man dressed in black skinny jeans with an arsenal of weapons strapped to his belt and back.

"Steve!" Jack searched around the room, as if expecting Caleo to step out from behind one of the frozen faces.

"Yeah?" Steve looked at Jack questionably with one eyebrow raised. He then put his hand on his hip impatiently when Jack didn't respond. "The truck is leaving, I suggest you get outside with the others," Steve ordered.

Jack tilted his head to the side and smiled. *He doesn't recognize me.*

"Nor does he care who you are." Steve materialized a few feet away, leaning against one of the frozen soldiers; one arm draped across the man's back as he smiled at Jack. "Should I recognize you?"

"No, of course not." Jack ran his fingers through his scruffy beard and smiled back. *It's the beard.*

Steve teleported again, appeared a few feet away from Jack, leaned forward, and squinted his eyes. "You do look kind of—" Jack pulled the trigger on the cuff gun and backed away slowly as Steve buckled forward. "You stupid son of ..." a knife hit the ground by Steve's feet, shortly before he dropped beside it, spasming under the pulsing of the cuff that Jack had embedded into his thigh.

"Where is Caleo?" Jack screamed at Steve, but he just spasmed on the ground, glaring up at him. "Were is he?" Jack kicked Steve in the gut and raised the gun threateningly.

A look of recognition crossed Steve's face, and it almost looked like he was smiling. "The human. I was wondering where you had disappeared to. Thought you might have been dead."

"Where is Caleo?" Jack kicked him again.

"I thought I would have to have your sister replace you, but ... Well, she's useless in her condition."

"My sister?" Jack stopped and looked down at Steve, anger bubbling out. "You better not have touched her!"

Steve smiled up at Jack. "Don't look at me. I didn't do anything to her." Steve laughed

He's just trying to throw me off. Jack pointed the sidearm at Steve's chest. "Where is Caleo?" Jack asked again.

Steve smiled up at him and chuckled.

"Behind you, dumb ass!"

Jack turned reflectively at the sound of Caleo's voice, and his bright blue eyes came into focus just as something hard smashed against the side of Jack's head, knocking him to the ground beside Steve.

"Shoot him!" Steve yelled angrily.

Jack looked up at Caleo to see a pistol aimed down at him and a sad look on his face. "What are you doing? It's me!" Jack pleaded as he slid away on his backside.

Caleo lowered his gun and tilted his head to the side, giving Jack a confused look. "Do I know you?"

"Shoot him!" Steve yelled again as he forced himself to his feet, fighting the pulsing of the cuff. "Just shoot the human. We don't have time for this, we have to go."

"It's me, Jack ... you're my ..." Jack stopped. Brother was not the right word anymore and he couldn't bring himself to say it. "We're family. We've known each other our whole lives. We were in diapers together." He went to climb to his feet, but stopped when Caleo raised his gun, aiming it at his head again.

Caleo shook his head, looking even more confused than a few second ago. "My family died. I killed them when I was a baby. I've seen the newspapers."

"No, Caleo. We lived at the Purple Rose Inn with Grandma!" Tears streamed down Jack's face as he stared at the clearly frustrated Caleo. *He doesn't remember us? Why wouldn't he remember us?*

Steve started chuckling as he removed the gun from Caleo's hand and aimed it at Jack. "Remember? Why would the Angel remember you?" Steve winked down at Jack. "I will not let him be tricked by your lies human."

"Smear?" Caleo's voice was barely a whisper, but Jack caught it and smiled.

"It's not the length that counts," Jack offered.

"What?" Caleo said as his and Jack's eyes met. Jack smiled, hoping Caleo would show the hint of recognition he was desperately searching for, but it only showed his sadness.

"Would you just shut up?" Steve raised the gun a little higher, aiming it at Jack's head. "He isn't going to fall for your tricks."

Jack watched as Caleo stepped in front of the gun protectively. "Steve, don—"

"He is lying to you!" Steve shouted and Jack could see his angry face staring him down from over Caleo's shoulder.

"I'm not lying! What's going on? Why don't you remember me?" Jack asked Caleo, not daring to move for fear he might unintentionally scare him and get shot.

"Because you never existed," Steve retorted with a snort.

"But what about my dreams?" Caleo whispered back.

Jack jumped to his feet. "What dreams?" Caleo sighed and looked over his shoulder at Jack. "I—"

"It doesn't matter. Get this thing off me and let's go!" Steve grabbed Caleo and pulled him toward the door.

"No!" Jack charged Steve, shoving him into the wall. "You're not taking him away from me again!"

Gunfire rang out and Jack had to duck down as pieces of the ceiling rained down around him.

"Caleo!" Jack turned around to see Caleo had taken cover behind a row of chairs on the other side of the room.

"Human!" Steve yelled and Jack turned around to see Steve crouched down beside him pulling at the cuff attached to his chest. "Get this thing off me!" he grunted, as a dark red stain formed on his T-shirt around the cuff.

"No!" Jack shoved Steve away and turned back to Caleo. He saw that a thick layer of frost was forming around his hands and spreading outward across the tiled floor.

"Ahh!" Steve screamed as he continued to pull at the device. "Look, you see that frost? He's getting worked up. We got to get out of here before he flash freezes the whole room. One bullet hits him and we are all dead."

Jack looked over at Steve and back to Caleo, whose bright blue eyes stared back at him. Jack knew he was fighting for control.

The lights dimmed and Jack looked around the room for a dark shadow. "Alix is here." He cursed as he spotted the shadow drifting along the side of the room in Caleo's direction.

"What? Where?" The excitement in Steve's voice caught Jack off guard. He looked over his shoulder to see Steve smiling as he ripped the cuff free from his chest, taking a good portion of the skin with it, and slammed it to the ground.

"The shadows, he's in the shadows." Jack pointed to the spot across the room just as Alix stepped out from the darkness and smiled down at Jack.

"Ah, Jack, I knew they would come for you eventually," he said in his velvety calm voice.

"Actually, we came for—" Steve started to say, but Alix cut him off abruptly.

"Leave us. Go after the prisoners, round up every one of them," Alix ordered, never taking his eyes off Steve as he spoke to his troops, which were now surrounding them. A clatter of footsteps and Jack could see all the Blessed guards leaving through the nearest exits. When the boots fell silent and the doors closed, Alix opened his arms and smiled down at Caleo for the first time. "You must be Caleo. You've got quite a—" In the blink of an eye, a shadow wrapped itself around Alix's arm in the shape of a round shield just as a knife struck it; embedding itself a few inches deep. As if the knife was no more than an annoying fly, Alix continued, "... legend for yourself." The shield vanished in a wisp, disappearing into the shadows, and the knife dropped to the floor.

Jack looked at Caleo, who had stood up and was slowly backing himself towards him and Steve. Another knife flew across the room, and again it was stopped by a shield pulled from the shadows.

"Steve, let's go," Caleo said, panic in his voice as he reached his arm back for Steve's hand. Unfortunately, he only grabbed air as Steve threw another knife.

Jack sprung forward and grabbed Steve's arm. "You're not leaving without me."

Pain exploded in the side of his knee as Steve kicked him, and he crumpled to the floor screaming in pain.

"What was that for?" Caleo bent down and put a hand on Jack's back like a child being comforted by its mother. Jack could feel the cold biting at his flesh under Caleo's palm, but he leaned back into it, welcoming any physical contact that let him know Caleo was real and alive.

"We're not leaving!" Steve said, not bothering to look down at Caleo as he stared at Alix.

"And what are you hoping to accomplish here? Why have you been trying to get my attention so bad that you needed to kill so many humans?" Alix's voice was calm and didn't have a hint of fear or anger as he took a few steps closer.

Steve smiled widely. "You got my message then?"

"You blew up New York. I think that was a bit of an overkill on sending me a message." Alix took another step forward and the shadows followed right on his heels, blacking out the lights above.

"*You* blew up New York?" Caleo gasped, looking up at Steve in shock. "You said he did it."

Steve puffed out his chest with pride, as if he was a villain about to reveal his master plan, but he never took his eyes off of Alix. "Well, you—"

"Shut up!" Alix boomed, cutting him off. "You are nothing but a splinter in my finger, an annoyance at best. Just tell me what the hell you want already and be done with it! You know the creed. You can't kill me without killing yourself. If I die, you die. So just tell me what this is all about."

Jack shook his head in confusion. "Creed? What creed?"

"Shut up, human!" Steve screamed, clearly frustrated, before turning his attention back to Alix. "There are two Angels now. I'm betting that the creed no longer applies as long as one of you stays alive."

"Maybe, but are you willing to take that risk?" Alix got his answer a split second later as Steve drew his gun and fired, emptying his gun's clip. He then dropped the empty gun and pulled another one from his belt.

Jack tried to stand, but his knee wouldn't hold his weight, and he crumpled back to the floor screaming in pain. *I've got to get Caleo out of here.* He looked up at Caleo, who was looking back at him, confusion and worry in his features. He kept glancing between Steve, Alix, and himself.

Pain erupted across Caleo's face and he screamed out in agony as he collapsed, landing on top of Jack.

"Caleo, what's wrong?" Jack asked frantically as he tried to push himself off the ground, but his hand slipped in something wet.

"Steve!" Caleo cried as he rolled off Jack onto the floor, his hand outstretched, reaching for him.

Jack looked down at himself and saw that he was covered in blood. *What happened?* He looked at Caleo and saw three deep gashes in his back. Ignoring his own pain, Jack rolled over and applied pressure to one of the wounds with the palm of his hands, hoping to slow the bleeding as Caleo continued to reach out for Steve.

"Steve, we have to go!" Jack screamed over another round of gunfire.

While still firing at Alix, Steve pulled another gun from its holster, and without looking aimed it at Jack's head. "Shut the—" Caleo's arm shot out and grabbed Steve by the bare skin of his leg. The second the contact was made, Jack's vision blurred out of focus and the emergency room was replaced by a small bedroom, with a twin size bed in the corner and plain white walls.

8

"Where are we?" Caleo asked weakly.

Jack turned away from the window he had been looking out and glanced down at Caleo lying face down, where he had been sleeping in a queen-sized bed for the last few hours. The blankets lay in a pile at the bottom of the bed and just a thin, white sheet had been pulled over Caleo's back.

"Well, according to the mail I found in the kitchen, Clarion," Jack said.

Caleo's head jumped off the pillow as he tried to look around the room. "Is this my old house? The one I killed my family in?"

Jack hobbled over to the bed and sat down. "I don't know. I know your mother lived in Clarion, but I don't know if I ever went to that house or not. Are you getting back your memory?" Jack asked, confused about how Caleo knew he once lived in Clarion.

Caleo shook his head. "Steve showed me a newspaper clipping from when I was a baby. It said it was the Clarion Ledger."

Jack tried not to look disappointed as he asked, "So you don't remember anything at all?"

"Not since about two weeks ago." Caleo looked back at Jack, a sad look on his face. "Steve said I must have hit my head or something."

He probably smacked you with the hammer. Jack picked up a bowl off the nightstand and held it out so Caleo could see its contents. "You hungry? I found a can of soup left in the kitchen."

Caleo shook his head in response. "Where is Steve?"

"I don't know. When we got here, it was just you and me," Jack explained, putting the bowl back on the nightstand.

"What? How could that be?" Caleo pushed himself to sit up but stopped, falling back to the bed when the pain proved too much.

"We were in the hospital, the room went all blurry, and when things cleared, me and you were in the room across the hall. I think it's someone's bedroom. It has a giant TV. About twice the size of the one we had in the living room."

Caleo weakly smiled back at Jack. "How long have we been here?"

"A few hours, tops." Jack pulled the sheet back slowly to uncover Caleo's back. The bed sheets he stole from the other room and used as bandages had large blotches where the blood had soaked through, but it looked like the bleeding was staunched. "I think the bleeding has stopped for now, but you probably shouldn't move too much."

"How bad is it?" Caleo tried looking over his shoulder, but it must have hurt because he gave up and collapsed onto the bed again.

"Pretty bad. They're deep." Jack ran his fingers across Caleo's bare shoulders to the back of his neck. "I tried to cauterize the wound using a spoon and the gas grill I found in the garage, but the spoon kept frosting over when it got close to your skin. So I layered a few towels across your back and applied pressure with my body until the bleeding slowed. I just wrapped you up and brought you in here about five hours ago."

"Five hours? I thought you said we have only been here a few hours," Caleo said, surprised.

"Okay, so it was more like half the day. You'll have to forgive me; I've been busy trying to keep you alive." Jack gently nudged Caleo in the arm.

"I wonder why Steve hasn't come back yet," Caleo murmured, worry creeping into his voice. "Did he go back to fight Alix?"

Jack shook his head. "Caleo, he was never here. I don't think he knows where we are."

"He has to know, how else would we be here?" The look on Caleo's face was one of terror and he tried to get back up again. "He can take me to John and he can heal me again, just like before."

Jack stood up, shaking his head and not bothering to pay attention to what Caleo was saying as he hobbled back to the window. *He doesn't even remember me. Why doesn't he remember me?*

"Why do you do that?"Caleo asked suddenly.

Startled, Jack looked over at Caleo. "Do what?"

"You do realize that you are talking, right?" The look on Caleo's face was almost comical, and Jack had to smile.

"What do you mean?" He hobbled back over and sat down.

"You just said I don't remember you," Caleo said.

Jack tilted his head in confusion. "No I didn't. I thought it."

"You're thinking out loud then," Caleo stated, looking seriously at Jack.

"I'm not." Jack smiled down at Caleo and shook his head. *Am I?*

Smiling, Caleo nodded his answer.

Jack could feel his legs weaken at the sight of the smile he had wanted to see for so long. "I guess I'm going to have to be more careful of what I'm thinking from now on." Jack chuckled.

"And singing," Caleo added, his smile getting bigger.

Jack couldn't stop looking down at Caleo. It all felt like an odd dream. *God how I have missed that smile.* Caleo's smile vanished and his cheeks reddened with embarrassment. "Sorry, I can't help the singing." Jack turned away from the window and hobbled to the door. "Try to get some sleep. I'm going to look around the house and see if I can find anything useful."

"Try the shower." Bewildered, Jack looked over his shoulder at Caleo.

"Do I smell that bad?" Jack lifted up his arm and sniffed experimentally. *It's not that bad.*

Caleo shook his head. "You're covered in blood. You kind of look like a serial killer."

Jack snapped his head up and glared at Caleo. "I thought you said you didn't remember who I was?"

Caleo's eyes widened as he looked back over his shoulder at Jack. He pushed off the bed and tried to sit up. "I . . . I . . ."

Jack pointed at Caleo, laughing. "I was just joking; I'm not a serial killer, buddy, calm down before you reopen your wounds."

Caleo looked a little relieved, but kept eyeing the window as if he was going to try to bolt at any moment.

"I already tried the sink when we first got here, but it didn't work. I'll see if I can get cleaned up though. Maybe they got some baby wipes or something." Jack looked down at the dried blood on his chest and shorts. "Never know, maybe I can even find some fresh clothes. If I'm lucky."

"If you find anything in my size, could you bring me a set? It seems some pervert has taken mine."

Jack smiled softly. "I swear, I am not a pervert either, I had to—"

Caleo winked over his shoulder at Jack. The gesture took Jack by surprise and cut him off. "Yeah, yeah, whatever you say, captain perv."

Jack walked out of the room and down the hall to a small bathroom. *Did he just wink at me?* He turned the knob to the sink, but again nothing came out. Frustrated, Jack pulled a towel off a rack behind the toilet and tried wiping the blood off. The towel came away red with dry blood, but it didn't seem to help. *Is Caleo actually flirting with me?* Jack threw the towel in the sink and left the room, heading down the hall and into the living room. A flat panel TV sat in the corner with an oversized sectional lining two of the walls. A potted plant, dead and dried, sat by the window.

"Maybe the kitchen will be more promising." Jack turned and walked into the kitchen. Mouse droppings covered the old, worn countertops, glass covered the floor next the back door, were someone must have broken in looking for supplies. The refrigerator appeared so out of place with the rest of the room it almost seemed comical with its artwork still stuck to the door for all to see.

"Great." Jack looked down at the glass from the window then to his bare feet as he treaded carefully over to the fridge and pulled open the door. He backed up as the smell of the rotting, moldy food assaulted his nose. Quickly he glanced over the shelves till his eyes found five bottles of water, stashed behind a nearly empty case of orange soda. Holding his breath, he grabbed the water and soda cans, and put them into the empty sink next to the fridge before kicking the door shut.

Carefully Jack carried his loot into the living room and deposited it on the floor before heading into the extra bedroom. He side-stepped a large, dark spot on the carpet, it was Caleo's blood from when they first teleported here. Glancing around, he saw the blue and green covers from the bed that he had thrown across the room so he could get the sheets to use as a bandage. On the wall were some posters of a lady with pink hair screaming into a microphone, but he had no clue who the singer was.

Jack opened the closet and stepped back. "Of course! Out of all the houses Steve could send us to, we get the pretty, pretty princess house." He grabbed a hand full of pink blouses and tossed them to the floor. "Thank God!" He pulled a pair of jeans from its hanger. "Jeans are jeans, right?" He held a pair up to his waist. They looked to be about the right size, so he dropped his shorts and slid them on. Jack buttoned the pants and started laughing as he checked his appearance in the mirror. "I think these are classified as really low rise skinny jeans. I would get arrested for wearing this out in public." He slid out of the pants and threw them to the pile of pink shirts.

Disappointed, Jack went to shut the door, but something got in his way and the door reopened revealing a fluffy pink robe. Shrugging, Jack pulled the ugly thing from its hanger on the door, slid it on, and tied the sash. "Do teenage girls really wear pink like this?"

Looking on the top shelf of the closet, he smiled when he saw a game of Monopoly. Thinking he and Caleo could maybe play a game while they waited for Steve to show up, he grabbed the box and turned to leave, but stopped when he heard something hit the floor. Turning, he discovered a shoe box had fallen to the ground, spilling its contents. "Crystals and candles! Thank whatever gods you were into lady." Quickly he picked up all the candles, a box of matches, and the Monopoly game, and ran from the room happy to present his find to Caleo.

"Caleo, I have Monopoly and candles. We can—" Jack froze in the doorway when he noticed that the bed was empty. *Did Steve already come? Why didn't I hear him?* Jack saw a bloody towel on the floor by the bed. "Caleo?"

"In here," Caleo called from the bathroom.

Rounding the corner of the room, Jack saw Caleo struggling to stay standing as he leaned against the doorframe to the master bathroom.

Jack ran to Caleo's side and helped him get back into bed. "What are you doing?"

"I had to pee." Caleo laid on his side and smiled weakly up at him as Jack pulled the sheet up to cover his nakedness.

Jack retrieved the candles where he had dropped them on the floor, lit one, and placed it on the table next to the bed. "Why didn't you call for me? I would have helped."

Confused, Caleo looked up at Jack. "Why would I call for you? I just met you, and you think I would ask you to help me pee?"

Jack took a step back, feeling the sting from the words. "But we have known each other our whole lives. I've seen you naked more times than I can count."

Caleo shook his head, embarrassed again. "You may have known me, but I have no clue who you are other than from the dreams, and I don't even know if those are real."

"Dreams?"

"Secondly," Caleo said, changing the subject, "you're in a pink robe."

Jack looked down at the robe and smiled. "What's wrong with my pink robe? It looks like something Steve would wear."

"Sorry, buddy, a mystery man in pink, helping me pee? Yeah, that might get a little awkward." Caleo smiled, looking down at the bed.

"I was just going to help you get to the bathroom, nothing more." Jack struck another candle and placed it on the other side of the bed next to Caleo. "Secondly," Jack said, mocking Caleo, "pink was pretty much the only option in that room ... and just for the record, skinny Jeans are not sexy at all. I have no clue how Steve can wear them."

"You didn't think that maybe there could be any clothes in here?" Caleo offered, pointing to the two dressers in the room. "I think I would have checked in here before I put that thing on. Besides, I think you would look better in a bright, sunny yellow."

Jack looked back at Caleo in surprise. "You remember the dress?"

"Dress?" Caleo's smile widened. "You wore a dress?"

Jack stuck his tongue out at Caleo. "You wore the pink one."

Caleo's smile vanished. "Yeah right. You're just making that up. Check the dressers."

"You've become awfully bossy lately." Jack pulled open a drawer and yanked out a pair of giant granny panties. "I think I found you a new pair of shorts." Jack held them up so Caleo could see them. "At least they're not pink."

"I think I'll pass," Caleo announced, his smile returning.

Jack walked over to the next dresser and pulled the second drawer open, hoping to avoid looking at more oversized underwear. "Well, we have Nascar or a camo shirt with a picture of a dear head." Jack held them up for Caleo.

Caleo snubbed his nose up at them. "Nothing plain?"

"Not that I'm offering. You make fun of the pink robe and you have to pick between Nascar or deer head." He waited for

Caleo's response, but when nothing came he added, "There are a lot of pink shirts in the other room."

"Nascar!"

Jack tossed the shirt onto the bed beside Caleo, and pulled open the next drawer. "Well, it looks like we are going to need a belt. Size thirty-eights." Opening the bottom one revealed sleeping pants. "And the winner is ..." Jack pulled a pair of green and red cartoon themed sleeping pants out and threw them on the bed for Caleo before grabbing a pair of green plaid for himself.

Jack automatically dropped his robe to the floor and slid on his pants. When he looked up, he noticed Caleo watching him. "Sorry," Jack said, frowning as he remembered that Caleo didn't know him. "You've seen me naked a thousand times growing up, but I guess that wasn't the same guy you are now."

Caleo looked down at the sleeping pants on the bed his cheeks reddened with embarrassment again. "I take it there wasn't any with Nascar on them?"

"What, you're afraid someone will see you in a non-matching set?" Jack turned around and started searching the drawer again for anything Nascar looking.

"So I take it you didn't find any water?" Caleo asked. When Jack looked back, he saw Caleo trying to slide on his pants as gingerly as possible, keeping his back stiff. Jack wanted to offer to help, but as soon as he thought it Caleo gave him a worried look.

Jack turned back around to give Caleo his privacy and ran his hands over his chest causing more dried blood flaked off. "Four bottles, but we will need that for drinking if we are going to be here for a while."

"The toilet flushed. I wonder why that water is working," he said, sounding like he was gritting his teeth from the pain.

"It's because the water the toilet flushed with is in ... the back Tank!" Jack looked over at the bathroom door in the hallway. "Caleo, you're a genius." He ran out of the bedroom and into the bathroom, where he pulled off the lid to the back tank of the toilet. The water smelled a little stale, but it still looked pretty clean. He pulled open the cupboard under the sink looking for some soap, but only found a container of bleach, which he quickly uncapped and poured a little in. Dipping the towel in the water, he proceeded to clean the blood off.

Five ruined white towels later, Jack was clean. He retrieved the drinks from the living room and returned to the bedroom. There, he found Caleo fully dressed, sitting with his back against the headboard. A game of Monopoly was set up in the middle of the bed with a big candle in the center of the board illuminating the game.

"I'm the hat," Caleo announced patting the bed beside him for Jack to sit down.

He always picked the hat. Jack smiled to himself. *Maybe he is remembering.*

Caleo tilted his head to the side as if confused. "You're doing it again, aren't you?"

"What?" Jack took a seat at the opposite side of the bed, picked up the boot, and placed it on go.

"Can you tell me what I was like? I mean, before I lost my memory," Caleo asked, picking up the dice and rolling them onto the board.

Jack looked up at Caleo, his white face seeming to glow behind the candle light. "What do you want to know?"

"I remember how to play this game. I was able to set up the board without looking at the directions, and I know that money goes in the center for the person who lands on free parking, even though the rules don't say that ... but I can't remember ever playing the game a single time."

Jack picked up the dice and took his turn. "We used to play this game every Friday for about two years. Back when Grandma decided that we needed a family game night. Jillian would always be the banker, and you and I would get accused of cheating all the time. We were usually guilty as charged, but we would argue with her till our faces turned blue. We even had this ... this routine ... we called it operation clean up. Where one of us would spill something and while everyone was looking at the mess the other would take some money out of the bank or put a house on their property."

"So you're saying we're cousins or something?" Caleo asked, sounding a little disappointed.

"No, my mother worked at your grandmother's Inn. We have always called her Grandma, but there is no blood relation. When my parents died, Grandma took us in and we have lived together since."

"Oh. I thought there might have been something else between us." Caleo looked down and counted his money in his hands.

"No, nothing like that." Jack then looked to the window to hide his face. *I was in love with you, but I was too chicken shit to say anything. Crap!* Jack chastised himself for even thinking that when he knew Caleo seemed to be able to hear what he was thinking, and quickly said, "Me and my sister were kind of adopted into your grandmother's house.

Even through the candlelight Jack could see Caleo smiling. "You were in love with me? Why would you be afraid to say anything? Is it because I am the Angel?"

"What? No. You didn't even know about the whole Angel thing back then. Would you stop reading my mind?" Jack stood up and walked to the window to hide his embarrassment.

"I'm not, you're talking out loud," Caleo protested with a smile, "and don't change the subject."

Jack took a deep breath and released it. "I was confused. I didn't understand how I felt about you until someone spelled it out for me and when I did, I didn't know what to do. I loved you, you were my best friend. What if I said something and you didn't like me that way? I didn't want that to happen, and it wasn't as if I had any competition at the time. So I decided to just let things happen and see if time would present an opportunity."

"Have you seen you? You look like a football jock. Other than your scar, you look like you could be an actor or model. Why wouldn't I go for you? I was gay then, too, right?"

Jack's hand came up, hiding his scar as he turned back toward the window, where he glared angrily at his own reflection from the dim candlelight. "It was complicated," Jack barked.

"Complicated how?"

"Well, for one you seemed to be ashamed of being gay and never told anyone, not even me. I guess I was afraid that if I told you how I really felt you would hate me or things would get awkward between us."

"I sound like a wimp," Caleo huffed.

Jack shook his head and sat back down on the bed. "No, you were strong and witty, with a never back down attitude. I was the wimp. I was too busy trying to be what everyone wanted me to be that I forgot to stand up for you ...With you," he corrected himself, "and you never held that against me." *I didn't deserve you.*

"I'm here now." Caleo reached his hand out and cupped the side of Jack's face before leaning forward and tilting his head to the left as if to kiss him.

Jack's lips met Caleo's briefly before he pulled away and jumped out of the bed. "No, no this isn't right."

"Jack, I'm here. It's okay," Caleo said disappointedly as he leaned back against the headboard.

"No, you're not him." Jack paced the floor nervously. "You're not my Caleo. I mean, you look like him, you are him ... but you're not him. Grrrr!" Jack pulled his hair in frustration.

"But I'm still me."

"You're not the Caleo I fell in love with," Jack said. Unsure what to do, he went and stood next to the window, looking out into the blackness. "You're not my Caleo."

"What if I never get my memory back?" Caleo asked, sounding worried and frustrated. "What if I'm afraid of losing who I am now? Do I exist if your Caleo comes back or do I just disappear, forgotten?"

Jack couldn't stop the tears from flowing down his cheeks. "I won't stop till I find him. There has to be a way. I found you, now I just need to find a way to fix whatever Steve has done to you."

"Steve? Steve hasn't done anything to me. He found me last month nearly beaten to death by the Blessed. He has done nothing but protect me."

"You were in the school in Butler over eight months ago with him. I saw you with my own eyes. That's how I knew you were alive." Jack punched the wall, infuriated. "He is using you! I don't know how he is screwing with your memory, but he is using you." Jack stormed out of the room and collapsed with his back to the wall just outside the bedroom door where he cried himself to sleep on the floor.

Jack woke up to the sound of something breaking in Caleo's room. Jumping to his feet, he ran in to find Caleo lying on the floor, trying to pull himself back up.

"Are you okay?" Jack asked, running to his side.

"No. I think I split my back open again," Caleo said angrily as he pushed Jack's offered help away, pulled himself back to his feet, and slowly disappeared into the bathroom.

"Do you need any help?" Jack asked, taking a step forward, torn between giving him his privacy and making sure he was okay.

"I'm fine," Caleo barked and emerged a moment later. He slowly made his way back to the bed. "Where the hell is Steve? Did he say when he was coming back?" Caleo asked grouchily as he crawled into the bed face first.

"I told you I didn't see Steve; it was just you and me when we got here." Jack glanced out the window. *I wouldn't let him take you away again even if he brought an army,* Jack thought bitterly.

"He has a guy named John who has the ability to heal. You know how nice that would be right now? I wouldn't be in pain!" Caleo finished, screaming the last part.

Jack nodded gruffly and turned to leave. "I'm going to check the neighboring houses for some supplies and hopefully some more water."

"Jack?" Jack froze at the door and looked back at Caleo, who stared at him with his mouth open, as if he wanted to ask a question but didn't know how. Finally he said, "If Steve comes back, I won't let him leave without you."

"Thanks." Jack smiled and left the room.

"Get your head on straight, Jacky. We need to—" Jack shook his head as he opened the back door to the house and stepped outside. "We? First thinking out loud, now I'm referring to myself as a we. Next I will be coveting after a ring ... I'm going to be headed to a nut house for sure once they rebuild it." Hopping the wooden fence into the neighboring yard, Jack grimaced at the sight of a grimy in-ground pool in desperate need of attention. "Gross! I guess I'm not going to get to go swimming anytime soon."

Slowly Jack made his way to the back door. "The window is broken, not very promising." He reached up for the door knob and felt a hard poke to his back.

"Where did you come from?"

Jack jumped at the sound of a deep voice behind him and spun around, coming face to face with the barrel of a rifle.

The tall, beefy, bearded man holding the gun shoved it against Jack's chest. "Hands up! Who are you and why are you here?"

"Just looking for supplies," Jack announced louder than he intended, backing away from the man. "I am unarmed."

"Boy, I can see that. Now just come away from my door." The man nudged the gun to the left, motioning for Jack to move in that direction.

"I was just looking for something to eat, maybe some water," Jack said, trying to sound calm.

"Jim, just send him away. He just a boy." Jack turned his head to see a middle-aged woman standing in the doorway with her hand on her hip. *His wife.*

"Yeah, she's my wife, what of it?" Jim nudged Jack closer to the pool with his gun. "You want me to just let him go? Do you remember the last guy we let go?" The woman flinched and backed away from the door at her husband's words.

"I was just looking for food. My friend is injured and we were just resting while he heals. We can leave right now if you let me go." Jack took a step back towards the fence and the man raised his gun defensively.

"Friend? How many of you are there?" the man grunted, motioning for Jack to move closer to the pool.

Shoot! I shouldn't have said that. Now he knows Caleo is injured. Jack looked at the fence; it was a good ten feet away and Jim was blocking his path. "Look, just let me go. We won't tell anyone you're here, and we won't come back. I just want to get home to my sister." Jack glanced over his shoulder. He was only a few feet from falling into that disgusting pool. *Oh God, is that a body?* Jack thought, seeing what looked to be a face at the bottom of the cloudy green water.

"Jim, there are trucks coming down the road!" the woman yelled from inside the house. "Jim!"

"Trucks?" The man shoved the gun barrel at Jack. "I thought you said—"

"They're not mine." Jack took a step closer to the left in an attempt to start getting around the man. *The Blessed, they found us. How the heck could they have found us?*

Jim looked up at Jack, his face reddening with anger. "Who are the Blessed?"

The woman reappeared at the door. "Jim, I think it's the army. They're finally here to help," she said excitedly, pulling the door open and staring out at her husband.

"Army?" The man glanced over his shoulder at the sound of multiple vehicles screeching to a halt in the front yard. He glared at Jack nervously, then his eyes darted to his wife as he tried to decide what to do.

"You have other problems. Just let me go," Jack tried again, and with his hands up he slowly started to work his way around Jim so that his back was to the fence.

"Jim, they stopped outside. Should I let them in?" she yelled.

"No!" Jim looked back at the house then to Jack before making a gruff noise and waving Jack off with his gun. Running into the house, he said to his wife, "Get in the crawl space and for the love of Pete keep your trap shut, woman."

Jack wasted no time; he ran and vaulted over the fence landing in a flowerbed on the other side. *That can't be the Army. It's the Blessed, somehow they know where we are.* He ran inside the back door cursing as the broken glass cut into his feet. He stopped dead in his tracks when he saw Caleo ripping the shelves out of the refrigerator. "Caleo, what are you doing? We have to get out of here." Jack motioned for Caleo to run with him out the door, but he kicked the last bits out the fridge and turned to Jack.

"Good, you're here. Get in." Caleo grabbed Jack by the wrist and pulled him toward the open fridge.

His hands are freezing. Jack pulled his arm away and stopped. "We can't hide in a fridge, they will find us. We got to run! Let's go!"

"There is no time, they are here. I can't do my thing if I have to worry about killing you. Now get in." Caleo held the door open and motioned with his hand for Jack to climb inside.

He's not going to hide! He wants me to while he what? Fights all of them? The sound of glass breaking drew Jack's attention to the door to see two soldiers standing there, guns drawn. Before Jack had time to react, two cuffs were buried in his chest and he crumpled to the ground, convulsing under the pulses.

"Run!" Jack screamed.

Jack watched helplessly as the two soldiers shot again, hitting Caleo in the chest with the cuffs. Caleo just charged them, grabbing both guns by the barrels before the soldiers even had time to react.

"Jack! Get in the fridge now!" Caleo screamed over his shoulder as he grabbed both of the men by their face.

Jack flicked his eyes to the fridge and tried to extend his arms, but the pulsing from the cuff kept making his muscles contract and he couldn't move. He looked back up at Caleo, whose Nascar shirt now had patches of frost forming around the cuffs and the fabric seemed rigid and frozen. He let go of the men's faces and Jack could see that they were now frozen solid.

The pulsing in Jack's cuffs abruptly stopped and he scrambled for the fridge, gasping for breath. He crouched down inside, scrunching up into a ball.

When he looked up, Caleo was closing the door and tossed him the control to the cuff. "Stay in there till I let you out." Caleo slammed the door shut just as Jack heard the front door being kicked in.

What happed to the boy who got beat up in school? Jack pushed his head back against the wall and listened as a man screamed in pain, a few guns were fired, and then a bunch of people screamed.

"Caleo! I don't think it's working, it's getting mighty cold in here." Jack slid up so he was sitting on the balls of his feet. The walls of the fridge felt like a giant ice cube and Jack couldn't stop shivering. "Caleo!"

The door opened and Jack was immediately surrounded by a thick layer of blankets. "Let's get you outside where it's warmer." Jack shrugged the blankets down around his shoulders and looked around. In the kitchen five Blessed soldiers were frozen solid, a thin layer of ice covered their face and hands.

"You did all this?" Jack asked, shaking his head at the sight. "When did you become so bad ass?"

"There are thirty more in the living room. I'm surprised they didn't send a few Leeches. There are always Leeches leading the dogs." Caleo pulled Jack to his feet. "You're shivering, let's go." Caleo led Jack out the back door and into the yard.

"I thought you only remembered the last two weeks? How many fights could you have had in the last two weeks?"

"Six," Caleo said flatly. "It's been a busy week."

Six? What the hell is Steve doing to him? "We should go scavenge what we can from the trucks and get out of here," Jack said, desperately trying to stop his jaw from shivering as he pushed open the fence and made his way to the front yard.

"Jack, wait. You need to get warm, and we can't go anywhere; Steve will be back here any minute." Caleo hobbled over to a nearby lawn chair and quickly sat down. "I don't think I can stand much longer anyway." Caleo rolled his head back and looked like he was ready to pass out at any moment.

"Caleo?" Jack ran to him as Caleo fell forward and collapsed on the ground. His bandages were stained dark red with fresh blood and Jack saw a few cuffs attached just over the bandages. "Caleo, wake up!" He slapped the side of Caleo's cheek to get his attention. When he didn't respond, Jack ran to the front yard where three trucks were pulled into the neighboring driveway, engines still running. *They have to have a first aid kit in one of these trucks.*

Jack ran to the first truck. "Damn it, where is the first aid kit?" He slammed his fist down on the seat when he couldn't find it. He opened the glove box. "A gun, why would they have a freaking gun and no first aid!" Pulling the gun out, he shoved it into the waistband of his pants.

Jack slammed the door closed and went to run to the next truck when he noticed movement out of the corner of his eye. Grabbing his weapon, he ducked beside the front tire.

Peeking around the front end of the truck, Jack saw nothing. *I don't have time for this,* he thought and readied himself to jump out, firing at the first thing that moved.

A man screamed in pain behind him; Jack whirled around and pulled the trigger. "Nolan!" Jack yelled, dropping the gun to the ground as he registered that he had just shot Nolan in the chest. "What? Why would you be stalking me?"

Nolan grunted, holding his hand over his chest as a big smile spread across his face. Slowly he removed his hand and Jack watched as the bullet wound sealed itself back up, leaving flawless tan skin through a hole in his T-shirt.

"You shot me," Nolan said, gasping for air as he smiled down at Jack. "I saved your life and you shot me."

Jack looked down to see Nolan towering over the body of a dead uniformed man, whom Jack presumed was a Leech. Jack looked back up at Nolan, unsure of what to say.

Nolan laughed and clapped Jack on the shoulder. "You're getting sloppy. Jillian will be so disappointed."

"Caleo's bleeding, he needs help!" Jack said, ignoring Nolan's comment.

Nolan ran past Jack and went straight for the backyard without saying another word. A gunshot suddenly filled the air.

"Caleo!" Jack flew through the fence as fast as he could, his thoughts racing. *Was that Nolan? Why would he shoot Caleo? What if it was a shape shifter?* As he rounded the corner, he saw Caleo curled up in a ball, crying on the ground. Nolan was crouched beside him, a hand resting on his shoulder and a dead man lying on the ground a few feet away, a bullet hole in his head. Jack ran to Caleo, pushing Nolan aside. "Are you okay?" When Caleo didn't answer, Jack looked up at Nolan for an explanation.

"I don't know!" Nolan growled. "I killed the Leech and he absorbed the—"

"I don't give a rat's ass!" Jack yelled, shaking Caleo by the shoulder. "Tell me what's wrong with him?"

"Would you just shut up and listen to the man." Jack turned to see Paris's mother standing beside him, hands on her hips. He looked around for Paris, but didn't see her anywhere. "He is trying to tell you your friend is healed. The dead guy was a Leech and now your friend is as good as new. So stop your blubbering and let's go before more of them show up."

"Caleo?" Jack peeled off the bandages on Caleo's back to reveal flawless, milky white skin. "Caleo, what's wrong? Talk to me."

"He remembers." Jack's head snapped up at the sound of Steve's voice and spotted him standing on the roof of the house, looking down at them. "This happens every time he absorbs a Leeches' essence. It heals his mind and he remembers everything he's done the last few months."

"He remembers me?" Jack went to wrap his arms around Caleo, but he was climbing to his feet, his eyes filled with anger.

"He remembers a lot more than that," Steve said happily.

Caleo wiped the tears from his eyes and glared up at Steve. "I remember all the people you made me kill!" Caleo screamed.

"I can make that go away, just like I always do," Steve offered, extending his hand. "Come back with me and you won't remember any of this."

"If you ever touch me again—" Caleo screamed

"You'll what, turn me into a popsicle?" Steve snapped his fingers and men rushed into the backyard; some armed others clearly trying to intimidate by showing their powers.

Jack looked over at Nolan, who had taken up a defensive stance on the other side of Caleo and was eyeing either a Leech, who was holding a fireball in his hand, or the man beside him who seemed to be glowing a shade of green. "What do we do?" Jack asked as he took Caleo's other flank and sized up an overly large man with a scaly snake like skin. *How the hell am I to take him out?* Jack looked at the man to the left of snake man and shook his head. "A freaking lion! You turn into a freaking lion?"

The lion's lips curled back into what Jack took as a smile.

"Don't let him scare you, he's a big pussy." Paris's mother smiled at Jack before taking a few steps forward to stand in front of Caleo.

Steve laughed at the sight of the phantom standing in front of Caleo protectively. "And what are you going to do? You're not even here. You're probably hiding in some attic nearby, waiting till the coast is clear for you to run away like you always do."

Paris's mother vanished and a specter image of Steve appeared beside him on the roof. "Not in an attic." The image leaned in toward the real Steve and smiled. "But I'm close enough to kill you," it warned.

Jack watched as Steve nervously glanced around. "You're bluffing."

The ghostly image of Steve patted him on the back, nearly knocking him off balance, then took a step back, laughing. "Do I look like a dishonest man to you?"

Steve jumped back and pulled his gun, aiming it at the ghost. "You're just a ghost, you can't touch me." Steve fired three shots into the image of himself only to have them pass right through the image undisturbed.

Steve's doppelganger melted into Paris's mother and she raised her hand, displaying a grenade pin hanging from her pinky finger. "Thorn's essence had a mighty kick to it. All that energy, I have learned I can do a lot more than touch people."

Steve looked down at his belt for a fraction of a second, trying to locate the armed grenade. Suddenly he vanished without a word, leaving all his clothes behind on the roof top, where they fell into a heap next to the smiling specter.

Paris's mother appeared beside Jack once again, and in a flat, indifferent voice said, "Duck."

Jack dropped to the ground just as the roof exploded, sending bits of shingles raining down on his head.

He was pulled to his feet by a ghostly arm. "You may want to get up before the fighting starts, my dear boy. I suggest you run like hell."

Four gun shots rang out and three of the Leeches fell to the ground. Jack looked around and saw Paris hunched down behind a window inside the house.

"Jack, take Caleo and run!" Nolan yelled as the contents of the neighbor's pool poured through the wooden fence and engulfed a Leech. He whipped a fireball at Caleo, hitting the ground by his feet, which erupted into a wall of flame four feet high.

Without hesitating, Caleo ran through the fire, extinguishing a path as he headed for the front yard.

Jack took a step to follow, but was knocked to the ground by something heavy landing on his back. "Caleo!" Jack screamed as he felt teeth sink into his left calf.

A roar vibrated the air around Jack and the teeth around his calf released their grip. Jack crawled as fast as he could away from the beast that bit him. *Why did it stop? Do we have a lion on our team now?* Jack glanced back over his shoulder to see a terrified looking lion hissing up at something near the house. It tentatively took a step forward, only to jump back as a nine foot scaly tail slammed against the ground inches from Jack's feet. A roar filled the air again, vibrating everything around. Jack looked up to see the specter image of a T-Rex towering over the house as it challenged the lion to test how solid it was.

Jack felt someone grab him from behind and pull him to his feet. "If you don't start moving I'm going to kill you myself."

"Paris! Holy crap, is that thing real? How the hell can you make a freaking T-Rex?" Jack began limping to the front of the house with Paris's assistance.

Paris smiled at Jack briefly before shooting the lion in the head with her gun. The T-Rex vanished only to be replaced by Paris's mother. "We have to get you out of—" She let Jack fall to the ground and raised her gun as the fence exploded inward and a Hummer plowed through the yard, taking out two Leeches on the far side of the yard. Next, it turned back around and stopped beside Jack and Paris.

"Get in!" Caleo yelled from the driver's side.

"Nolan, it's time to go!" Paris's mother yelled as Paris shoved Jack into the back seat and climbed in after him. Jack looked out the window. Nolan was standing in the middle of the yard in a pure liquid form; his hand appeared to be shoved down another man's throat, and he was on the ground, thrashing madly.

"Is he drowning that guy?" Jack asked, but both Caleo and Paris ignored him. Paris threw her gun out the window and her mother's ghost caught it, firing at two approaching Leeches.

"Nolan, now!" Paris's mother shouted again. Nolan's head perked up and he turned his head toward the Hummer. A thick fog rose from the ground around him, blurring everything in a white cloud.

"Where is he?" Caleo asked impatiently from the driver's seat, looking over his shoulder and trying to see through the dense fog.

"I don't know, I can't see anything." Jack rolled down his window, hoping it would help him see something in the mess.

Paris's mother appeared in the seat between Jack and Paris. "If he shows up naked again, I swear he will be drinking his own blood."

A pound at the passenger's side door made everyone jump. Jack turned to see both Caleo and Paris had drawn their guns and were pointing them at Nolan, who was pulling on the handle to open the door. "Unlock the door!" He pounded on the window again.

"Right!" Caleo hit the button and Nolan pulled the door but nothing happened. He tried again, but the door was still locked. "You have to wait till the door unlocks before—"

"Oh for Christ's sake!" Nolan let go of the handle and held his hands up in surrender, a pair of jeans hanging in his grip.

Paris rolled her eyes as Caleo unlocked the door again. "Just leave him!" Paris's mother snapped as Nolan opened the door. "Well at least you stopped to put on your underwear this time," she said flatly as she looked down at Nolan's blue boxer briefs. "I swear, if it wasn't for the fact that I am a lady, you boys would run around as naked as savages."

"You know it's a little hard to stop and get dressed when people are shooting at you." Climbing in, Nolan slammed the door shut.

"What man would get undressed for a battle in the first place?" Paris's mother shot back.

Caleo slammed on the gas and jetted out into the street and down the road.

"Is everyone all right?" Nolan called back over the seat.

"Yeah." Jack looked back over his shoulder to make sure they weren't being followed. When no one else spoke, panic gripped Jack's heart. "Caleo?" Jack whipped around to see Nolan and Paris turned in his direction, a worried look on their faces.

Caleo looked back between the seats. "I'm fine. You're the one bleeding all over the floor." He glanced down at Jack's leg before turning his attention back to the road. "We need to get him bandaged up before he loses too much blood."

Nolan turned as much as his big frame would let him in the car. "Paris, search the back and see if you can find anything to use as a tourniquet."

"I'm fine. Let's just worry about getting—" Jack looked down at his leg, seeing all the blood for the first time, and felt a sudden light headedness at the sight of the dark blood pouring down his calf. "I think we are going to need to patch this up."

"Jack, are you okay?" Caleo called from the front seat, but Jack was afraid to open his mouth to respond. He was suddenly very cold and he could tell that Paris was doing something with his leg, but had no idea what it was.

☽✳☾

Jack's eyes flew open and a soft gray blur obstructed his vision. "Ahh, what the heck?" He reached above his head and felt cold stone beneath his fingers. He closed his eyes, trying to remember what was happening.

"Are you okay?" Jack looked up to see Caleo's face looking down at him with a smile.

Oh, how I have missed that smile. Jack rubbed his face, feeling embarrassed when he realized by the look on Caleo's face that he'd said it out loud again.

"Why do you do that? Say everything you're thinking. Did they do something to you at the hospital?" Caleo brushed Jack's hair out of his face, tucking the long strands to the side.

Jack looked around, taking in his surroundings. They were tucked up under a bridge with a small river below them. He glanced back up at Caleo, who was obviously waiting for an answer as he ran his fingers over Jack's scalp, which was resting on his lap. Jack laughed to himself for a moment, taking in the bliss. When Caleo gave him a questioning look, Jack said, "I truthfully don't know. I don't think they did anything. They treated me really well there. Three meals a day, TV, hot showers. They pretty much just left me in the room by myself for weeks at a time with no one to talk to. Every so often Alix would come talk to me about you or Thorn."

"Thorn?"

"Did you know that he actually made every one of the plants around the Inn? Not just the purple roses, but also the apple trees. That's why they're the only apple trees that produce fruit all year round in existence. The grass is special, too. It actually puts off a chemical that kills off clover and other weeds."

"So it was just you in a room by yourself for the last year?"

"Pretty much."

"No wonder you're insane." Caleo turned his head to hide his smile. "You were bored. I don't think my brain would have survived the first Bon Jovi day marathon."

"Hey! I didn't even think I got to Bon Jovi." Jack sat up and shoved Caleo playfully. "It's a good idea though. Where were you when I had *Raspberry Beret* stuck in my head for like a month? Where were you then? Huh?"

Caleo shook his head and shifted uncomfortably. "Apparently, not knowing who I was and murdering hundreds of people."

Jack frowned for bringing the subject up and glanced down at the river. "I don't understand how. Did you bump your head or something?"

Again Caleo shook his head, but this time he refused to look back at Jack. "Stan." He said the name as if it was a curse.

Jack stared at his left leg, pulling at the white cloth to try to get a better look at the damage. "So this Stan, he is a Leech I take it?"

Caleo nodded again.

Jack grabbed Caleo's chin and steered his face so it turned toward his own. "It's okay, I am here now." Jack wiped Caleo's tears away with his thumbs. "I'm not going to let anyone take you away from me again."

Caleo pulled his face away from Jack, stood up, and walked down the ramp to kneel beside the water. "Don't you understand? He took everyone, hell everything, away from me. He made me forget my whole life. I didn't even know you existed. He turned me into a killer."

"Caleo." Jack slid down the ramp and climbed to his feet. His left leg screamed in pain and threatened to give way as he hobbled after Caleo.

"Jack, you don't understand. I had no one. I was alone. Steve dropped me in the middle of a battle and, and ..." Caleo looked at Jack, tears streaming down his face. "I killed so many people! I had to or they would have killed me."

Jack moved closer, but stopped when he noticed a thin layer of ice spreading out across the river near Caleo's hands.

Caleo must have noticed Jack's pause, because he looked down at the ice and smashed it with his fist. "I'm a monster. A killer!"

"No you're not." Jack came forward a step. "I have loved you my whole life. You are the kindest person I have ever known."

"Jack, stop. I don't want to hurt you. I can't control this!" Caleo held up his hands to show the frost covering the palms.

Jack didn't stop his slow hobble. "You can. This isn't something new. You're the Angel. You were born with this. You don't have to be afraid of hurting me."

"But?"

"But nothing. I'm not afraid. I know you. You've had this power your whole life, and could have killed me at any moment growing up. Any of the times you were scared or mad your power could have kicked in. But it didn't ... you didn't let it."

"I can't control this!" Caleo said again as he slid away from Jack, but stopped when his hand hit the water.

"I don't think you have to. Your power is part of you." Jack reached out and cupped Caleo's face in his palm. "And I think it doesn't want to hurt me anymore than you do." Puzzled, Caleo looked up at Jack, then stared down at his frost covered hands. "That's why you couldn't use your power when we were attacked at the car last year. Your power didn't want to hurt me … you didn't want me to get hurt." Jack reached down, grabbed Caleo's hand, and pulled it to his chest over his heart.

"I don't understand." Caleo tugged his hand back and glanced down at it. Even Jack could tell the frost had vanished by the look of surprise on his face.

Jack lifted Caleo's chin so he was looking him in the eyes. "There isn't a single part of you that wants to hurt me. Your subconscious won't let your power harm me." Jack pressed his lips against Caleo's, kissing him fully. *This is my Caleo.*

Caleo took a step back, his cheeks reddening.

"I'm sorry!" Jack blurted out, reaching for Caleo's hand.

"No, I …"

Jack dropped his hand. *I shouldn't have done that. He doesn't feel the same way.*

Caleo shook his head.

He is mad at me. I shouldn't have, Jack thought, chastising himself.

Caleo jolted his head up.

"Crap!" Jack covered his mouth with his hand, trying to stop thinking out loud.

Caleo let out a little laugh before saying, "I'm not mad."

"You're not?" Jack glanced up to see Caleo smiling.

"No." Caleo sat down at the edge of the bank and patted the ground beside him for Jack to follow suit.

Jack eyed the back of Caleo's head as he slowly maneuvered his way down beside him. *So does this mean he—* Jack stopped when Caleo turned to look at him again.

"You really don't realize you are talking out loud, do you?" Caleo asked, chuckling.

"I'm starting to." Jack brushed his long hair away from his face, tucking it behind his ear. "I don't understand what is wrong with me."

"You have been brainwashed." Jack jumped at the sound of Paris's mother's voice, and looked across the river to see her phantom sitting in the very center, water lapping at her dress. "They have a Leech that gets into your head. He's called the interrogator. He makes people spill their secrets by asking them questions. His power causes that voice that everyone has in their head to spill out of their mouth, like word vomit. Every time that voice in your head says something, it comes pouring out of your mouth without you even knowing. It's a very clever gift."

"Really? I can ask you anything and you will have to answer it?" Caleo asked, his smile returning as he playfully punched Jack's arm.

"No," Jack answered quickly, not even bothering to think about the question. "Change the subject." Caleo's smile widened, but before he could say anything, Jack asked, "Where is Nolan?" He nodded at Paris's mother. "And where are you?"

A pair of gloves dropped onto Jack's lap. He looked back to see Paris walking back up the bank behind them to the road above.

"You left these in the truck, before you decided to do a strip tease in the middle of the street for the Blessed." Paris's mother coughed, as if suppressing a laugh, and walked across the water to stand in front of Jack. "I replaced the battery pack while you were passed out over seeing a little blood."

"A little blood? I was mauled by a tiger!" Jack pointed to his leg for emphasis.

"Lion," Caleo corrected flatly, as if it was somehow a housecat compared to a tiger.

Jack threw his hands up dramatically "Nearly eaten by a lion!"

"Eaten? That's barely a mark," Caleo teased, "try having your back ripped open by shadows."

"He practically chewed off my leg," Jack complained.

"Scratched!" Paris's mother corrected. "His teeth never touched you."

"Whatever, it had really big claws."

Rolling her eyes, Paris's mother threw up her hands. "Does that make you feel manlier? Fine, you got a little scratch from a big old kitty cat. Your sister would be so impressed."

"Not anymore." Jack hung his head in mock disappointment.

"Good, cause it only needed two stitches. You sissy," she barked.

Caleo leaned over and whispered in Jack's ear, "I like her."

"She made a pretty convincing ghost of you," Jack whispered back as he slid his hands into the gloves and flexed his fingers, smiling at his invention.

"What's that?" Caleo reached over and turned Jack's hand up, revealing the four metal prongs sticking out of the palm.

"It's my power. With this I am on even ground with you Leeches." Jack stretched out his fingers and an arc of electricity jumped between two of the prongs.

"Cool! But it's still no match for me. Electricity doesn't seem to affect my powers like other Leeches."

Bewildered, Jack looked up at Caleo. "Really? Why not?"

"It's because he isn't a Leech. He is a different breed all on his own," Paris's mother announced.

"It hurts like heck, but has no effect on my powers."

Jack thought back to Caleo getting shot in the kitchen and how it barely affected him, when he himself was curled up on the floor.

"You boys better get some sleep. When Nolan gets back, we are heading out." Paris's mother didn't even wait for a response before vanishing.

Caleo stood up, dusting off the back of his pants, then extended a hand down to help Jack up. "Let's get you something to eat. We found food rations in the back of the Hummer in some kind of self-heating container. I'm sure you would love to figure out how it works."

Jack took Caleo's hand and climbed to his feet. "Really? Is it mechanical or chemical?"

"I would say chemical. It says it's some kind of beef, but it didn't taste like any cow to me."

Jack smiled. "I meant the heating device."

Caleo helped Jack back up the ramp and they sat down, their heads almost touching the bridge above them. Caleo dug into a duffel bag on his right, removing a pouch and a bottle of water. "Just add the water and it heats right up."

Jack poured the water into the bag and watched to see if he could figure out how it worked. When the bag became too hot to hold, he sat it next to him, disappointed that it didn't reveal its secrets.

"You're giving up that easily?" Caleo joked, taking a swig from the bottle of water.

"Once we get back home I will tear one of those suckers apart." Jack smiled to himself. *It's so good to have him back.* He looked up at Caleo, expecting to be made fun of, but he was looking down at the river, pretending not to have heard him. However, the side of his lip tilting up in a faint smile told Jack he had.

Jack caught movement out of the corner of his eye and instinctively started getting to his feet, ready to run.

"What moved?" Caleo asked, searching for danger.

Jack looked back at Caleo to see him holding a gun, looking around for any signs of trouble. "You saw it, too?"

Caleo stood up and walked out from under the bridge. "No, I heard you say 'what was that' and jump up."

"There, that shadow!" Jack pointed to a blob moving across the ground.

Caleo shaded his eyes as he looked up. "Jack, calm down, it's a turkey buzzard flying overhead."

"Are you sure?" Jack hobbled out and looked up to see the bird flying high above, and he suddenly felt stupid.

"Yep, I am pretty sure," Caleo said sarcastically, "but it might be an eagle or something. You want me to shoot it down?"

Jack shook his head and returned to his meal.

"Is everything okay?" Caleo sat down next to Jack, who was spooning the meat substance into his mouth quickly. "Jack?"

Jack chewed, swallowed, and wiped his mouth on his bare arm. "I am trying to keep my brain from spilling out my thoughts. You don't know how frustrating this is. I don't want people hearing everything I think."

"Don't worry, we'll figure out a way to fix you." Caleo pulled a Blessed army jacket out from under the pack and threw it to Jack before he laid down with his head on the equipment pack using it as a pillow. "We better get some sleep. Nolan said he wants to leave as soon as he returns."

Jack quickly scarfed down the rest of the food. Scrunching the jacket up into a ball, Jack rested his head on it as he laid down, making sure to keep his back to the cement wall of the bridge. *I can't wait to get home and sleep in my own comfy bed.*

"If you still have a bed. Jillian probably gave away all your stuff by now," Caleo said, yawning.

"Fat chance. With the baby on the way and all, she has more than likely confiscated it in the name of the royal child." Jack couldn't help picturing the baby wearing a red velvety diaper with a crown on its head.

Caleo bolted up straight, staring at Jack in shock. "What? Jillian's pregnant?

Jack smiled, remembering how he felt when he learned the news. "I just found out the other day. She should be almost ready to pop, too."

"But who is the father?" Caleo shook his head, a smile beaming across his face. "Man, I have missed so much. I can't believe she is pregnant."

Jack frowned, knowing that he couldn't lie with his condition, so he just let the words spill out. "We found Mike hiding out at the school and ..." Jack paused, not wanting to continue.

"Jack, I think me finding out that I have super powers and the town blowing up kind of dissolves the whole being picked on in school thing. Besides, if he tries anything again I will freeze his butt off."

"He's dead," Jack said flatly, then explained, "Mike didn't like the fact that Jillian is with a Leech, and when I was out trying to convince Paris to help track you down. He ... forced her, and she shot him and Bruce."

Jack looked up at the bridge above and concentrated on not crying.

There was a long pause before Caleo said, "So Jillian is dating a Leech? How did that happen? Anyone I know?"

Jack was so caught off guard by the question that he couldn't help bursting out laughing. "Stinky! She is dating Stinky!"

Caleo was laughing so hard he snorted. "Stinky? That perverted kitten was a Leech?"

Jack nodded, smiling as he thought back to the days where Mickey would try to follow Jillian into the woods while she changed.

"I feel like we should have known that all along."

"I know, right?" Jack shook his head at how much things had changed.

"We're having a baby!" Caleo yelled triumphantly into the air.

Jack sprang up and glanced around for any sign of trouble. When nothing sprang out at them, he looked over at Caleo. "Stupid much? We're in hiding you know."

Caleo lay back down, and Jack explained as much as he could remember about what had happened after Caleo's accident. Suddenly he heard Caleo snoring softly, so he just laid still and watched the shadow of the turkey buzzard circle around a nearby tree. "Something isn't right about that shadow," Jack whispered to himself.

Caleo moaned in his sleep a few feet away and kicked lightly.

"Just like a little puppy." Jack smiled as he readjusted the coat he was using as a pillow so he could see Caleo sleeping.

"No, it wasn't me," Caleo whined, and his body seemed to spasm.

"Must be a bad dream," Jack said, noticing the drop in temperature. He huffed out a lungful of air and watched the white cloud rise into the air in front of his face.

"I'm sorry." Caleo thrashed as if fighting away an invisible blanket. "I'm not a murderer."

Jack picked up his coat and scooted across the ground to lay behind Caleo. "No, you're not. I am here now. Nothing is going to touch you," Jack whispered in Caleo's ear as he wrapped the coat around Caleo's shoulders and pulled him into his arms, resting his own head on the supply bag right behind Caleo's. Softly Jack sang in Caleo's ear, and slowly Caleo's body relaxed into Jack's arms.

"I love you," Jack whispered, then softly kissed Caleo on the back of the head before closing his own eyes, happy to have him back.

9

Jack woke with a start when Paris shook his shoulder. "What's going on?" Jack looked up at Paris for an answer, but she had a finger pressed to her lips, telling him to be quiet. *Must be trouble.* Jack looked around. *Where did Caleo go?*

Paris put her gloved left hand over Jack's mouth and pointed to the road above with her other hand.

"Is there danger?" Jack mumbled, looking up at the road above. "Is Caleo up—"

Paris cut Jack of with a quick poke of her index finger to his ribs.

"Crap!" Jack whispered before forcing himself to bite down on the jacket he had been using as a pillow to stop his thought vomit. Concentrating on keeping his mouth tightly closed around the jacket, Jack looked around and spotted Caleo on the other side of the bridge tucked as close to the road as he could get. The sound of cars in the distance drew Jack's attention back to the road above. *We're sitting ducks here.* Jack received another poke in his side and rolled his eyes, knowing he was going to have to be more careful from now on.

The trucks rolled over head. "Don't stop, don't stop," Jack whispered through his clenched teeth. The envoy of trucks pulled across the bridge, one after another, and Jack counted eight as they passed overhead.

Without warning, they all came to a halt. Jack could hear boots hitting the ground above. A man's voice instructed the men to, "Spread out search the area!"

Jack looked back to Caleo, who was running for the water where Nolan waited with outstretched hands in water form. "What's he going to do?"

Jack felt Paris's hand grab his arm, yanking him to his feet and down toward the water. Caleo was just grabbing Nolan's hand when pain shot through his leg, causing him to stumble forward and land flat on his face.

Paris let go of his arm and turned, her face registering fear as five darts embedded themselves into her clothing. She crumpled limply to the ground.

Caleo screamed and Jack looked up to see he was trapped under an unconscious Nolan on a dry river bed.

"Jack!" Caleo screamed, his arm stretched out as if he could reach Jack if he just stretched a little more.

"Where's the water?" Jack had barely thought the words before a huge wave crashed down on him, sending him rolling through the water as it rushed back for the riverbed. He thrashed as he desperately tried to grab Paris's arm. He bumped against something solid, knocking the air from his lungs. Disoriented, he kicked his legs, trying to figure out which way was up. His lungs burned as he flailed about. A hand grabbed a hold of his foot, and as if someone turned gravity back on Jack fell into a thick slosh of mud.

He looked back and smiled as he saw Caleo lying on top of a nearly submerged in the mud nude Nolan, with Paris lying right beside him.

"Where are we?" Jack looked up noticing the water flowing all around them, encasing them in a bubble at the bottom of the river. He could see Blessed agents shooting down towards the water, but none of the cuffs, bullets, or darts made it through the surface.

Jack looked back down at Caleo. "Are you doing this?"

Caleo nodded. "I don't know how, but I think I am. It's like I'm connected to the water. I can feel it and move it like it's an extension of my body. I know I can move it just like I know how to move my little toe. It's awesome!"

"We need to get out of here before they decide to go for a swim!"

Caleo grinned mischievously. "They already tried that. It didn't work out the way they planned." Caleo pointed up. Two uniformed men stood on the water as if it was made of stone.

Jack shook his head in amazement. "Well, we still need to figure out a way to get away from them, right?"

Caleo's smile widened. "I have an idea."

Before Jack could even ask what the plan was, the bubble encasing them elongated, forming a tunnel that was big enough to crawl through. Caleo let go of Jack's leg and wrapped his arm around Paris's waist, pulling her tight to his body.

Jack sunk his hand in the mud and pulled himself forward. The mud was slick but his arms sunk in, making it hard to move. "We can't crawl through this!"

"Do you remember five years ago, when we went to that water park?" Caleo yelled, excitement clearly evident in his voice.

"I got kicked out of the water park for going head first down that one slide." Jack looked back and had to stop himself from cursing as a wall of water came rushing through the tunnel.

"It's going to be a lot like that! I hope this works!" Caleo screamed as a wall of water blasted him from behind, propelling him and Paris forward on top of their Nolan surf board. A split second later they slammed into Jack and rocketed down the river; the tunnel elongated in front of them as the water rushed in, propelling them forward.

Jack watched as the tunnel veered—left, right, and then left—dodging rock after rock at lightning speed. "This is awesome! I wonder why Nolan never thought of this."

"Probably because it takes so much energy," Caleo yelled back, sounding out of breath and exhausted.

"How far do you think we've traveled?" Jack asked, trying to look up through the water for any landmarks that could tell him where they were, but everything was a blur under the water.

"I don't know, but I can't keep this up much longer." No sooner than Caleo said the words did the tunnel collapse in on itself.

Surrounded by water, Jack kicked off the bottom of the river bed and surfaced, expecting to see Blessed soldiers surrounding them, but the banks were clear. *Caleo?*

"Here!" Caleo called, sounding desperate.

Jack turned to see him a few feet away with Nolan in one arm and Paris in the other, barely keeping their heads above water. Jack quickly swam to his side and took Nolan's weight, swimming the short distance to shore.

Caleo collapsed, gasping for air the second he was on dry land. "I am never doing that again."

Jack pulled the naked Nolan onto the bank and dropped him unceremoniously in the dirt as he smiled at Caleo. "That was the best waterslide I have ever been on." He looked up the river.

Not seeing anyone following, he turned around, surveying his surroundings. A few houses were scattered around the river, but it looked like they were in the country. "We should probably get as far away from the river as we can before it gets dark."

"Just let me catch my breath." Caleo sat up and looked at Nolan. "I wonder how they found us."

"I'm guessing they tracked us somehow." Jack pulled a dart from Paris's neck and examined it between his fingertips. "Did he bring anything back with him from the Hummer?"

Caleo pulled a dart from Nolan's neck and threw it into the river. "I don't think so. He got back about a half hour before they found us."

Jack pulled another dart from Paris's chest and looked at it. "I think this one still has stuff in it." Jack laid the dart down by his feet and removed the remaining two, examining them to make sure they were empty before throwing them into the river with the others. "I don't think they were trying to kill us."

"Why do you say that?"

"They weren't shooting bullets." Jack stood up, walked down to the river, and started washing off some of the mud from his arms. "I'm hoping these are just some kind of sleeping drug and it will wear off soon." He looked down at Caleo, who was trying to remove a cuff from Nolan's chest, and walked over to touch the cuff with the back of his glove. The cuff retracted, rolling off Nolan's chest, and Caleo smiled at Jack appreciatively. "Please tell me he has clothes somewhere?"

Caleo looked down at Nolan, then back up at Jack and grinned. "Is that jealousy?"

"Yes," Jack said, unable to stop himself, but he quickly tried to cover his thought vomit with, "I have been trying to get a six pack for months and he does it effortlessly."

Smiling, Caleo turned and reached into a backpack near Paris, pulling out a pair of wet shorts and a T-shirt. "I grabbed his pack before running to the river." He then knelt down by Nolan's feet and started to thread his feet through the shorts like it wasn't a big deal.

Jack turned around. He knew Caleo was just doing what needed to be done, but he didn't want to see it happening. Biting back his jealousy, he tried to change the subject. "Did you happen to grab a gun?"

"No," Caleo said, sounding almost ashamed.

Jack immediately wanted to take back the question. *He thinks I'm mad at him. Why did I even ask such a stupid question? I was sleeping on a whole case of weapons and I didn't get them. Am I really that jealous?*

Jack felt Caleo's cool touch on his arm. "Jack, it's okay. It's all done; he is dressed and there is nothing to worry about. Now what do we do?"

Jack looked back over his shoulder at the still unconscious Nolan. "We need to get back to the Inn, but I'm not sure how we're going to drag that elephant cross-country."

"How long do you think it will take for them to wake up?" Caleo asked, staring at the river, and Jack could tell he was looking for any signs of the Blessed.

Jack shrugged and looked up at the nearest house. "Maybe they will have a car or something we can steal."

"Or a boat!" Caleo pointed to a small canoe beside the house.

"Do you really think that we can all fit in a dingy? I don't even think it will float with him." Jack pointed back over his shoulder, smiling.

Caleo stood up and started toward the house. "He isn't that big."

"That's what she said!" Jack blurted out before he could stop himself. Picking up the dart, he wrapped it in Nolan's wet T-shirt and shoved it into his pocket as he ran after Caleo.

Caleo snorted. "I wasn't talking about that."

"It's nothing impressive if you ask me." Jack shrugged, limping behind Caleo.

Caleo looked back over his shoulder, a mischievous smile playing on his face as he raised a single white eyebrow. "What, you looked?"

Jack hobbled a little quicker as Caleo waited. "Well, it's not like he's modest. I swear that guy will come up with any excuse to get his clothes off. Oh, no, the Blessed are coming! I better get naked so I can turn into water."

Caleo turned around and started walking backwards. "This coming from the only member of the swim team who still wears a Speedo to all the matches."

"Wearing a Speedo is different. It still conceals what should be hidden."

"Not by much," Caleo snorted.

"And I only wear if for swimming," Jack continued, pretending to ignore Caleo's comment.

"And underwear," Caleo added.

"Fine swimming and sometimes underwear, but—"

Caleo held up his hand. "Oh and sometimes around the house just because you were too lazy to get dressed into real clothes."

"I was getting ready for a swim meet and my pants were in the dryer." Jack couldn't help but smile. "The point is ..."

"The point is, if you got it why would you be shy about it?" Caleo turned back around and approached the front of the boat as Jack hobbled to the back.

"No, the point is ..." Jack stopped and looked up a Caleo. "Wait, did you just say that I got it?"

"No. Now you're just putting words in my mouth." Caleo smiled.

Jack picked up his end, and they started their way back to the river. "Fine, since you think it's so sexy, next fight I'm going to strip butt naked and run in guns a blazing."

Caleo raised an eyebrow. "I dare you!"

"You may need to fend the bad guys off for a little bit; it takes us mere mortals a few extra seconds to shed all our clothes before doing battle."

Caleo smiled, dropping his side of the boat into the water. "One look at you running into battle and everyone on the battlefield would die laughing."

Jack dropped his end in the dirt and looked up at Caleo. "Ouch, that kind of hurt." Jack smiled playfully. "Vampire."

"Dog," Caleo jabbed back as they both grabbed Nolan and deposited him into the boat.

"Albino deer." Jack grinned thinking of the last ridiculous names he heard someone at school call Caleo.

Caleo smiled back at Jack as they laid Paris on top of Nolan in the boat, but Jack's smile vanished quickly as Jack remembered Mike was the one who had called him that.

"We should probably get going," Caleo said awkwardly.

"Yeah." Jack pushed the boat into the water. *I ruined the fun. I am such a dumbass.*

Caleo laughed and Jack looked up to meet his eyes. "No doubt about it." They shoved the boat into the water and followed it in.

"So how far do we go?" Caleo asked, hanging onto the back of the boat as it drifted down the river.

"I don't know. I guess until those two wake up or we find a landmark we know." Jack let go of the boat, floating back to drift beside Caleo so they wouldn't have to talk so loud. "I wasn't awake when we got out of the Hummer, so I don't even know what river this is." Jack kicked his feet up through the water. His pants were weighing him down, but even so he was just excited about swimming again. He submerged and came up to spit a mouth full of water at Caleo.

Caleo wiped the water from his face and said, "I believe it's the Clarion River. It empties into the Allegany, I think."

Jack nodded, knowing most streams, creeks, and rivers ended up in the Allegany around here. "Well if we are on the Clarion, we'll hit the Allegany, then follow that down to interstate sixty-eight. We can probably steal a car and take that home."

"We just have to hope that we aren't attacked," Caleo joked.

"We're not that lucky." The boat rocked and Jack looked over the edge to see Paris starting to stir in her sleep.

"I just wish I knew how they found us back there," Caleo murmured, looking up at the sky as if he was looking for a helicopter or plane.

"Maybe there was some kind of tracking device in the bag," Jack suggested. "It was their supplies, it would make sense that they would track them.

"And back at the house?"

Jack shrugged. "I have no idea."

☽ ✳ ☾

Jack pushed the boat up onto the bank and looked down at Nolan and Paris through the pouring rain. "I think we need to find a place to hide out for the night." The sound of thunder overhead forced Jack to duck his head again.

Caleo came up beside him, shielding his eyes from the heavy rain as he looked toward the small town just over the embankment. "Do you think that's safe?"

Jack shook his head. "I don't know. The storm came out of nowhere. Maybe it's Leech made."

Caleo looked up at the sky. "Do you know of any Leeches that can control weather? That would take a lot of energy to maintain it for this long."

Jack glanced back at Nolan, remembering the downpour he caused to help him and Jillian escape. It didn't last very long, but it was enough to hide them while they ran and hid. "They have an Angel on their side, too. I think anything is possible."

Jack climbed the embankment. There was an old, two-story house a few yards away and he pointed to it. "There. Let's get them inside."

"It's going to be hard to carry him that far. If it's even possible," Caleo yelled over the downpour, and Jack turned to see Caleo pointing at Nolan.

"I thought you said he wasn't that big." Jack limped back down the hill to Caleo. "Can't you just float him up there?"

"Float him?" Caleo asked, confused.

Jack pointed down at the river. "You know, like in the boat. Do something Leechy?"

Caleo shook his head. "I've been trying for the last few hours. I can't, it's gone. Whatever it was that gave me Nolan's power is gone."

Jack bent over and motioned for Caleo to grab Paris's feet. The second Jack put his hand on her wrist, Paris's eyes flew open. She kicked Caleo hard in the stomach, and twisted Jack's wrist, sending them both to the ground. Jack pushed himself out of the mud, feeling something press against his throat as a foot stomped down on his back, forcing him back down into the mud.

"Paris!" Jack yelled, struggling to free himself from the boot that held him in place. He heard Paris breathing hard above him, then she pulled the knife away and removed her foot. Jack pushed off the muddy embankment and gingerly climbed to his feet as he saw Paris running to the back porch of the house. "Are you all right?" Jack asked, looking back at Caleo, who was still sitting on his butt in the mud looking shocked.

"What's her problem?" Caleo tried to get up, but stopped with a strange almost embarrassed smile on his face.

Confused by the look, Jack asked, "What?" He looked around, trying to figure out what Caleo was doing.

"I think I froze my pants." Caleo tapped the side of his pants to show the fabric was as stiff as a board. "Should this be embarrassing?"

Jack smiled as he extended a hand to help Caleo up. "I won't tell anyone."

"Thanks." Caleo took Jack's hand, and after some breaking in the fabric around the knees Caleo was on his feet.

"Except maybe Jillian," Jack added, laughing.

"What? Why does she have to know?" Caleo whined, attempting to wash the mud off the back of his pants in the rain.

"I've been gone for eight months, and I am sure he told her that I stripped in the middle of the street for the Blessed army,"

Jack said, pointing down to Nolan. "I need something to help draw the attention away from me." Jack slapped Caleo on the back, shoving him toward the bottom of the boat. "Besides, you owe me for all the months you were gone and I had to deal with her alone."

"Fine, but you will have to do my chores for a week," Caleo said, reaching down and grabbing Nolan's feet.

"Chores? We aren't even back yet and you're thinking about how to get out of chores?"

"Do we have a deal?" Caleo motioned for Jack to grab Nolan's hands, but Jack just looked down at Nolan and shrugged.

"If he attacks me, I'm going to knock your boyfriend flat on his ass." Jack held his modified gloved hand up so Caleo could see that he was still wearing it.

"He's not my boyfriend," Caleo said sharply, and Jack looked up to see an almost hurt expression underneath the locks of wet white hair that hid his eyes.

What did I do? Reaching down, Jack grabbed Nolan by the arms. "I think it would be easier to drag an elephant," Jack said, trying to lighten the mood he had obviously spoiled.

They picked up Nolan, and dragged him out of the boat and toward the house.

They made it about halfway before Caleo said, "And electricity? Really? Even I know that's a bad idea in a rain storm." His voice was strained from the effort of keeping Nolan off the ground.

"Doesn't he like water or something? We could always just leave him here and he would thank us for it when he woke up."

"I don't think it works like that." Caleo dropped Nolan's feet at the bottom step to the porch and stretched his back.

"Looks like she let herself in." Jack nodded toward the open door with a glass window shattered out of the frame.

"Would've been nice if she helped get Nolan in," Caleo grumbled, picking Nolan's feet up again and they lugged him up the few steps to the porch.

They went through the door, swung Nolan onto the couch, and deposited themselves into the two empty recliners with grateful sighs of relief to be out of the storm.

"The thing about Paris is she doesn't like," Jack paused, as if searching for the right word, "direct human interaction."

"What the hell is going on?" Jack turned at the shrill sound of Paris's mother yelling from the bottom of the steps.

"I was just telling Caleo how you don't—"

"I don't give a shit about that! How the hell did I end up on a boat in the middle of a monsoon?" Paris's mother flickered out of existence.

"You were shot by the Blessed and *we* rescued *you*!" Caleo shouted, grinning at Jack for support.

Jack shook his head, trying to hide a smile with his hands. "She will kill you," he warned.

Jack stepped in front of Caleo as a very disheveled Paris stormed down the stairs, gun drawn. "Paris don't!" Jack pleaded his hands up, attempting to keep Paris as far away from Caleo as possible. "He was just joking around. We've had a long day, and we are all tired. That's all, he didn't mean anything."

Paris lowered her gun, glared at Jack, and then pointed at Caleo. "Don't think that just 'cause you're the Angel and all that I won't shoot you between the eyes and leave you to rot," Paris's mother growled, standing right behind Caleo. "You wouldn't be the first Angel I killed either," she said proudly as Paris turned and disappeared back up the steps, glaring at Caleo the whole way.

Caleo looked at Jack briefly and Jack could see the mischief in his eyes as he turned around. "I saved your life and you threaten to kill me?"

Paris's mother put her hand on her hip. "Don't make me come back down there and show you it wasn't a threat."

Jack grabbed Caleo's arm and pulled him back. "Caleo," he whispered as Paris's mother flickered away again. "Don't push your luck. We need her," Jack pleaded. "We need all the help we can get right now."

Nolan groaned on the couch and Caleo turned his attention to him. "Nolan? Are you okay?" He knelt beside the couch and shook Nolan gently. "Nolan, it's me, Caleo."

"Great, the giant is awake," Jack mumbled.

Caleo looked up disapprovingly and threw Jack's own comment back in his face. "We need all the help we can get right now."

Jack rolled his eyes, turned, and limped out of the room, walking into the only bedroom on the bottom floor. "Please have a descent pair of jeans." Jack walked straight to the closet. "No whammy, no whammy, no whammy." He pulled the door open and stepped back, appraising its contents. "Oh, praise Jesus!" He grabbed the first pair his hands could find and looked at the tag inside. "Thirty-two and men's. It must be my lucky day!"

Jack, careful not to hit his injured leg, peeled out of his wet sleeping pants and threw them to the floor, getting the first look at his wound. "Small scratch my butt." He poked at the still spongy white flesh and wondered if the bacteria from the river water was going to cause an infection. "Two stitches? Try six. At least it's not bleeding, though." Carefully, Jack hobbled into the attached bathroom and looked in the medicine cabinet for any peroxide or antibiotic ointment.

Finding none, he limped back into the room, peeling off his soaked T-shirt tossing it to the floor with the sleeping pants. He lay down on the bed, under the sheet, and left his leg exposed to the air in an attempt to let it dry out. He heard Caleo and Nolan talking excitedly from the other room, but couldn't make out the words. "Stupid Nolan," Jack grumbled as he heard Caleo laugh. He pulled the pillow up around his ears and closed his eyes. "Why does it have to be him? If it's got to be someone else, why couldn't it be someone younger? Maybe not as muscular." Jack felt the bed shift under him, and he opened his eyes to see Caleo sitting beside him. *Shoot!* Jack let the pillow fall back to the bed and looked up at Caleo's angelic face hovering above his.

"You do know that just because you cover your ears doesn't mean others can't hear you," Caleo whispered softly.

Jack felt his cheeks get warm from the embarrassment. "I hate this stupid ... whatever this curse is. That's what it is, a curse!" Jack declared and lifted his head, expecting to see Nolan standing in the doorway, but instead the door to the room was closed.

"He is on the porch keeping watch. He told me we should go get some rest, so we can head out once the storm passes. He also said something about getting too much sleep already today so he wasn't tired." Caleo lay down beside Jack and smiled playfully over at him. "And I don't think it's a curse. I kind of like it."

"I bet," Jack grumbled. "I can't hold a single thought inside my head and it's giving you all kinds of ammo to throw back at me later. It's worse than being drunk. I'm a mess. Between this and the scars, I—"

Caleo put his index finger over Jack's mouth to stop him. "I like it because I finally know how you feel about me. No more deflecting with jokes, or silence. I know what you think of me." Caleo leaned forward and kissed Jack on the forehead. "And I don't care about your scars. You got them defending me and I couldn't think of anything sexier." Caleo kissed the side of Jack's face where the scars were the most prominent.

Frowning, Jack reached up and felt the bumpy texture of his cheek.

Caleo smiled, pulling Jack's hand away. "I love you."

Stunned, Jack stared at Caleo. He had said he loved him a hundred times over the years, but this was different. *He loves me.*

Caleo nodded, biting his lower lip nervously.

Tears began to stream down Jack's face as he leaned forward and kissed Caleo's lips. "I love you."

Smiling, Caleo pulled away, his cheeks red. "Didn't we have a conversation today about being naked all the time?" Caleo lifted the edge of the sheet playfully.

"Hey." Jack yanked the sheet out of Caleo's hand and tucked it under himself. "My grandmother always preached no fooling around till there's a ring on my finger."

Caleo laughed. "I think my Gran might have mentioned the same thing to me, but I believe it was," he coughed before continuing in a stern impression of his grandmother's voice, "if you bring a girl home pregnant, you better have put a ring on her finger. Seeing as how you are a boy."

Jack shook his head, not ready for such a big step. "I think you left out the threats of death and castration." Jack pointed down at the wet clothes piled on the floor, changing the subject before his stray thoughts gave Caleo any false hope that something would happen. "My clothes were all wet, and I wanted to let my lion bite air-dry a little before I put my jeans on," Jack said, making sure to emphasis lion bite part. "Wait? How are you dry? " Jack asked, noticing that Caleo was still dressed in his pajama bottoms and shirt.

"Nolan. He sucked the water out of my clothes and—" Caleo stopped.

Jack figured he must have said what he was thinking again and started laughing. "I'm sorry, it just sounds horrible."

"You're such a dork." Sitting up in the bed, Caleo sucker punched him in the arm.

"A sexy dork?" Jack asked, pulling Caleo back down on the bed beside him and wrapping his arms around him.

"I wouldn't say that." Caleo laid his cheek against Jack's chest, and he couldn't help but shiver at its cool touch.

"Not nice." Jack closed his eyes, humming to himself in an attempt to keep his mind from spilling his thoughts. Caleo traced patterns into Jack's chest and stomach with his cold index finger, laughing when he made Jack shiver.

☽＊☾

Jack opened his eyes to the sound of Caleo's laughter. The room was completely black except for the moonlight coming through the window. Quickly Jack felt for his pants at the bottom of the bed and slid them on; grabbing his gloves from the nightstand just in case, he slipped out of the room and down the hall. The back door was closed, but Jack could see the two silhouetted figures of Caleo and Nolan in the backyard through the window in the living room. *What are they doing out there?* Jack crept up closer to the window and looked out, keeping to the side so no one would see him.

Caleo was holding Nolan's hand, large spouts of water spiked out of the ground all around them, throwing huge orbs of water into the air only for them to explode and rain down on them. All of the sudden Nolan turned transparent and Jack saw his clothes fall through his liquid body to the ground below. "That stupid son of a—" Jack stopped when Caleo did the same. "That no good rotten piece of crap. He thinks he can steal Caleo away from me by playing in the rain he has another thing—"

Jack felt a hand on his shoulder and whipped around, ready for an attack, to find Paris standing right behind him. Shocked that it was actually her touching him and not her ghost, Jack looked around and saw her phantom standing a few feet away at the bottom of the stairs.

"Does this mean you're going to kill me?" Jack asked with a smile.

Paris just smiled and her mother answered, "I like you, Jack, so at this moment . . . no."

Jack couldn't help but chuckle.

Paris pointed with her chin out the window, and Jack looked to see Nolan still in liquid form dancing with a liquid Caleo under the moonlight. Their forms melding together then breaking apart, but always staying joined at the hand.

"Do you want me to kill him?" Paris's mother asked brightly.

Jack smiled and turned to look at her. "Can I get a rain check on that? I think we may need the jerk to survive this."

"He chose you kiddo. I heard him tell Nolan that just a few minutes ago," Paris's ghost said softly, walking up and standing on Jack's other side. "And how could he not? With those big, brown, puppy dog eyes and that—"

Jack smiled, feeling self-assured. Still looking out the window at Nolan and Caleo, he asked. "And that what?" Jack egged her on when he realized Paris didn't finish her statement. When no reply came, he looked over his shoulder to see that her phantom had disappeared. "Paris?" Jack turned toward where Paris was standing and stumbled back at the sight of a sword sticking out of her chest. She crumpled forward, gasping. Jack caught her and gently lowered her to the ground where she laid on her side.

"Paris? Stay with me." Jack slapped the side of her cheek. Blood dripped out of the corner of her mouth onto the floor as she tried to cough. "Just hold still. Everything is going to be fine." He pulled the sword out of her back and tried to apply pressure to both her back and chest. *I need help.*

"Don't," Steve said and Jack turned to see him reclining back on the couch. "I'm not going to hurt you. I just came for her essence," he said flatly.

Paris's mother appeared beside Jack, looking down at Paris. "Let go, Jack. It's okay."

"I can't," Jack cried.

She smiled weakly. "You can't save everyone, baby. I have lived a long life. It's time for me to go be with my ghosts. Mother has been waiting a very long time."

"Would you hurry up and die already? I am very busy," Steve said, his sarcastic boredom dramatically played out by tapping his watch.

"No! I need you," Jack pleaded, ignoring Steve.

Paris's mother reached up and cupped Jack's face. "Give them hell for me kid." She reached down and pulled his hands away. Seconds later, the phantom faded and the silver that was her essence snaked its way from her body to Steve's.

Jack didn't even bother looking up. He knew Steve was enjoying himself absorbing her essence and it made him want to puke. Slowly he pushed himself off the ground glaring at the man.

"Wow!" Steve said, jumping off the couch as if he was a kid with a new toy.

"Why?" Jack stammered, trying to put together why Steve would just kill her like that.

"Why? I am a Leech. She had Thorn's energy and now it's mine." Steve teleported across the room, appearing behind Jack to sit on the steps. "It's that simple. She was no longer a use to me. She had something I wanted, so I killed her. And man did she have power!"

Jack glanced out the window, contemplating smashing it to alert Caleo and Nolan.

"Don't! I'm not going to kill you. I actually need your help," Steve admitted, still sounding like a boy who just got his first kiss.

Jack glared at Steve and balled his fist. "You're not laying a finger on Caleo."

Steve waved his hand dismissively. "If I wanted Caleo, I would have him by now." He pointed out the window with a smile. "Right now he is keeping my brother in line and has already played his part. So he just needs to stay out of the way until I'm ready for him to finish the plan."

Plan? What plan is he talking about? Jack glanced around for anything he could use as a weapon and spotted the sword by Paris's body. *Can't get to it quick enough.*

"You, on the other hand, have been problematic." Steve pointed over to Paris's body. "All you had to do was follow the pretty little girl's instructions and everything would have been over by now."

Jack turned, backing away from Steve into the living room. "Instructions?"

"Yes. You, the human, were supposed to see the Blessed mistreating your human friends at the school. You would have found out about the rest of the world still being alive and well, and convinced them that the Blessed are not helping save humans like they said they are and—"

"Have you lost your mind?" Jack spat. "You did all this so that I would tell the government the Blessed are bad?"

"There was more to the plan. But if you want to boil it down to make it sound like nothing." Steve folded his arms across his chest and looked disappointed that he didn't get to finish explaining his master plan.

"What the hell does all this mean? Why go through all this just to get the humans after the Blessed? You didn't have to blow up half the country for that."

"Is it really that hard to see? The Blessed are all that stand in my way of me being a god among men. With Alix dead, the Blessed will be gone and I can do what I want."

"That's your rule the world speech? You killed thousands of people. Just so you can ... what? Oh, that's right! Do what you want?" Jack shook his head. "You're insane."

"Don't you see? Without the Blessed, I will be in charge. I can—"

"Do what you want?" Jack said, feigning boredom as he tried to buy himself more time. "Yeah, I think I see you're psychotic." He looked behind himself; he was only a few feet from the door. *If I make it outside Caleo and Nolan will see me and can help.*

"All you have to do is get your part of the plan back on track. Go to the government, tell them all about how the Blessed treated the people at the school, and convince them that Alix isn't their ally."

Jack took another step backward. "Why would I do that? You were behind the attack at the school. You're the one behind the whole thing. You're the cause of all of this."

Steve smiled proudly as he said, "Because, human, right now I don't need your precious Caleo. However, if you don't cooperate I will have to come up with a new plan involving your boyfriend fighting Alix one on one, and we saw what happened the last time."

"You won't touch him!" Jack growled.

Steve drew a knife from his pocket. "I think it's time for you to start learning your place in the new world I am creating." Steve took a step forward, then teleported the remaining distance to Jack. He punched Jack the face with the hilt of the knife, knocking him to the ground from the unexpected blow. "That's where all humans will be, crawling on their hands and knees to serve me." Steve kicked Jack across the face, sending blood gushing from his nose.

Jack spat blood and wiped his nose on the back of his forearm as he glared up at Steve.

"One week to get your ass south across the war line and to the government. If not, I hunt you down, kill your boyfriend, your sister, her kitten, and your baby niece."

"Niece?" Shocked, Jack looked up at Steve. *He saw Jillian? Maybe he's trying to trick me. There is no way Jillian would have let him see the baby.*

"I know where you live, dumbass. Don't forget one week and I—"

Jack sprang at Steve, wrapping his modified gloved hand around Steve's throat as he slammed him against the wall.

Steve laughed. "Is this the part where you tell me if I harm one little hair, blah, blah, blah? I got news for you. I can get there a hell of a lot quicker than you can, and this little stunt may just get you front row tickets to watch a demonstration."

Jack flipped the switch on the glove with his thumb and Steve's eyes went wide with surprise as electricity passed through Jack's gloves and into his throat. Steve's body tried to collapse under the pulsing but Jack held him in place, constricting his finger and pressing him harder against the wall. "Just die already!" Jack screamed, punching Steve in the stomach with his free hand.

Jack felt a hand grab his shoulder and he let go of Steve's neck, spun around, and hit the intruder square in the chest with an open palm. Not even bothering to look to see who the man was as he fell to the ground, Jack turned back around and started savagely kicking the unconscious Steve as hard and as fast as he could. "You won't hurt my family anymore!" Jack straddled over Steve's lifeless form and ground his gloved palm into the side of Steve's head, praying that the electricity would due permanent brain damage before whoever Steve's reinforcement was got back up and stopped him.

"Jack!" Caleo's voice rang through Jack's head, dissolving the maddening rage. He looked up at the shocked look on Caleo's face and pulled his hand away from Steve's head.

Jack climbed to his feet, not taking his eyes off Caleo's face. "He killed Paris. He threatened to kill Jillian and ..." Jack collapsed against the wall, his bad leg unable to hold his weight anymore. "Our niece."

Caleo's eyes widened and Jack could tell he wasn't sure how to take the conflicting emotions, because he himself was having them. Drained, Jack let himself fall to the floor. *I have a niece.*

"We have to get moving," Nolan said and Jack finally noticed that he was crouched on the floor beside his brother, a red welt on his bare chest. "There's a car in the garage, the keys are in the ignition. If we hurry we might be able to get clear before the Blessed show up."

"They found us?" Caleo asked, panicked as he looked up at Nolan.

Nolan pointed down at his brother. "If he found us, they can't be far behind."

"Fine, but we're bringing Paris. We can bury her when we get home," Jack said, sliding himself back up the wall where Caleo helped him out to the garage.

"You're bleeding," Caleo said, looking over at Jack.

Jack blotted at his nose with the back of his glove. "It's not too bad, I'll live."

"I was talking about your leg." Caleo pulled Jack to a stop and got down on his knees so that he could look at the bite wound.

Jack squinted through the dimly lit garage and made out the outline of a minivan. "It's only a thirty minute drive, tops. We can deal with it when we get home." He hobbled toward the van, ignoring Caleo's protests.

Caleo ran ahead, pulled open the back door, and helped Jack inside where Jack propped up his leg on the seat. Just as he was pulling up his pant leg to get a better look at the stitches he knew he ripped open, Steve's bloodied, smiling face emerged through the van door.

"What the hell is he doing?" Jack said, reactivating his glove as he waited for Steve to try something.

"Relax," Nolan said, shoving Steve into the front seat and slamming the door shut. "He is tripled cuffed, unarmed, and tied secure with handcuffs. Plus, you have the gun." Nolan tossed a pistol through the back door where it landed on the seat beside Jack's leg. "If he tries anything, just shoot him."

Jack picked up the gun and glared at the back of Steve's head. *It would be so simple just to kill him now. Me, Caleo, Jillian, and the baby could disappear and never have to worry about any of his crap again.*

"Are you dreaming? You really think the Blessed are just going to let you walk away? I am the best chance of survival you got," Steve said, not even bothering to look back at Jack. When Jack said nothing, he continued, "You have been watching the TV at the hospital. Did you see any mention about Leeches?"

Jack thought back on all the hours of news he watched, all the footage of the recovery in New York City. *They called them terrorists, not Leeches,* Jack thought.

"Exactly, and how many survivors were interviewed? None! They're saying that there are no survivors. And that's true because there are no survivors, because the Blessed are not letting anyone talk about what's happening. They don't want the world knowing about us."

"There's no way the government would allow that. Just shut up before I shoot you." Feeling queasy, Jack leaned his head back against the window.

"Once they capture Caleo, you are all dead. They will come in and burn everything down with one big explosion and say it was a suicide bomb when they were capturing the terrorists."

"I said shut up," Jack drawled lazily. "Can't you see I'm trying to ignore you."

"Your only hope of surviving is to go to your humans and blow the lid off all this."

Jack started humming *Dancing in the Moonlight*, trying to keep his mouth from exposing his thoughts. *Why would the government hide this? Are the Blessed controlling them? They are afraid that the humans will ... what? Be afraid, demand action. How will they decide who is a Leech and who is human?* Jack looked up at Steve, who had shifted in his seat to stare at Jack. "A witch hunt."

"Damn straight!" Steve said, his smile back on his blood covered face.

"Wait, you're wanting a witch hunt?" Jack asked, confused.

"Why not? Humans start attacking Leeches, Leeches get tired of playing by the Blessed rules, and Alix becomes an enemy of both sides. Once he is dead, who will the Leeches rally behind to fight the humans? Well, me and my army, of course."

"But the humans will be after you, too."

"Let them, it will be the perfect opportunity to start putting you guys back in your place." Steve wore a smug look on his face as he smiled at Jack.

"I'm not going to help you," Jack spat, pressing the gun against the side of Steve's head.

Steve laughed and turned his head so the gun pressed into the center of his forehead. "You really think you have a choice. You're dead either way. My way and your family can stay alive; as long as they stay out of the way that is."

Jack pulled the trigger and the gun clicked empty. He pulled the trigger three more times and it clicked empty again and again. "Son of a bitch gave me an empty gun!"

"Come on. He didn't let you kill me in the house, did you really think that he was going to give you a loaded gun to kill me out here? If my brother wanted me dead, he would have killed me by now." Steve leaned away from the gun. "Funny thing about brothers, we may hate each other and it may seem like we are trying to kill each other, but that's just how we say I love you."

"Just shut up already." Jack flipped the gun around and hit Steve over the side of the head with the butt of the gun.

"What the hell was that for?" Steve screamed.

Jack swung the gun again and Steve's head lolled to one side, just as Nolan and Caleo entered the garage. Caleo was carrying a backpack over one shoulder and a cuff gun in his hand.

Nolan had a large bundle wrapped in a blanket thrown over his shoulder. Caleo sat in the backseat and threw the backpack on the floor by Jack's foot as Nolan put what Jack assumed was Paris in the back of the van and opened the garage door.

"What happened to him?" Nolan asked, opening the driver's door and sliding behind the steering wheel.

"I couldn't get him to shut up so I used the gun." Jack looked up at Nolan's face in the rearview mirror; he was smiling, but didn't return Jack's gaze.

"You shot him?"Caleo jumped forward in his seat and checked to make sure Steve was still breathing.

"Nope, turns out this is more of a club than a gun." Jack aimed the gun at the windshield and pulled the trigger again to demonstrate.

Nolan slammed his door shut, started the car, and rolled down all the windows in the front of the van before putting the vehicle into reverse and backing out.

"Wait? We're letting the blind man drive?" Jack looked behind them as they just barely missed hitting the mailbox before Nolan put the car in drive and sped down the road.

"Jack, relax. It's still raining so Nolan can see better than we can." Caleo reached over and put his hand on Jack's.

Jack smiled at the now familiar cold in Caleo's touch and entwined their fingers together as he complained, "He doesn't even have the lights on."

"Believe me, he doesn't need them. You wouldn't believe the detail he can see. It's amazing," Caleo said excitedly.

Jack rolled his eyes and began singing softly before any jealous thoughts could escape his head. "A long, long time ago ..."

"The only way I can describe it is like running your fingertips over an object." Caleo ran the tips of his fingers of his free hand down Jack's arm to his knuckles in an attempt to give Jack a visual of his point. "But it's so much more than that, you're doing it to everything around all at once and ..." Caleo flicked Jack in the ear with his free hand.

"What?" Jack asked, trying hard not to smile. "I'm paying attention. I can sing and pay attention at the same time."

"Really? American Pie? There is no way you can sing *American Pie* without giving it your full attention. I know you, Jack Barely."

Jack couldn't help but smile at Caleo's attempt at changing the subject. "And what song would you recommend? It has to be one that I can sing and devote my attention to your conversation while still pleasantly keeping my thoughts in my head."

"Well we are driving home to see our niece," Caleo said, and Jack couldn't help but feel proud at the word niece.

"So you're thinking about a song about going home? As long as it's not *Sweet Home Alabama*." Jack looked at his shaggy reflection in the mirror. *I'm going to need a haircut once we find a place to settle down for a few weeks. Maybe we can find a way to get past the Blessed and reenter civilization.*

"Find a place to settle down?" Caleo asked, alarmed. He must have realized that Jack was only thinking the words and quickly added, "What's wrong with *Sweet Home Alabama*?"

"Look guys, why don't we forget the song. Jack, you're bleeding. Caleo, look in Steve's bag and see if there is anything we can use to wrap it up until we get back to the Inn," Nolan said, turning his head so he faced Caleo.

Would you just shut up and watch the road. Jack watched as Caleo's eyes widened in the moonlight and he slapped a hand over his mouth. "Sweet Home Alabama ..." Jack sang softly as he cursed himself for not being more careful with his thoughts.

"Don't go through my bag!" Steve said, appearing to spring awake and trying to wiggle free of his bounds.

"Well, look who's awake." Nolan nodded to Caleo to go ahead and open the bag.

"I was never asleep. The human hits like a girl." Steve smiled at his brother before turning to face the road ahead, suddenly seeming disinterested now that Caleo was digging through his bag.

"What's in there?" Jack leaned forward and tried to look into the bag, but it was still too dark to see much more than the outline of a few guns.

"I don't know, maybe a few guns and ammo. It's too dark to see much more." Caleo pulled out a handgun and sat it on the seat between him and Jack.

Nolan reached one of his arms back between the seats and held his palm up for Caleo to grab. "Use my power."

"Or turn on the light and take a look." Jack reached up and pressed on one of the reading lights. "See, the mere mortal has options, too."

"What's this?" Caleo pulled out a flat electronic device the size of a cell phone and turned it on.

"Just a GPS tracking device," Steve said casually. "Nothing you need to worry about."

Jack took the device from Caleo and stared at the screen. It showed their location as a blue dot with a red triangle moving down the road. "So this is how your friends will find us?"

"My friends?" Steve laughed. "My soldiers know where I'm going."

"Cut the crap. What's the device for?" Nolan growled at his brother.

"Device? I think you're getting old, brother. You need to keep up with the lingo. This here gadget is what the kids call a GPS. It stands for Global——"

Without warning, Nolan thrust out his arm and clocked Steve in the jaw.

Steve shook his head for a moment before extending his jaw a few times. "Did you see that, human? That's how you hit like a man."

Jack flipped the device around and the red triangle pointed the other way.

"Steve?" Nolan growled.

"I picked it up off a Blessed soldier that was tracking you." Steve leaned back against the door and poked his head out the window. "You're going kind of fast on wet roads. Is that wise? I wouldn't actually know, this is actually the longest I have ever ridden in a car in years."

"So this is tracking us?" Jack looked down at the GPS device and frowned knowing the answer before he even asked it. "Who are they tracking?"

"Well that would be you, human. My guess is they implanted it under your skin while you were living it up in your penthouse apartment." Steve stuck his head back out the window and howled joyfully into the night.

Jack felt his skin crawl, and he started feeling around for any kind of lump that could be the tracker.

Nolan passed a knife back between the seats. "Caleo. His right thigh, mid-way down."

"You want me to cut it out?" Caleo looked at the knife and Jack could swear he went a few shades whiter than his already eggshell complexion.

"My thigh?" Jack unbuttoned and slid out of his jeans as if they were covered in spiders. He felt gingerly for any kind of abnormality on his thigh that would tell him where the tracker was embedded. "Caleo, help me," Jack pleaded.

Ignoring the knife, Caleo grabbed Nolan's arm and took a deep, gasping breath. "There!" Caleo put his finger in the back of Jack's leg, about six inches above the back of his knee.

Jack ran his fingers over the spot and felt a small bump about the size of a pimple. "Are you sure?" he asked.

Caleo looked up at Nolan who nodded his head.

"Fifty bucks says he's going to pass out before the knife even touches his skin." Steve looked over at Nolan with a smile. Then, disappointed in not getting a response from anyone, he began to watch Jack eagerly.

"Someone shut him up before I shoot him." Jack grabbed the knife from Nolan and took a deep breath as he positioned the point of the blade over the bump.

"Why don't you make me, Sally? What are you going to do, hit me again? I'm so scared of your girly punches," Steve mocked.

Without warning, Nolan punched Steve again. "You should really let Caleo—"

Jack screamed in pain as he shoved the tip of the blade into his skin. "Caleo, can you see if the blade is touching the—" Jack gasped in pain as the van hit a bump in the road. "Whatever this stupid thing is!"

"I don't know!" Caleo said, leaning his head down and trying to look under Jack's leg.

"Nolan!" Jack yelled. "Is the knife touching this effing thing?"

Nolan reached back and stuck his fingers into the blood around the wound. "Yes. It's there. You're on it."

Jack clenched his teeth in pain. "Caleo, if I pass out, kill him." He nodded toward Steve and gave a week smile. Gritting his teeth, Jack grabbed the knife by its medal blade with his gloved hand and flicked it on with his thumb. Electricity arced up the blade and Jack howled in pain, letting go of the knife.

"Check the GPS," Jack said between gasps for air.

Caleo picked up the GPS off the floor where he had dropped it and looked at the screen, shaking his head.

"Is there still a blue dot and red triangle?" Jack asked, trying to hold as still as possible so the knife wouldn't do anymore damage then it had already done.

"Yes. They are—"

Jack didn't even wait for Caleo to finish before he grabbed a hold of the knife blade again and screamed as he pushed it in deeper. Electricity arced off the knife singeing the hair on the back of his leg, causing Jack to cry out in pain.

"Jack." He felt Caleo patting him on the cheek and opened his eyes.

"Did it work?"

"Yes. Look, the blue dot is gone." Caleo passed Jack the GPS device to show him.

Jack squinted at the screen and smiled weakly. "Thank you, Jesus." He laid his head back down and groaned. "I passed out, didn't I?"

"Yes you did!" Steve announced happily from the front seat.

"I thought I told you to kill him!" Jack looked up at Caleo to see him smiling. "It's not funny. I wasn't joking."

"You were only out for less than a second," Caleo retorted, leaning back in his chair and looking exhausted.

"No one is killing my brother," Nolan announced from the front seat.

Steve looked over at Nolan and smiled. "Aww, that's so sweet. My brother still loves me."

Nolan ignored Steve's statement and continued, "I'm taking him to the Blessed myself. Maybe if we give them him, Alix will back off Caleo."

"You're taking me to the Blessed?" Steve looked over at Nolan as if he had been stung. "They're going to kill you, too. You know that, right?"

"Maybe." Nolan shrugged.

"What about our pact?"

"And what pact would that be?" Nolan looked over at his brother and actually smiled.

"The one where we promised to make each other's lives miserable to the day I kill you."

Nolan snorted. "You wouldn't kill me. You would get bored if I was gone."

"Bored? I think you over estimate your worth. I'm already bored, hence the blowing up the world and causing mass chaos."

Jack smiled up at Caleo, ignoring the two arguing in the front seat. Caleo ripped a piece off his own shirt to bandage Jack's leg. "Does that count as a battle?" he asked weakly.

Caleo wrapped the cloth around Jack's thigh and tied it tight. "Technically your pants were still on. They were just pulled down."

Jack pulled back up his pants, wincing as the jeans brushed against the fresh wound. "Fine, I will do better next time."

"Don't you blame this on Mom!" Nolan shouted, nearly shoving Steve out of the window.

"Don't make me pull this car over you two," Jack said, hoping to disrupt the fight. "I'm all for throwing Steve out of a moving van, but if you are just planning on kicking the crap out of him, can we at least pull the car over so we don't wreck and kill us all?"

"That probably wouldn't be a good idea with those cars following us," Steve said unconcernedly.

"Car!" Caleo and Jack said in unison, both looking over the seat to see only the blackness of the night.

"Great, he's playing with us," Jack groaned.

Caleo turned around and kicked the back of Steve's seat. "You stupid lying piece of crap!"

"He's not. They caught up with us about three minutes ago. They're about a mile back," Nolan said casually.

"A mile back? And you were planning on telling us this when?" Jack turned back around, pulled a gun from Steve's bag, and checked the clip for ammo.

The van picked up speed as Nolan said, "I think they just realized your tracker is off, they're catching up."

Jack glanced back to see the outline of an SUV less than a football field away. "I thought you said a mile!" He aimed his gun at the back window and tried to line up his shot with where he believed the driver would be.

"Wait till they are closer," Nolan commanded.

"Don't I get a gun? Or at least stop and let me out?" Steve playfully whined from the front seat.

Jack rolled his eyes and glared at the back of Steve's head. "Can't we just shoot him now?"

"Get ready," Nolan barked.

Jack turned to see Caleo beside him crouched behind the seat with his gun aimed out the back window. Lights flashed on behind them, bathing everything in a blinding white glow.

"Now!" Nolan yelled

Jack and Caleo opened fire and the back window shattered out.

"Aim for the lights!" Nolan yelled over the gunfire.

Jack squeezed off the rest of his ammo and reached down to reload as a volley of return fire blew out their back tire. The van lurched to one side, but Nolan kept it upright.

"Jack!" Caleo yelled as another SUV rushed past them and kept going down the street.

"Where are they going?" Jack ducked as he slid the new clip into his gun, then turned around and shot at the truck behind them again. "Oh shit! There's a bridge up ahead!" Jack turned back around, putting his head between the seats. "Get off this road. There's a bridge up ahead. They're going to trap us."

A truck pulled up beside them on the left as the SUV rammed them from behind, causing Jack to fall back into the seat and land on Caleo.

"It's too late, we're trapped," Nolan said, swerving and scraping against the truck beside them.

"We have to," Jack said, thinking about how high the bridge was from the ground below, then cursed knowing he was too late as the van bounced, announcing that they were now on the bridge.

"Can we jump the sides?" Caleo asked and Nolan just shook his head.

"It's too far down."

The truck beside them rammed into the guardrail.

The SUV came into sight, sitting sideways in the middle of the bridge, blocking both lanes of traffic.

"This is the time you turn these cuffs off so I can get the hell out of here!" Steve said, sounding panicked for the first time as he struggled with his restraints.

"Buckle up!" Nolan said.

"My hands are tied! You . . ."

Jack ignored Steve and turned to Caleo; who appeared to be fighting to keep his power under control. "This is stupid." Jack looked at Caleo. "Grab Nolan, turn to water, and get away!"

"Brace yourselves!" Nolan yelled as the van accelerated.

Jack looked up to see Nolan stretching his arm out in an attempt to help hold his brother in the seat. Caleo's hand wrapped itself around Jack's just as the van rammed into the side of the SUV. Jack flew forward on impact and braced himself for the pain, but none came. Instead, it was replaced with a feeling of vertigo and weightlessness. Jack opened his eyes and realized he was submerged in water.

Jack kicked wildly to the surface of the water and gasped for air. "Caleo!" he screamed as he looked around in the dim light.

"Here!" Caleo said, coughing. Jack turned around to see Caleo a few feet away and Nolan dragging a struggling, cursing Steve toward the shore.

"What happened?" Jack looked around and smiled when he saw the purple rose bush in front of a rock that looked like a grave marker next to a cliff in the dim morning light. "We're at the cave!"

"I figured if I could use Nolan's power just by touching him, why wouldn't I be able to do the same with Steve's?" Caleo announced happily.

Jack closed the distance between him in Caleo in a few steps and embraced him in a bear hug. "You're amazing! We're almost home!" Jack laughed as him and Caleo crawled onto the rocky riverbank and laid down on the large flat rock they used to sit on months ago.

"Almost home." Caleo sighed contentedly.

Jack sat up and looked down at his soaked jeans, wondering if he was ever going to be able to keep a pair of pants dry. "Yeah," he said, both excited and sad that they wouldn't be able to rest for long.

"But we're not staying, are we?" Nolan asked and Jack looked back to see him towering behind them.

Jack glared up at Nolan for trying to make him out to be the bad guy. "We can't," he said flatly, afraid to see Caleo's disappointed face.

"What? Why not? The Blessed don't know where the Inn is." Caleo's words were almost pleading and Jack hated the fact that Nolan wasn't taking the lead here when Jack knew he was thinking the same thing.

Taking a deep breath, Jack looked over at Caleo to see the same brave kid he had fallen in love with, a kid who wanted more than anything to be normal, to live a normal life. But he wasn't normal, he was something far better than that. Jack smiled softly knowing he couldn't keep his thoughts to himself and said, "Don't give me that puppy dog look." He nudged Caleo with his elbow. "We can't stay. The Blessed are swarming all over and closing in around us. It's only a matter of time before they find the Inn, and who knows what Alix got out of my head? We need to find a way to get through them. Maybe we can head south where they were unaffected by all of this. Electricity, food, fresh clothes; we could start fresh and start over where no one knows who we are."

"Won't work!" Steve yelled from somewhere in the distance behind them, but Jack didn't even bother to turn around.

"Maybe even eat at a real restaurant. A nice juicy hamburger sounds great right about now." He knew it was a slim chance of escaping the Blessed without a fight, but he didn't see any other option except to run and hide again.

"A hot shower would be nice," Caleo added with a smile as he looked up at the sky, daydreaming.

"They've got the border to the south guarded! You've seen the maps, Caleo! The second you step fifty miles near human population they will be on your ass," Steve yelled.

Jack looked over at Caleo's face and knew Steve was telling the truth. "Fine, then we head north up into New York. I have seen the TV. They are cleaning up the mess up there. I'm sure we can blend into the work crew for a while. New names, new identities, we can even give you a normal name if you want. How do you like Dan?"

"Not a chance!" Steve yelled.

Fed up, Jack turned and glared at Steve. "Then what would you recommend?"

Steve smiled. "Following the plan. You go south and talk to the government. Causing chaos around the world, drawing Alix out so I can kill him, and letting the Leeches take their rightful places as rulers of this world."

Jack rolled his eyes and went to respond, but Nolan beat him to it. "That's your big plan? You did all of this just because you want to enslave the humans and become ... what some kind of ruler of the world?"

"Not ruler of the world. I'm just planning on taking most of Pennsylvania, maybe Pittsburgh, Erie, and a few surrounding cities." Steve leaned back against the cliff wall and smiled contently. "You can govern Butler for me if you would like, brother, but Scarface over there will be my personal slave."

Nolan calmly walked up to his brother and sat down beside him. "You are the very reason the Blessed exist. They are not here to play governor. They were created to protect the humans against people like you." Nolan kicked off his left shoe and pulled off one of his wet socks to reveal his mark on the sole of his foot.

"That's a lie. The Blessed are there to protect the Angel. Even a new born Leech is told that," Steve spat.

Smiling, Nolan bunched up his wet sock and turned to Steve.

"Don't even think about putting that in my mouth!" Steve turned his head away, but Nolan grabbed him by the chin, pried his jaws apart, and shoved the sock in.

"That is just a part of the legend. The Angel isn't one of us. He was designed to kill us. Unlimited power sent to destroy our kind."

Steve murmured something angrily, but Jack couldn't make it out and just smiled, watching Steve gag on the sock as he tried to spit it out.

"We were supposed to be protectors of the human race. Saved by Archangel Samael, or the Angel of Death as most call him, to become guardian angels for the living. Saved by our power so that we can protect others from the same fate."

Jack looked over at Caleo in wonder, but Caleo looked as confused as he was by the story.

"We became corrupt over time and started seeking power for ourselves. The human race was enslaved and we became kings. That was until divine intervention stepped in and the Archangel Samael was forced to bind his life to the blood of a mortal, creating the perfect weapon against us. He was designed to kill us, all of our strengths with unlimited power, and the kicker is we can't kill him."

"Why?" Caleo asked, and Jack found himself looking over at Caleo, wondering the same thing.

"If we kill off the blood line, we kill off the Arch Angel and very magic that keeps us alive. The Archangel Samael lives in your blood. We kill him, we kill the very thing that spared us from death and gave us our powers."

"Bullshit!" Steve mumbled clearly through the sock.

"Don't believe me? It's all in here." Nolan pulled a thick, leather book from a backpack. *The Book of the Guardians*, or as we are called now *The Book of the Leeches*."

Caleo climbed to his feet and hurried over to Nolan as Jack gingerly stood up, the pain from the knife wound in the back of his thigh screamed and the stitches from the bite pulled as he hobbled over. He had just caught a glimpse of a figure of an Angel, a golden halo hovering above its head, its wings spread out majestically standing over a screaming baby with a golden tattoo glowing on its forearm, when Nolan slammed the book shut.

"We better get going," Nolan said, looking back over his shoulder at Jack with a challenging smirk. "You okay to walk that far?"

"It's only about a mile or so," Jack said, accepting the challenge as he thought about each excruciating step. "I can manage." Without waiting for the others, Jack started hobbling into the woods, hoping to get a head start and not slow them down too much.

"You guys go ahead. I'm going to put Steve in the cave and I will catch up," Nolan called.

Jack stopped and looked over his shoulder. Caleo was rushing over to catch up with him, but Nolan was standing beside Steve with that brown leather backpack slung over his shoulder. *What is he up to?* Jack looked back at Caleo when he realized he had spoken out loud and saw Caleo shrug indifferently. "You're just going to leave him here?" Jack yelled back to Nolan.

Nolan smiled. "Well, I can't take him into camp. Your sister already shot him once and swore to kill him next time she saw him."

Grumbling, Jack turned around and started heading through the woods, whistling the theme song to the Andy Griffith show so he wouldn't share any of his thoughts out loud. *If the Archangel Samaul lives inside of Caleo, how is it that people are still dying? If Caleo dies, does that mean that all the Leeches are just going to fall over dead?* Jack shook his head, dismissing the thought. The thought of Caleo being dead brought back that empty feeling again as if he had lost his soul. *If Alix is still the Angel, does that mean that the power is actually divided somehow? Caleo still gets tired. That doesn't seem like unlimited power to me.*

Caleo came up beside him. "Let me help." He lifted Jack's arm up and placed it over his shoulder so he was taking some of the weight off his injured leg.

"Thanks," Jack said before picking his whistling back up where he left off as him and Caleo trudged through the woods.

"What do you think she is like?" Caleo asked.

Bewildered, Jack looked at him. "Who?"

"The baby," Caleo said.

The look of excitement on his face made Jack want to laugh. "I don't know, don't all babies look the same? Alien eyes, squashy faces and chubby cheeks."

"I don't know. I mean, I imagine she will be special. Well, she has your genes, so won't she look like Jillian and you did when you were babies?"

"I guess so. I don't really remember what we looked like, though. I have seen the photos but I don't." Jack stopped as he heard the sound of a stick breaking under a thick bush in front of them. "Did you hear that?" Jack whispered as he looked through the trees for any sign of movement.

"We are close to the Inn," Caleo suggested.

"Hello!" Jack called into the woods.

"They are not going to answer until you're surrounded," Nolan called casually, walking up behind them. "Walk to that stump up ahead and wait. Someone will come out to take our weapons and escort us into the base."

"Base?" Jack asked as he watched Nolan walk past them and head right for the stump, where he stood patiently waiting. Jack and Caleo started forward and Jack looked around, picking out a few armed men hiding behind trees. Movement in the trees above his head caused Jack to look up just as a small black furball came flying out of the branches, landing at Jack's feet.

"Mickey!" Jack said joyfully. "Man, I never thought I would be so glad to see your furry little butt. Where's Jillian and my niece?"

Mickey looked up at Jack and tilted his head to the side as if confused then meowed.

"Hey, Stinky," Caleo said timidly as he bent down to pet the kitten.

Mickey hissed, scratching a warning in the air, then took off in the direction of the house. Without waiting for permission from the armed men, Jack pushed ahead; he and Caleo ran straight for the house. They passed two wide-eyed kids that couldn't be older than thirteen, who were holding their guns pointed at Jack as they ran between them.

"Who are all these people?" Caleo asked as they passed by three more men who appeared worried at their arrival.

Jack looked over at a man he thought he recognized from the school but wasn't sure. "Some I think were at the high school. I'm not sure about the rest." They stopped as they cleared the woods and saw the huge, eight-foot wall made of tree trunks sticking straight out of the ground. A man with a gun stood on a ledge above them, glaring down.

Mickey's meow drew Jack's attention and he turned just as the cat disappeared into an open door in the side of the fence. Ignoring the pain in his leg, he let go of Caleo and hobbled as fast as he could to catch up. As he rounded the corner to the door, he stopped in awe of how everything had changed. Little, one-room log cabins were everywhere. They were barely big enough to be called a shed and most didn't look tall enough to stand in, but it looked to be the start of a small town.

"Wow! When did all this happen?" Caleo asked, standing behind him.

Nolan walked past them both. "We've been busy since you been away." He pointed up the hill to where the old Inn used to be and Jack turned his head to see that a new, shingled roof had been laid over the basement. Jack's eyes stopped at the woman standing just outside of the small opening to the house with a plastic shower curtain hung over it.

"Jillian," Jack whispered as he staggered forward as fast as he could. He saw her bend down and pick up a fidgeting black kitten off the ground and cradle it in her arms. Mickey batted her hands away and jumped down.

"Fine. What's gotten into you today and why are you—" Jillian stopped talking and looked up. Her face wrinkled up as if she was trying to figure out who the man staggering toward her was. Jack saw her face brighten as she mouthed the name Caleo. She took two steps forward before screaming, "Jack!" and running as fast as she could into Jack's open arms.

Pulling her in, Jack hugged her tightly as he sobbed into her hair. "I've missed you so much."

Jillian pulled away and ran her fingers over Jack's scruffy beard before looking around at all the eyes in the village on her. "I will have someone bring a razor to you. That beard is not staying, and you need a haircut."

Jack glanced around and suddenly realized that everyone around had stopped what they were doing and were now watching Jillian intently. A few of the men had picked up weapons and looked like they were ready to spring into action and defend her. "I've been home less than a minute and you're complaining about my hair?"

Jillian let go of Jack and hugged Caleo. "It's good to have you home." She let go, took a step back, and smiled. "At least you look presentable. Definitely need a bath though," she said, wrinkling up her nose.

"It's only because I can't grow a beard," Caleo stated, smiling as he rubbed the light peach fuzz on his chin.

"Jillian?" Jack could tell his sister was stressed about something. The last time he saw her like this was when she was trying out for cheerleading their first year at Butler High.

"Do we get to see the baby?" Caleo asked, looking past Jillian to the little door beyond that led to the basement.

"After you get cleaned up," Jillian said, pointing to where a small stream now ran through the yard. "There are two bath houses set up over there." Jack followed the stream with his eyes and saw two wooden structures at the edge of the small town with the stream running under the wall and back out the other side. "There is soap and towels inside, I will have ..."

Jack looked back at his sister, but her words fell away as Mickey emerged from the small door to the basement carrying a little baby wrapped in a white silk dress.

"Is that her?" Jack heard Caleo ask, but he didn't wait for an answer as he hobbled passed Jillian and straight toward the approaching Mickey.

"I can't believe I'm an uncle. She is so beautiful." Jack reached out his arms for the baby, but Jillian stopped him.

"Don't you dare touch! It took us five weeks to get that fabric clean enough for today. You're not going to get it dirty now."

Jack held his hands up in surrender as he looked down at the little baby and cooed, wiggling a finger. *She's not alien eyed at all, look at those cute brown eyes.*

"Of course he doesn't have alien eyes!" Jillian said, laughing.

Jack cringed, thankful he didn't say anything hurtful out loud. Suddenly a thought occurred to him. "What's her name?"

"He," Jillian paused as if to let that part sink in, "doesn't have one yet. We were just getting him dressed for our new little tradition here. We call it the naming ceremony."

"He? But Steve said you had a girl," Caleo explained, beating Jack to the punch.

Jillian looked over at Caleo, obviously annoyed that she had to stop her story about the baby's big event. "I didn't realize that Steve was still alive." She glared over at Nolan, who was standing a few feet away quietly. "I shot him in the chest. I assumed he was dead when you dragged his body out of here."

"I didn't know till later that he was still alive," Nolan explained stiffly.

"But you let me think he was dead?" Jillian waited for a response but Nolan said nothing. "I assume you are wishing to stay here?" she asked.

Jack was in awe of Jillian's air of command and had to forcibly stop himself from even thinking 'Miss Bossy Pants'.

"If that is all right, ma'am."

"That is fine, escort Caleo to the showers and get some rest. You will take watch in ten hours," Jillian commanded before grabbing Caleo's hand and smiling. "When you get done, come see me so we can talk." She kissed him on the side of the cheek, then grabbed Jack's hand and led him to a wooden chair just outside of the basement door where Jillian helped him down into a chair. "Mickey, can you tell Marcy that we are postponing the ceremony till tomorrow morning and find me the razor and a pair of scissors, please?"

"Yes, dear," Mickey said and in one quick motion he deposited the baby into Jack's lap and pulled the white christening dress over his head, leaving the baby in nothing but a cloth diaper. "Hold him till I get back, will you?" He glanced up at Jillian with a smile and stuck out his tongue. "I can't carry the baby around with a pair of scissors in my hands. That would be dangerous."

Jack stared down at the little infant and smiled. "Hello little guy." He picked him up and looked down at those big, brown eyes that seemed to be studying him. "I'm your Uncle Jack."

"Uncle Jack just sounds so strange," Jillian said, kneeling down beside him.

Jack didn't even look at her, not wanting to take his eyes off the baby for a second. "Just wait till he calls you mom."

"That won't be so bad." Jillian cooed down at the baby.

"He's beautiful. When was he born?" Jack shifted his weight and winced in pain as he put more pressure on the knife wound. The baby in his arms screamed and Jack looked up at Jillian, terrified that he did something wrong.

Jillian reached down and picked the baby out of Jack's arms. "A week ago."

"Seven days? Wow, and you're up and moving?"

"I'm just happy everything went perfectly. You wouldn't believe how paranoid I was that something was going to go wrong."

"I can imagine. I am just glad I missed pregzilla Jillian," Jack said with a smile.

"I wasn't that bad."

"Yes she was." Mickey snorted as he came up behind her, holding a little car seat, which he sat on the ground next to Jillian.

"I was not!"

"You shot Steve without even finding out why he was here." Mickey handed Jack an electric beard trimmer and a razor before taking the baby from Jillian's arms and placing him in the seat.

Jillian smiled as if she was reliving the moment. "Anything out of that man's mouth is a wasted breath. I was just saving us all air."

Mickey looked down at Jack and changed the subject. "So how was prison? Did you meet anyone special we should know about?" He wiggled his eyebrows suggestively. "What's his name?"

Jillian grabbed the beard trimmer out of Jack's hand and pointed it at Mickey. "Stop it." She patted Jack on the shoulder and commanded, "Shirt off." As Jack pulled the still damp shirt off over his head, he heard Jillian whisper, "You know he is in love with Caleo."

"Hello, I'm right here you know?" Jack said, blushing at the mere mention of someone else knowing about his love for Caleo and speaking about it so casually.

Jillian turned the clippers on and ran them down Jack's head. "You haven't told him yet?"

"Yes, I told him," Jack hissed as he watched another strip of his hair fall to the ground.

"And?"

Jack bit his tongue and tried not to spill his thoughts out. "It's only been a few days," Jack said carefully.

"And what does that mean? First base?" Jillian prodded and Jack couldn't help but smile as he struggled to keep his thoughts inside his head.

"Oh? Someone made first base!" Mickey said triumphantly as he interpreted Jack's face. "Second?"

"Can we change the subject please?" Jack begged.

Jillian turned off the clippers and brushed off some of the hair on Jack's back. "I have been watching this soap opera for eighteen years now. So I missed a few episodes. Forgive me, we haven't had power until about three months ago. Don't I deserve a little recap of what I missed?" She stuck out her lip to show Jack her pouting face.

"You have power?"

"Yeah," she said, holding up the clippers with a look that called Jack stupid without her having to say the words. "The boys brought back some solar panels on one of their scavenging trips. It's not enough to power everything, but it gives us light and a little extra." Jillian turned on the trimmers again and went to work on Jack's beard. "In a few days we are hitting that Home Warehouse store near the old Shop-Mart in New Castle. Mark says he may be able to get some indoor plumbing." She flicked the shaver off again and picked up the electric razor.

"Wait? Can we get back to this Jack rounding the bases thing?" Mickey asked, smiling down at Jack with his arms folded across his chest.

"We can't stay here that long," Jack said, trying to keep his voice calm as he met Jillian's eyes.

"You're leaving again?" Jillian asked, confused. "But you just got here."

Jack shook his head and explained why they had to leave as soon as possible. When he was done Jillian looked upset, but said nothing as she turned on the razor and silently finished shaving his face.

When she'd finished, she handed Jack back the razor and said, "I am going to lie down for a minute, I don't feel well." She turned to Mickey and put her hand on his chest. "Can you look at Jack's leg? I think he's bleeding."

"Jillian?" Jack went to stand up, but wasn't quick enough with his leg and Jillian was already down the stairs before Jack was out of his seat.

"Let her go," Mickey said softly. "She's just going to deal. Give her a few minutes to wrap her head around things and she'll be fine." Mickey took a step closer to Jack and whispered, "When are you wanting to leave?"

"A day, two at the most. The Blessed are—"

Mickey held up his finger to his lips and looked around to make sure no one in the town was listening. "I will get her ready as soon as I can. Just let her have this naming ceremony thing and she will be more level-headed about everything."

Jack nodded his agreement, knowing that Jillian would be easier to deal with after the event was over.

"Now let me see that wound." Mickey pointed to the dark red smudge on the seat where Jack had been.

"It's fine," Jack said, looking at all of the people running around the town. *I wonder what's taking Caleo so long.*

"Forget it. Your sister will kill me if I don't at least look at your leg. So drop trou and turn around."

Jack glanced around. Everyone seemed to be doing their own thing; an elderly man and woman were tending to a few children, while everyone else seemed to be working on the cabins or in a large garden. Even the guards on the wall kept their eyes outward. "Okay, they're not that bad, though. My calf is already stitched, but my thigh might need one or two." Jack unbuttoned his pants. Taking one last look around at the kids running around nearby, he glanced down at Mickey who was adjusting the pacifier in the baby's mouth. "Are you sure you want to do this here?" Jack motioned to the kids playing no more than a few yards away.

Confused, Mickey stared at Jack and then at the kids. "Oh yeah, don't worry about them. With what we have been through, these kids have seen it all." He looked back down at the baby as Jack unzipped his pants.

I wish I would have looked for underwear back at that house, Jack thought as he dropped his pants.

"What?" Mickey looked back up at Jack. "Woah! I was talking about blood. Why wouldn't you be wearing a pair?"

Jack turned away and yanked his pants back up. "I have been shopping out of people's closets for the last few days. It's not like I could run out and buy any."

"And you didn't think to at least look for a pair of underwear?" Mickey hissed.

"It seemed gross and it didn't seem that important," Jack admitted.

"Not important? That should have been the first thing out of your mouth when a doctor asks you to drop your pants."

Jack rolled his eyes. "You're a nurse, not a doctor."

"I don't care. You almost scared all the children in town. Any one of them could have been scarred for life." Mickey picked up the baby carrier and started for the stairs. "Head for the bathhouse. I'm going to grab my doctor's bag and you a change of clothes with underwear and I will be right down."

"Nurse's bag," Jack corrected as he limped away toward the bathhouses, avoiding the dirty looks the elderly couple tending the kids gave him.

When he got there, he heard Caleo and Nolan talking inside the first bathhouse. As he rounded the corner to where the door was, he heard Caleo say, "I can't just leave them. They're my family."

"You're the reason they're in danger. We need to head north and find a place we can lay low. I say hide in the mountains somewhere. In a few years things will calm down and we can come back. It will be easier to hide if it's just the two of us," Nolan said.

Jack took a few steps forward so he could see Caleo— standing in the stream, scrubbing at the dirt under his nails— through a gap in the curtain.

"But what about Jack? I can't just leave him," Caleo pleaded.

Nolan stepped forward into Jack's vision so that his body was inches away from Caleo's naked body. Jack shoved his fist into his mouth to keep from saying a word.

"He is mortal, Caleo. He doesn't belong in our world."

Caleo turned away at Nolan's words, but Nolan grabbed his hand and turned him back so that they were face to face. "He is going to get old and die, where we will stay young forever." Nolan smiled briefly before leaning down and capturing Caleo's lips in his own.

Jack climbed to his feet and ran into the other bathhouse, collapsing in the corner and shoving his shirt into his mouth to keep his thoughts from exploding out as he cried.

"Jack?" At the sound of Mickey saying his name, Jack looked at the curtain, but he didn't dare take the shirt out of his mouth with Nolan and Caleo so close.

"I ran into Nolan on the way down, and he said you were in here." Mickey stepped through the curtain and pulled it back in place. "Caleo ran past me and into the house so I guess he is excited to see the baby." Mickey turned around and looked down at Jack. "What's wrong?"

Jack pulled the shirt out of his mouth and looked up at Mickey ready to say nothing but "He kissed him," escaped.

"Kissed who?"

"Who do you think? Nolan and Caleo," Jack blurted out.

"Oh," Mickey said, looking back at the curtain as if he wanted to leave.

"You can go, I'll be fine."

Mickey walked into the room further and took a seat on the plastic bench someone had taken from a picnic table. "You know I can't." He placed the fresh set of clothes on the bench beside him and opened up his bag, pulling out a plastic pack that contained a surgical needle and thread. "Pants off, face down on the bench." He stood and patted the bench.

Jack stood up obediently and walked toward the bench.

"Now tell me, why would Caleo kiss Nolan?" Mickey asked softly as he slipped on a pair of rubber gloves and threaded the needle.

Jack winced at the words as if he was stung, but tried to cover by pulling down his pants over the bandage that was part of Caleo's shirt.

Mickey's eyes widened at the wound. "Who stabbed you in the back of the leg?"

"I did." Jack pulled the bandage free and tossed it into the stream. "There was a tracker in my leg and I had to cut it out."

"You did this yourself?" Mickey put the first stitch in and Jack gritted his teeth at the pain.

Jack nodded, keeping his teeth tight as he waited for the pain again.

"And the one on your calf?"

"A lion bit—"

A scream from the camp cut Jack off, and they both turned toward the door as gunshots erupted all over the town.

Jack barely had time to pull up his pants before two Blessed soldiers rushed in. Mickey slammed the first man into the wall before pulling a gun from the holster at his belt and unloading two shots into the man's back. Jack grabbed the next man and rammed his knee into his gut, throwing him into the stream where Mickey put a bullet in his head.

"Take it." Mickey threw Jack the gun. "I've got to check on my son and Jillian." Before the gun was even in Jack's hands, Mickey was a kitten and out the door.

Jack buttoned his pants and peeked around the corner to make sure no one was outside. He saw soldiers dragging people from their houses, throwing them to the ground and shooting them. He ran out from the bathhouse and ducked behind the other one just as two soldiers came running out. Jack shot both the men in the back of the head and went to retrieve their guns. As he was bending over, Jack heard the click of a rifle and turned to see a man standing behind him, gun aimed at his head.

"Jack?" the soldier asked.

Jack looked up at the man just as he removed his helmet and dropped it to the ground. "Larry?"

"You're part of the rebels?"

"These aren't rebels, they're the people I rescued from the school!" Jack yelled.

"Humans?" Larry looked towards the village and lowered his gun. "We were told it was a rebel base." Larry grabbed his walky-talky "Abort, they are civilians! I repeat, abort they are civilians."

A moment went by before the familiar voice of Alix came across the speaker. "We have what we came for, burn everything to ash." The soldiers all stopped firing as the retreat was sounded. In a wave they all melted back into the trees as pillars of smoke started to rise up from all the huts.

"Caleo!" Jack screamed, running for the house. He heard someone shooting in the distance, but didn't stop as he ducked inside the entrance to the basement and hurried down the stairs. "Caleo, Jillian?" He stopped at the sight of Mickey naked and crying, the body of Jillian pulled onto his lap. A large crimson blotch stained the front of her blouse and Mickey seemed to be sitting in a pool of blood.

"No!" Jack murmured. Suddenly his legs couldn't support his weight and he collapsed to the floor at the bottom of the stairs. "No!" Jack bellowed, refusing to accept the reality that Jillian was dead.

Mickey looked up at Jack, tears streaming down his face. "They took him! They took my son!"

"They took the baby?" Dumbfounded, Jack looked at the empty crib. "Why would they take the baby?"

Mickey didn't answer; he just looked back down and sobbed into Jillian's hair.

"Jack!" Larry called from the top of the stairs. "Your friend, the pale kid, I found him. He's dying."

"What? No, he can't be. Why now?" Jack scrambled up the stairs as fast as he could. When he reached the top, he found Larry crouched over a shirtless Caleo, who was lying in a pool of blood, gashes and cuts all over his body.

"He's still breathing, but he's losing a lot of blood. I don't know if he—"

Jack pulled his gun and shot Larry through the back of the head before he could even finish his words. I'm sorry." Jack knelt down next to Caleo, placing his hand on his back as he watched the deep gashes in his back shrink and disappear. Caleo's shallow breathing became normal.

Jack sat in the dirt, tears streaming down his face unsure of what to do. He heard the sound of approaching footsteps, but couldn't even find the strength to care who it was until the bare feet stopped in his vision a few feet away. When he looked up, a battered and bloody Nolan was standing above him. "Alix took the baby and got into a helicopter. I took out . . ."

Nolan kept talking, but Jack tuned him out. Uninterested in what Nolan had to say, he stared down at Caleo's bare skin. Moments ago, Jack hated Nolan for kissing Caleo. Loathed him for being able to give Caleo something that he couldn't. Despised Nolan because he loved Caleo and could spend an eternity loving Caleo when he would have to settle for just a lifetime.

Caleo groaned, bringing Jack back to reality. He groaned again, pushing himself up from the ground. When he saw Jack sitting beside him, he asked, "The baby?"

Jack shook his head, unable to hold back the tears. "They took him."

"They thought he was mine. Alix thought I was the father," Caleo cried as he pushed himself onto his feet. "We have to go after him."

Jack shook his head, unable to move. He knew he needed to get up. He needed to go get his nephew, but he couldn't move. "You can't," he said finally.

"What?" Shocked, Caleo looked down at Jack. "We can't just let them take our nephew like that!"

"Caleo," Jack said softly, reaching into his pocket as a plan took shape in his head. "You're dead."

"I don't understand." Caleo shook his head and looked at Nolan for help.

Mickey climbed the steps and dropped a backpack full of supplies by Jack's feet. "He's saying the Blessed think you are dead. You're not coming with us because you're safe now."

Caleo looked back to Jack as he climbed to his feet. "You can't just leave me. This is my family, too. I have every right to go after him."

Jack reached out and wrapped his arms around Caleo, pulling him in close. "I love you," Jack cried, fighting to keep his mind from spilling his plan. He pulled Caleo's lips to his own and shoved the dart he had pulled from Paris's chest into the side of Caleo's arm. His body went limp almost immediately, and Jack slowly lowered him to the ground where he kissed him on the forehead. "I just want you to be safe." Jack looked up at Nolan. "You keep him safe. Take him to the mountains and hide. I don't care what you do, don't come out till you know it's safe. Tie him up if you have to."

"I will," Nolan grunted. "What are you going to do?"

"I will get my nephew back." Jack scooped up the bag and started for the woods. "Or die trying."

"How? You don't even know where their base is?" Nolan yelled.

Turning around, Jack took one last look at the remaining parts of his former life burning down. "I know a man who said he could draw them out!" He turned back around and saw Mickey in cat form, sitting on a rock and watching the buildings burn. "She wouldn't want us to wait around. We have to go get your son back."

10

"Jillian, are you down here?" Caleo called as he pushed open the door that lead into the basement and stopped at the top of the stairs, suddenly feeling like he was walking into someone else's house and not the one he had grown up in. "Can I come in?" he asked awkwardly as he looked down the old steps.

"Of course, I'm just changing the baby." Jillian's voice sounded stressed, but Caleo dismissed it and descended the stairs two at a time. When he reached the bottom, he saw Jillian standing over a small crib, which was next to a mattress lying on the floor in the back corner of the room.

Slowly Caleo crossed the room, taking in the small loveseat in the corner and the rugs that hung from the ceiling to floor dividing the large basement into rooms. "Wow. You guys have been busy. I didn't think there would be enough left of the place to rebuild after the fire." Caleo looked up at the light hanging from the ceiling as the bulb dimmed.

Jillian picked up the baby and sat down on the edge of the bed, where she patted for Caleo to join her. "It's been hard. For a while we just had a leaky tarp over our head, but some of the camp pulled together and built a roof."

Caleo sat down beside her and casually reached out to touch the baby's tiny foot. "It's amazing. How did you get all this stuff?" he asked, but his attention was now solely devoted to the little baby and he didn't catch her response. Slowly Caleo traced a wrinkle in the baby's foot, marveling at how tiny it was. The baby kicked his feet and Caleo pulled his hand back. He saw that the baby was smiling up at him with big brown eyes, and Caleo couldn't help returning the smile as he wondered if the baby had somehow inherited the Barely's contagious smile.

"Earth to Caleo." Caleo tore his eyes away from the baby to see Jillian smiling. "You want to hold him?" Without waiting for an answer, Jillian stood up and slid the baby into Caleo's arms and instructed him how to hold him.

"He's just so ..." Caleo stopped, speechless as his brain fumbled for a description that could describe the baby, but his mind was blank. Instead he asked, "So what name do you have picked out for him?"

"I have picked out a few, but we are going to wait, put them in a hat, and draw them in the morning at the ceremony. The first two will be his first and middle name," Jillian said excitedly, obviously wanting Caleo to ask about the naming ceremony.

Caleo wanted to know if she was going to give the baby her last name, Mickey's, or Mike's but he was afraid to breach the topic so he just cooed down at the little baby. "Don't worry, I won't let your mommy give you a crappy name like mine." Jillian coughed softly and Caleo looked up to see her smiling. "You didn't?"

"Your name's not that bad, I thought it would be cute." Jillian laughed

"You wouldn't!" Caleo said, looking up at Jillian. The baby made a small noise and Caleo felt something warm against his chest. He looked down to see he had thrown up. "Aah?"

"It's okay," Jillian said, taking the baby from Caleo's arms and wiping his mouth with a towel. "Put your shirt in the laundry basket. I'll get you one of Mickey's."

Caleo pulled the shirt over his head and tossed it to the bin. "I'm not going to let you name him Caleo."

"What, why not? I was thinking Caleo Barely had a nice ring to it." She raised her eyebrows to farther drive home the point that they were not just talking about the baby's name anymore.

Caleo shook his head, not taking the bait. "You're not putting him through all that torture. Name him something normal, like Tom or Greg or something."

"Oh come on, you're going to make me just come out and ask for details. I know Jack told you, and being that he is practically glowing with excitement I would say it went well," Jillian gushed.

Caleo thought about what Nolan had just said in the bathhouse and the kiss, and shook his head. *I'm not going to run away from Jack or Jillian, they are my family.* Caleo bit his lip, staring down at the baby in his arms. *But if I stay I am putting them at risk.*

"What is it?" Jillian asked, all the excitement gone from her voice.

Caleo looked up to see Jillian kneeling in front of him. "I ..." Caleo stopped, not knowing what he could do, but when Jillian slid a hand over his knee for reassurance he continued. "I don't want to leave."

"I don't either. We have food, walls, and guards here. I think it will be safer here then on the road," Jillian said, scooping the baby out of Caleo's arms and placing him into the crib next to the bed. "But Jack says it would be too dangerous if we stayed."

"Wait," Caleo said, surprised, "you guys are leaving?"

"Yeah, Mickey said we need to be ready to leave right after the naming."

The lights above Caleo's head dimmed and he looked up at them. "He didn't tell me we were leaving tomorrow."

"I'm sure he would have told you tonight. Things were just a little distracting with seeing his nephew and all." Jillian reached up and flicked the bulb with her finger tip. "These stupid compact bulbs, I swear if we didn't have to—" Jillian stopped mid-sentence, shoved Caleo to the side, pulled out a gun from under her pillow, and whipped around to aim at the shadows beside the stairs. "Who the hell are you?" she demanded.

Caleo jumped to his feet just as Alix emerged from the shadows, smiling. *How did he find me?* he asked himself as he stepped in front of Jillian protectively, but she shoved him out of the way and fired till her gun was empty.

"That's quite enough of that," Alix said casually as he waved away the shadow cocoon that had protected him from the bullets like it was smoke. "I just came for the baby. Hand him over and I will let the mother live."

"What? Why?" Caleo asked, but before Alix could answer Jillian had slid more ammo into her gun.

"Over my dead body!" she screamed and emptied the gun once more.

Again Alix's shadows protected him, and emotionlessly he said, "Fine." The shadows rippled behind him and three black spear like objects shot out, impaling themselves through Jillian's chest.

"No!" Caleo screamed as Jillian fell to her knees.

The spears vanished and Jillian looked up at Caleo, fear in her eyes. "Don't let him take my baby," Jillian cried as she fumbled to reload her gun, but it fell out of her hands as she slumped to the ground head first.

"You!" Caleo turned to confront Alix, raising his fists up like a boxer ready to fight. His hands turned snow white as frost covered his entire body. Caleo forced all the energy to the surface, ready to let loose and freeze the whole building. "Guard against this—"

"The baby?" Alix said calmly, smiling as he nodded towards the crib. Caleo's attention was drawn to the baby screaming behind him and he let his power slip away, knowing that he couldn't use it without killing him. "You see, your family makes you weak." Alix walked over to the crib and looked down at the baby. "That is why Thorn took your grand-father away from me. He said he was a weakness that others could exploit and he was right."

Caleo looked down at Jillian's gun lying beside her in a growing pool of blood. *If I could just get to it I could ... what shoot at him and have it do nothing again? I have to try something.* Caleo thought, infuriated that he had nothing to fight back with.

A scream outside followed by a bunch of gunshots drew Caleo's attention to the stairs. It sounded like a war was going on out there. *Oh God, the Blessed are attacking the camp!*

Caleo felt a sharp pain in his side and looked down to see Alix right in front of him, holding a black knife. "I am sorry, my boy. I wish I could have gotten to know you, but I can't risk the repercussions of someone finding out about you." He pulled the knife out of Caleo's side and let it evaporate into the shadows. "Don't worry, I'll make sure your child is raised like the king he is."

"No!" Caleo cried, blood crawling up his throat as he fell to the ground, clutching his side. "He's not mine. He's just a baby," Caleo pleaded, but Alix just stepped past him toward the crib. Caleo reached out and grabbed him by the foot. "Don't, please don't take him."

Alix looked down at Caleo, pity clearly showing in his eyes. "You're dying. This whole town is destroyed. There is no one left to help the baby. I will make sure he lives." He raised his hands and brought them together in a fist by his chest. The shadows in the room rushed forward and solidified into a spear. "I'm sorry," Alix said, driving the weapon into Caleo's back.

Caleo screamed in pain, unable to move as Alix ran over to the screaming baby's crib, snatched him up, and ran up the stairs. The spear in Caleo back vanished a few moments later and Caleo pushed himself up, ignoring the pain, and rushed for the stairs. His body screamed as he climbed the stairs on all fours. "Alix!" Caleo bellowed as he made it to the top of the stairs and stumbled out into the open air. "Alix! Get back here you coward!" he challenged as he staggered after the noise of the screaming baby.

Three gunshots registered, and Caleo turned to see two soldiers behind him with assault rifles raised. They fired again and Caleo felt hot pain erupt from his chest as bullet after bullet penetrated through his chest and exited his back. Caleo's world went black as he fell to the ground.

☽ ✳ ☾

Caleo groaned as his head spun; his body felt amazing and wondered, *Is this what dead feels like?* He opened his eyes, and groaning again he pushed himself up from the ground. He saw Jack sitting beside him and froze as a pit formed in his stomach. He knew by Jack's expression that he had already seen Jillian and the baby was gone, but he still had to ask, "The baby?"

Jack shook his head as tears streamed down his face. "They took him."

"They thought he was mine. Alix thought I was the father," Caleo cried as he pushed himself onto his feet. "We have to go after him."

Jack shook his head, his hands held in fists at his sides as he stayed kneeling. After a long silence he said, "You can't."

Shocked, Caleo looked down at Jack, but Jack's features were ashen and he looked to be staring into another world. "What?" Caleo debated pulling Jack to his feet and slapping some sense into him. "We can't just let them take our nephew like that!"

"Caleo," Jack said softly, and his eyes focused back on Caleo's as fresh tears streamed down his face. His lips quivered as he said, "You're dead."

"I don't understand." Caleo shook his head and looked at Nolan for help, but he seemed as confused as he was.

Caleo turned to the sound of approaching footsteps to see Mickey as he dropped a backpack full of supplies by Jack's feet. "He's saying the Blessed think you're dead. You're not coming with us because you are safe now."

Caleo looked back to Jack as he climbed to his feet. "You can't just leave me. This is my family, too. I have every right to go after him."

Jack reached out and wrapped his arms around Caleo, pulling him in close. Jack's voice was hoarse as he cried, "I love you," into Caleo's ear, then mumbled something that Caleo could not make out. Before Caleo could ask, Jack pulled Caleo's lips to his own, kissing him deeply. Caleo's mind went blank. He couldn't understand how everything in his world could be falling apart and this kiss seemed to make it all seem to lessen. A sharp prick in his neck and Caleo's eyes flew open. He knew instantly that he had been tricked and Jack had somehow injected him with a drug. Caleo felt his legs go limp as he fell into Jack's arms and he slowly lowered him to the ground. He saw Jack bend over through the drunken haze that was now his vision and felt his warm lips press against his forehead. "I just want you to be safe."

☽ ✳ ☾

Caleo opened his eyes and looked around. He seemed to be in the backseat of a small car; the leather in front of him was blistered and cracked, exposing the thin layer of foam underneath. *How did I get here?* He shook his head, trying to clear his mind. *Was I drugged?* He looked up at the sky through the open window above his head. *Jack!* he yelled, jolting straight up.

He feverously looked out all the windows for any sign of him as the memories came rushing in; Nolan kissing him in the bathhouse, running to find Jack but only finding Jillian in the basement, Alix appearing out of the shadows, Jillian opening fire and Alix killing her effortlessly, Alix taking the baby, running after Alix up the stairs right into Blessed guards who opened fire, and Jack saying good-bye. Caleo's eyes stopped on Nolan filling in a hole beside a large statue. *I'm at the cemetery.*

Slowly, Caleo pushed open the door and stepped outside. The sun was still high in the sky so he knew he was only out for a few hours. When he looked back down, he saw Nolan leaning on a shovel and wiping his brow on his torn, dirty shirt.

"Where's Jack? What happened?" Caleo asked as he approached Nolan.

Nolan shook his head. "I don't know. Wherever they went, they took Steve and the book."

"What? Why would he want the book or Steve?" Bewildered, Caleo looked down at the ground, but when he saw a small wooden cross on the ground he looked away. Fighting back tears, his brain put it together that he was burying Jillian. Caleo looked up into Nolan's eyes. "He was going for revenge, right?"

Nolan tossed the shovel to the side and planted the cross at the head of the grave. "That's what he said."

"And what are we supposed to do?" Caleo asked, thinking back to Nolan's plan of going into hiding for a few years and wondering how Nolan would react if he didn't want to go into hiding, if he wanted to find the Blessed and fight back instead.

Nolan looked over at the car parked a few feet away. "Well, the plan was to take you and go into hiding up in the mountains somewhere."

Disappointed, Caleo bit his lip. His brain desperately tried to come up with a plan to run away from Nolan and somehow catch up with Jack.

"But I don't think we have that choice now."

Confused, Caleo looked up at Nolan. "What do you mean?"

Nolan reached down and took Caleo's left hand into his own and Caleo gasped as he was suddenly aware of all the moisture in the air, all the details of the trees, rocks, and grass around him suddenly came into focus in his mind.

"I don't understand." Caleo had no sooner said the words then he noticed what Nolan had wanted him to see. "How did they find us? I thought we were supposed to be safe," Caleo whispered, trying to count the all the soldiers hiding just beyond the tree line.

"They must have been in Thorn's compound. I didn't see them till a few seconds ago." Nolan ran his hand down the side of Caleo's face. "You're going to have to be strong."

Caleo nodded somberly.

"I will distract them while you run. The keys are in the ignition. Don't stop till you know it's safe." Nolan smiled down at Caleo. "I'm sorry, kid."

"I'm not running," Caleo said firmly. "I'm tired of running. I'm tired of being afraid."

"Caleo, we can't do this right now," Nolan pleaded.

"I'm tired of the people I love dying." Caleo stepped back out of Nolan's arms and looked down at his frost covered hands. "You need to run," he said glaring up a warning.

"Caleo?" Nolan asked, taking a step back as the ground below Caleo's feet frosted over. "Not now, you can't take them all," Nolan said, grabbing Caleo by the arm and dragging him to the woods as fast as he could. Pulling his gun out with his free hand, Nolan fired six times. Three soldiers crumpled to the ground in their path and a man crying out in pain let Caleo know that another man was down to his left. "If we can make it to the cliff, we can turn to water and escape right down the side and into the river."

Nolan fired six more times into the woods before pulling Caleo to a sudden stop. "Here!"

Caleo pushed through the bramble and peered over the cliff, his heart stopping as he saw the exact spot he had hit only months before. "I can't!" He pulled back and looked up at Nolan in panic.

Nolan fired a few more times before his gun clicked empty. "You have to. There are over fifty guards in there, some of which are Leeches." Nolan extended his hand out to Caleo. "We're just going to turn to water and run down the side of the cliff. It won't hurt. I promise."

Caleo looked down at Nolan's hand wearily.

"You don't have a choice we have to run." Nolan said softly

Choice? I haven't had a choice in any of this, Caleo thought bitterly. *All I've been doing is running for my life. But what has that gotten me? They took my life anyway.* Caleo reached out and took his hand just as a bullet whizzed overhead. *I'm tired of everyone I love dying. I'm tired of having to hide.*

"Caleo!" Nolan screamed and Caleo looked over to see him already in liquid form.

A sharp pain stabbed into Caleo's arm and he knew he had been shot. "I'm not running!" Caleo screamed as he shoved Nolan over the edge of the cliff and crouched low to the ground, watching the surprised look on Nolan's face before he splattered against the cliff face and ran down to the riverbank to form three large puddles.

"You!" Caleo turned around to see that a wall of at least fifty soldiers had formed behind him. "Arms up," a man barked as two cuffs sunk themselves into Caleo's chest.

Caleo smiled at the man impishly and growled, "You should run."

The man stepped forward past the soldiers. "By the order of the Angel..." The man raised his hand level with his chest and a single wolf ran to his side, growling at Caleo. "...you are to be executed."

As if executed was a command, the wolf jumped at Caleo, pulling him to the ground. It let out a cry and stopped frozen solid, its teeth still embedded into Caleo's leg. Caleo kicked at the wolf attached to his leg and its jaw snapped off as the wolf toppled over the edge of the cliff.

"I am the Angel!" Caleo screamed as two more stabs of pain in his abdomen announced that he had been shot again.

"Take him—" The man didn't get to finish his statement as a blast of blue light erupted from Caleo's body, bleaching the color out of everything.

☽ ✳ ☾

"Caleo, are you all right?" Caleo looked up to see Nolan slipping his shirt back over his head as he towered over him on the ground.

"I'm fine," Caleo barked, poking his finger through one of the bullet holes in his shirt to feel the flawless skin beneath it.

They stood in silence for a moment before Nolan asked, "Now what?"

Caleo shrugged, not taking his eyes off the masses of frozen soldiers standing in front of him still poised to shoot him. "I don't know."

"Well we can't stay here. Alix will be sending reinforcements once he discovers what happened." Nolan crouched low to the ground and drew a line in the dirt.

"Let him." Caleo stood up and walked over to the man at the front of the soldiers. His hand was still pointing to where Caleo was just standing, his mouth opened in mid-shout.

"He will send his army to get you, millions of trained Leeches and soldiers all hunting you down."

"They won't have to hunt," Caleo declared. "I'm not running anymore." Carefully Caleo pulled the gun from the man's holster and tucked it into the waistband of his own pants.

"So what's your plan? Find my brother and fight with the rebels?"

Even though he could hear Nolan's sarcastic tone, Caleo didn't even look back at him as he pulled a frost covered cell phone from the man's pocket.

"No. It's time for me to do what I was born to do. What I was created for." Caleo flipped open the phone and looked at the screen. It had full bars saying the signal was good. It *must be a satellite phone*, Caleo thought as he brought up the call list.

"So now you want to be king of the Leeches. Do you think that will solve all your problems?" Nolan threw a stone over the edge of the cliff, clearly frustrated. "Why would you want to be king of the Leeches?"

"I'm not. I'm going to kill them all." Caleo pressed send on the phone as he looked up at a shocked faced Nolan.

"Tell me he's dead," a voice growled on the other end.

Caleo smiled at the sound of Alix's voice. "I'm coming for you, grandpa. The second you show your ugly face, you're dead." He closed the phone, not waiting for a reply, and tossed it over the cliff before turning back to Nolan. "Let's go."

The End
Of Book 2

Coming soon

Leech Book 3

NOLAN

Made in the USA
Middletown, DE
02 July 2016